UNSTUFF
YOUR STUFF

UNSTUFF YOUR STUFF

A MILLICENT HARGROVE MYSTERY

Mike Befeler

Encircle Publications, LLC
Farmington, Maine, U.S.A.

Unstuff Your Stuff Copyright © 2018 Mike Befeler

Paperback ISBN 13:978-1-948338-08-0
E-book ISBN 13: 978-1-948338-10-3

Library of Congress Control Number: 2018932722

This book is a work of fiction. All names, characters, places and events are products of the author's imagination or are used fictitiously, and any resemblance to actual persons, living or dead, or to actual places or businesses, is entirely coincidental.

Editor: Cynthia Brackett-Vincent
Book design: Eddie Vincent
Cover design: Beth MacKenney
Cover images ©iStock.com

Published by: Encircle Publications, LLC
PO Box 187
Farmington, ME 04938

Visit: http://encirclepub.com

Printed in U.S.A.

Dedication

To Wendy, my first reader and inspiration.

Acknowledgments

Many thanks to Wendy, my critique group,
Eddie Vincent and Cynthia Brackett-Vincent.

Chapter 1

Millicent Hargrove strolled toward her back door and glanced up to find the Big Dipper in the May sky. A jolt of elation caused her to increase her stride at being in her late sixties, healthy and alive. Pushing back a strand of silver hair, she sucked in a deep breath of the cool Colorado air.

Then a cloud swept across the sky to cover the pointer stars. Millicent paused as she remembered the three no trump bid from the bridge game earlier in the evening with her three best friends. Anyone watching would have seen a scowl replace her normal pleasant smile. How could she have been so stupid as to not pull clubs? She should have made that bid instead of going down two. Oh, well. That was the only setback of the evening. Otherwise she had been sharp and on her game, setting her opponents, Katherine and Allison, when they had bid a small slam, doubled and redoubled. Even her partner, Diane, had been surprised at her defensive play in that hand.

Her husband, George, would be waiting for her inside. He'd ask if she'd won at bridge and then go back to his stamps. A grin tugged at the corners of her mouth as she thought how she had married this good man who had never kept any secrets from her. A friendly, solid citizen who always loved and provided for her.

Another thought popped into her mind. Right before she left for bridge, George cut himself while peeling an apple. Sometimes he acted like such a big baby. He screamed, and she rushed into the kitchen to find him holding a bleeding finger. She retrieved a Band-Aid and fixed him up, in the process getting a drop of blood on her pants. She didn't want to change into a new

1

outfit, so she wiped it off the best she could. Fortunately, nothing showed against the navy blue. Then as he accompanied her when she stepped out the back door to leave for bridge, she stopped. "You need to clean up your den, George."

He turned red. "Quit bugging me about my den! You have the whole house in immaculate condition. Leave this one place alone."

Millicent put her hands on her hips. "George, don't raise your voice with me!"

"Then quit harping on my den!"

They glared at each other for a moment, and then Millicent exhaled and replied in a softer, calmer voice, "Okay, as long as you help keep the other rooms in order."

George hung his head. "I'm sorry I overreacted. I'll do my part with the rest of the house. I like my den the way it is." He gave her a kiss before she headed to the garage.

Now as she returned home, she instinctively reached for the doorknob. It would be locked. George obsessed over security and insisted that everything be locked at all times. She prepared to insert the key in the lock but out of habit still tried turning the doorknob first. To her surprise, the door opened.

She scrunched her eyebrows. How did George allow this to happen? Oh, well, maybe he was loosening up with their recent change in lifestyle. They both retired two months ago—George leaving the high-tech computer industry to work on his stamp collection and she giving up her job as a research administrator at the Boulder Medical Center to whip their house into shape. Initially she had been surprised at how much she enjoyed organizing, and the results looked marvelous. She sorted through forty years of family stuff, eliminated items no longer necessary and then redecorated to end up with a more comfortable, usable living space. After George's initial grumbling, even he admitted the house looked better. A month from now they planned to start traveling, first to visit their two kids and two grandchildren and then to take a European vacation. That would be delightful. After all those years of work, they now had time to see other parts of the world. Of course George had traveled a lot for his job, but Millicent rarely accompanied him on his business trips. She wanted to visit Europe, Japan and eventually go on a safari in Africa. What a change that would be from her quiet life here in Boulder.

She entered the house, closed the door behind her and called out, "George?"

No answer.

He was probably in his den, absorbed in his stamp collection. How that man could lose himself in those little pieces of gummed paper. He forgot all sense of time when he started into one of his projects. He could spend hours sorting through stamps, eliminating duplicates and mounting the ones he wanted to keep. Ironically, he followed much the same process she used in organizing their home. They applied similar sets of skills to their separate areas of interest. And she realized she should be grateful. He never went off drinking with the boys or causing trouble. Just occupied himself with his albums of United States stamps. She put her purse and keys on the kitchen counter. At one time their golden retriever, Gladdy, would have appeared to push a cold black nose against her leg, but three months ago Gladdy had gone to doggy heaven after succumbing to heart problems. Millicent gulped as her own heart missed a beat at the thought of this loss. What a wonderful dog. Always eager for an ear scratch, ready for a walk—the constant companion. She and George had considered getting another dog, but had decided to put it off until after some of their planned travels. No sense having a new dog and immediately sending it off to the kennel for a lengthy stay.

Millicent noticed that a light remained on in the living room. Maybe George had decided to read in there, but if so, he should have heard her when she called his name. Had he fallen asleep?

"George?" she called out again in a tentative voice.

Still no answer.

She shrugged and moseyed toward the living room, looking at the easy chair, but George wasn't sitting there. Then she scanned the room and found George.

Millicent put her hand to her cheek and screamed.

He lay splayed on the hardwood floor in a pool of blood with a knife handle protruding from his chest.

Chapter 2

Millicent had never been one to faint, but she gasped for breath, and her hands shook at the gruesome sight of the man she loved and what he had suffered. Then she heard the sound of breaking glass coming from the direction of George's den. Picking up a brass dog statue, she rushed into the hall and dashed into the den. The light was on and she could see the curtains by one window, swaying in the breeze. She darted over, separated the curtains and found the window had been smashed. She stuck her head through the opening and discerned a figure disappearing around the side of the neighbor's house.

She reached for the phone on George's desk and called 9-1-1.

*****

The paramedics arrived first, but could do nothing to save George. Then a police officer appeared and took her aside to ask some initial questions. Her whole body shook as if the knife had been stuck in her chest. The room started to spin. The only thought in her mind was that her world had come to an end. She took two deep breaths in an effort to steel herself to not play the part of the helpless widow. No, she would get through this awful thing without falling apart.

Another group of police technicians arrived, followed by a man in a dark suit who introduced himself as Detective James Buchanan. He steered her into the dining room and held out a chair for her.

She fell into the chair, thrust her throbbing head into her hands, and bit her lip so hard she could taste blood.

Somewhere in the background Buchanan's voice said, "Now, please tell me what happened here tonight."

Millicent squeezed her eyes shut trying to hold back her tears. "I . . . I came back from my bridge game. The . . ." She gulped. She wanted to be left alone. She wanted to sink into her bed and never get up again. "Oh, this is awful . . ."

"I know this is difficult, Mrs. Hargrove. Please continue."

She willed herself to gain control. She took a deep breath and slowly let the air out. "The . . . the door was unlocked—why did George leave it unlocked? He never does that. He locks me out when I run out to get the mail." She paused, realizing she was babbling. She took another deep breath, then another as the detective waited. "I . . . I yelled, but George didn't answer. I thought he fell asleep in his chair, but then…" She trailed off, the scene replaying in her mind, unable to stop her tears.

The detective got up, returning a few seconds later with a box of tissues. "Take your time."

She gulped, sat straighter and crossed her arms. She *would* get through this—for George, for the kids. Oh, God, the kids. What would she tell them? She shook her head, pushing that thought aside. Twisting a tissue between her hands, she continued. "He was lying on the floor . . . There was a knife. Then I heard glass breaking. In George's study. I . . . I ran back there and saw someone running away." Tears were flowing freely down her face as she stopped and once again buried her face in her hands.

"Describe the person you saw through the window."

"I . . . I didn't get a good enough look. Without any nearby streetlight, I could only make out someone running."

"Could you tell if it was a man or woman?"

Millicent sat up and wiped her tears with the tissue. "No . . . not distinctly. I had an impression of it being a man."

"Tall or short?"

She pressed her hands to her temples, trying to bring something useful to mind. "Nothing struck me one way or the other."

Buchanan held the box of tissues out for her again. She took one and blew her nose loudly. She tried to force a smile to thank him, but her lips wouldn't move the right way.

He put the box back down. "Was the person you saw thin or heavy set?"

She shook her head trying to loosen the cobwebs. "Again, no impression."

"Did anyone have a grudge against your husband?"

Millicent paused to think. "No, everyone liked George. He had many friends from his business days, always helped neighbors and volunteered at our church. I can't think of anyone who would do such a horrible thing to him." Her pleading eyes turned to Buchanan. "Why would anyone do this awful thing to George?"

Buchanan met her gaze. "Now, please bear with me, Mrs. Hargrove, because I have to ask this question. How was your relationship between you and your husband?"

Millicent's mouth dropped open, but then she straightened, determined to pull herself together. "We had a good marriage, if that's what you're asking."

He nodded. "Did you notice any strange behavior from your husband recently?"

"No, he seemed to be settling into the life of a retired businessman."

"Enough questions for now. I'll have a victim's advocate come be with you."

Millicent shook her head. "No. I don't want that."

"We need to carefully inspect the house tonight. Do you have someone you can spend the night with?"

Millicent thought for a moment, trying to figure out where she could go. Her mind swirled in confusion. "I . . . I guess I could stay with one of my friends." Who should she contact? "M . . . maybe Katherine Pepper. She's a short drive away. I . . . I'll give her a call." She stood up and stumbled toward the kitchen telephone.

Buchanan held out an arm. "Please sit back down. Don't touch anything right now. Here, you can use my cell phone."

Millicent slumped back down in the chair. She took the cell phone and stared at it for a moment as if it were some strange object from space. What was Katherine's number? She couldn't focus. She waited for the pain in her chest to ease. It didn't, but she finally could think clearly enough to remember the number she called almost daily. She punched the keys, made a mistake and started over. It rang and was answered. "Katherine, this is Millicent . . . no I'm not calling to brag about that hand when I set you. Something horrible has happened and I need a place to stay tonight . . . no, George hasn't done anything, he's . . . he's . . ." She mustered all her strength to suppress a sob. "He's . . . dead . . . Katherine, are you there?" Millicent pulled the cell phone away from her face and stared at it. Then she looked up at Buchanan. "She must have dropped her phone and disconnected."

"Call her again," Buchanan suggested.

Millicent's lips quivered as she poked in the numbers again. When Katherine answered, she said, "Don't hang up on me this time . . . I understand, you were shaken up. So am I. Can I come spend the night at your condo? . . . good . . . I'll be over soon."

She went to hand the phone back to Buchanan, but he said, "You can put it down on the table."

Millicent set down the cell phone where instructed.

"I wouldn't suggest you drive right now, Mrs. Hargrove. I'll have one of the officers give you a ride."

"That's . . . that's a good idea. I'm too upset to drive myself."

Buchanan signaled a policeman over and explained what he needed to do. Then he turned back to Millicent. "I'm glad you have someone to stay with. Please meet me back here at nine in the morning. Get some sleep and we'll talk further at that time."

*****

Katherine Pepper, her curly blond hair immaculate as always, smothered Millicent with a hug at the door. "Lord a mercy, what happened?"

After the sobs subsided, Millicent gave her the *Reader's Digest* version and then asked if she could make two phone calls. "I need to break the news to my children."

Doing everything she could to control her despair, Millicent called her son, Jerry, in Indianapolis and daughter, Karen, in Memphis. After tears on all ends of the phone, both children promised to fly out the next day.

Millicent was glad her kids would be with her. It was just the worst possible reason to bring them back to Boulder.

Chapter 3

The next morning Millicent threw the borrowed nightgown in the clothes hamper and changed back into her clothes from the night before. In her confusion she forgot to even comb her hair. She tried once again to hold back the tears, but when she saw Katherine in the kitchen with her perfect makeup and not a hair out of place, she broke into uncontrolled sobs.

Katherine held her as she convulsed from the memories of George's body lying on the floor.

Finally they separated and Katherine took her hands. "Sugar, you need some good southern hospitality for what ails you."

Millicent dried her tears. "I can't believe George is gone. And what horrible person killed him?"

"Bless your heart, you've been through a heap of trouble. Don't worry your pretty blue eyes. I'm sure the police are working on trackin' down that polecat."

Millicent dabbed at her eyes once more. "Thanks for being here for me. I promise not to lose control again."

"Goodness gracious, not to worry. That's what friends are for. Now, let's get some vittles into you." Katherine handed her a steaming cup of coffee and set a bowl of bran flakes on the table.

Millicent wrinkled her nose at the cereal. "How can you eat this stuff?"

"Now, now, Millicent. At our age this helps keep us regular."

"I may be sixty-eight but I'm not ready to eat cardboard. My system does fine with real food—pancakes, bacon, eggs, toast."

"Would you rather have tofu eggs?"

Millicent rolled her eyes. "You and your health kicks."

"Ever since Ralph divorced me, my diet has improved." Katherine patted her slightly protruding stomach. "I can't eat whatever I want and stay slim and trim like you. I've even given up the grits."

Millicent took a bite of cereal and decided that nothing would taste good today anyway. She sighed heavily. "I have to work things out with the kids, take care of the funeral and get rid of the house."

"Get rid of the house? Hon, you love that place and have fixed it up so nicely. Why not keep living there?"

"I can't after seeing George's body there. I didn't sleep much last night, but I decided one thing. I'm going to sell the house and move into a condo like you did. But I'm still not going to eat horse food like you do."

Katherine put her hands on her hips. "Some thanks to little ol' me after I put you up for the night."

Millicent stepped over and gave Katherine a hug. "And I'm grateful for your hospitality but don't force feed me Boulder's alternative to real food."

*****

Katherine dropped Millicent off at nine, and Millicent made her way through the media frenzy to meet Detective Buchanan inside the door.

Willing herself to not focus on the image from the night before of George's body, she had enough presence of mind to inquire, "Are you a descendant of President James Buchanan?"

"Not that I know of, ma'am."

"Probably just as well. He didn't do anything to stop the pending Civil War and was one of our worst presidents."

Buchanan gave an indulgent smile. "Thanks for the history lesson."

"You're welcome." As Millicent regarded his face, she thought at least he wasn't named Millard Fillmore.

"Mrs. Hargrove, now that we've had a chance to check through the house,

I'd like you to accompany me to see if you notice anything missing or out of place."

They walked through all the rooms ending with George's den. She hadn't noticed anything that had been taken, but something seemed different here. She looked thoughtfully around the room and then snapped her fingers. "That's it. The one decorative accent that George allowed me to put in this room—a stainless steel vase. I don't see it here."

Buchanan smiled. "We found it out on the lawn. Someone used it to break the window. Your fingerprints were all over it, Mrs. Hargrove."

"Well, that makes sense, since I put it in George's den in the first place." She paused for a moment. "How did you know they were my fingerprints?" Then she nodded. "I get it." She shook her right index finger at Buchanan. "You matched the fingerprints from your cell phone that I used last night."

Buchanan gave a sheepish grin. "I can't put anything over on you, Mrs. Hargrove. But I'd like you to look at one other thing. Let's go into the kitchen."

They entered the kitchen and Buchanan said, "Please check all your cutlery."

Millicent opened the knife drawer and looked inside. "There's one knife missing." Then it struck her. "That was the murder weapon, wasn't it?"

"Yes. And we only found your fingerprints on it, Mrs. Hargrove."

Millicent drew back in horror. "You're considering me a suspect?"

"We always have to check out family members. Most homicides are committed by people who knew the victim."

"Well, I certainly didn't kill George, and I do all the cooking. Of course my fingerprints would be on the knife. For all of George's good points, he never lifted a finger to help in the kitchen. And I'm sure your murderer wore gloves so he didn't leave any fingerprints."

"Around the house we found yours, George's and an unidentified set of prints."

"Probably from Anna who comes once a week to clean the house. I'll give you her phone number so you can contact her."

"One last thing, Mrs. Hargrove. I see you're still wearing the same clothes as last night."

"That's right. I didn't think to grab anything else before going to Katherine's."

"Why don't you go up to your room and change now. Bring the clothes you're wearing back down for us to check."

*****

On her way to Burn's Funeral Home to make arrangements for after the autopsy, Millicent thought over what Detective Buchanan had implied. She was a person-of-interest in George's murder. She knew she didn't kill him, but a suspicious detective could draw a different conclusion with her fingerprints on the murder weapon and the vase. She could believe Buchanan's mind had gone through this scenario: The wife comes home from bridge, stabs her husband, throws a vase through the window to make it seem like an intruder and calls 9-1-1. But when they test her clothes, they'll find no blood from George. Then she remembered the cut she had tended for George that evening before going to bridge. A drop of blood had fallen on her pants and she had partially wiped if off. The police would find that as well.

Chapter 4

Millicent succumbed to the whirlwind of confusion, which enveloped her over the next two days. Between her children, Jerry and Karen, arriving with their spouses and her two grandchildren, finalizing funeral arrangements and packing her clothes and necessities to stay with Katherine temporarily, all seemed a blur to her. The frenetic activity helped take her mind off her troubles, so she didn't have to brood over the murder of George.

Once the police completed their dusting and inspection of the house, Jerry replaced the windowpane in the den for Millicent. She appreciated having a son who could fix things.

When she sat down with the minister at Flatirons Methodist Church, she maintained her composure as they discussed a simple service with eulogies to be given by family members. When the minister asked if she would like to address the congregation, everything finally collapsed in on her. Millicent broke into uncontrolled sobs.

"You don't have to speak if you don't want to," he said, trying to reassure her.

She wiped tears from her eyes. "No, it isn't that. I do want to say something. But it suddenly struck me that I won't ever see George again. And on top of him dying, to be murdered so brutally."

"There will be times like this ahead. There's nothing wrong with crying." He handed her a tissue from a box readily available on his desk.

She blew her nose. "I know, but I tried to control myself so well."

"You aren't expected to control yourself. You can let yourself go."

14

And she did. She let out wails that must have even surprised the minister. When she had completed her crying jag, she took a deep breath, dabbed her cheeks with the fifth tissue she had consumed and turned to the minister. "All right. I'm ready to get back to the plans."

*****

They proceeded with the service before the autopsy was completed, and it went as well as could be expected. Millicent sat in her black dress surrounded by her children and grandchildren. Friends of hers and George's packed the church. She stood up at the appropriate time and thanked everyone for coming and proceeded to eulogize the one man she had ever loved, describing what a good citizen, businessman, husband, father and grandfather he had been. After she sat back down, the tears again flowed freely. Jerry and Karen both hugged her, and she was ever so grateful for the warmth and support of her family.

At the reception in the church meeting hall afterwards, she shook hands and hugged all the other grievers and even managed to eat a few spring rolls from the buffet to maintain her energy. Her bridge group hovered around her as if anticipating they would need to catch her fainting body. She finally told them to go mingle as she could take care of herself.

Her son's wife Nancy and two kids, twelve-year-old Stacy and ten-year-old Drew, approached Millicent after she had shooed her bridge group away.

Stacy gave her grandmother a hug. "I'm going to miss Grandpa."

Millicent hugged her back. "So am I, dear. So am I."

"I'm going to miss him too." Drew sucked on his lip.

Millicent gave Drew a hug. "Yes, and he loved the two of you so much."

Drew wriggled away. "Grandpa started teaching me about stamps. Stacy says they're yucky, but I think collecting stamps is awesome."

That gave Millicent an idea. "Maybe, you and your dad can work on stamps together, Drew."

"Cool." Drew dashed off to the food table.

Millicent smiled as she watched him grab two cookies. Ah, the resilience of youth.

Her daughter Karen came up and gave Millicent a hug. They stood the same height—a respectable five-foot-six. "What a nice eulogy you gave."

"I didn't think I could finish it without breaking down."

Karen held her close. "And I want to thank you, Mother. Since I came here, you haven't once asked me when I would be giving you grandchildren."

"I guess I've been distracted."

Karen leaned over and whispered in Millicent's ear. "Actually, we've decided to seriously try."

Millicent put her hand to her mouth. "Oh, my. What a pleasant surprise."

"I'm only thirty-six so there's still time." Karen kissed her mother on the cheek and then went over to join her husband Hal by the buffet.

Millicent scanned the crowd. She knew nearly everyone here—her friends and George's business associates. They had all come to pay their respects to George and to comfort her. She felt tears forming in her eyes again. *Pull yourself together*. There would be time for crying on her own later. She looked around the room again and noticed an unfamiliar man standing off by himself. He appeared to be in his forties, tall, and anorexic thin, wearing a black suit and white shirt. He nibbled on a carrot stick as intently as if seeking his only sustenance for the day. She decided to go over to introduce herself and find out who he was. She moved toward him, but he seemed to notice her and darted into a crowd of people by the buffet table.

At that moment another man she didn't recognize approached her. He had powerful shoulders, a stern face and exuded an air of confidence. He clasped her right hand in both of his. "Mrs. Hargrove, may I speak with you in private?"

She looked around him and couldn't spot the tall, gaunt man. "I suppose."

He placed a hand on her back and steered her out the door to the porch of the church meeting hall. "I have something for you." He reached inside his suit coat and pulled out a business envelope which he placed in Millicent's hand.

16

She arched an eyebrow. "What's this?"

"It's a check for you. It represents some special compensation for your loss. And its tax free."

"Are you with an insurance company?"

He gave a wan smile. "No, but I represent a government agency that George did some work for."

Millicent winced. "He never mentioned that. What kind of work?"

"I'm sorry, it's classified. Let's just say that the government is very appreciative of what George did and wants you to be compensated accordingly."

Millicent twiddled the envelope and then looked more closely at the man. In addition to his powerful build, he had a firm jaw, dark brown eyes, a full head of black hair and stood with his feet planted like he planned to block advancing rushers to protect a quarterback. Millicent didn't know what to make of him or his gift of a check.

"One other item, Mrs. Hargrove. Have you by any chance found a signet ring in George's belongings?"

"No. I haven't seen a ring."

He snapped out a business card and handed it to her. "If you do, would you be kind enough to send it to the address on this card." With that he turned and headed to the curb. Millicent stood there dumbfounded and watched as he opened the door of a black sedan and drove away.

She finally looked at the card. It had no person's name or phone number. Only the words, "Regent Agency" with a post office box number in Denver.

Before she had a chance to open the envelope, her bridge group descended on her again. "Who was that man speaking with you?" Allison Petrov asked.

"I don't know. Someone who George used to work with."

"Why didn't you introduce him to me?" Katherine asked.

"In the confusion I . . . I didn't even get his name."

"He's too young for you, Katherine," Diane Cooney said, smoothing out her conservative suit that matched her dark tinted hair drawn back in a bun.

Katherine patted her coiffure. "They're never too young, dear. Even though you're happily married, it doesn't mean the rest of us can't be looking."

*****

Only after she left the church while sitting in the backseat of the rental car driven by her son, Jerry, did Millicent remember the tall, thin man. She never did get a chance to find out his identity. *Oh well.* Now she had this envelope that the government man had given her. She tore it open and removed the check. Looking at the figure, she gasped. It was enough money to purchase a condo outright.

Chapter 5

Millicent and her two kids returned to the house while her grandkids went off with her son-in-law and daughter-in-law to hike in the foothills. She wandered around in a daze, still trying to put George's death in perspective. She couldn't fathom George being murdered. Who would do such a gruesome thing to a caring and loving person?

Her thoughts were interrupted by her daughter, Karen, asking, "Do you want to come spend some time in Memphis with me?"

"No, dear. I want to stay in Boulder. And I have my bridge friends who will help me through this." Suddenly something George had told her several months ago popped into her head. She turned to her son, Jerry. "I just recalled something. George said if anything ever happened to him, I should look through his United States stamp collection with you."

Jerry's mouth fell open. "That's strange. Dad called me two months ago and during the conversation made a cryptic statement. He said if he died to get together with you and something regarding a zeppelin and an album. I asked him what he meant and he said to remember it and talk to you if the time ever came."

Millicent bit her lip. "At the end your father left a number of strange puzzles. Let me get the stamps, and let's take a look." She retrieved the United States stamp albums from the bookshelf in the den, and she and Jerry sat down to look through them. "This collection must be valuable. I'm sure your father would want you to have it, Jerry. Besides, Drew expressed an interest in stamps, and it might be a good project for you two to work on. Karen, do you have any objection if I give this to Jerry?"

"No, Mom. I'm not interested in stamps. You can save me your doll collection."

"I'll pack that up for you here soon. When I move out of the house, I need to get rid of lots of things."

"You're not going to keep the house?" both kids replied in unison.

"That's right. I don't want to live here any longer. I have enough money to buy a condo, so I'm going to clean things out and move as quickly as I can."

"I can't believe you'd give up the house," Jerry said.

"It's time for a change. I want my happy memories of your father, but I don't want to remain in the house where I found his body. That's why I'm staying at Katherine's condo until I get a new place."

"If that's what you really want to do," Karen said with a catch in her throat.

"I know you're both fond of your childhood home, but it's time for me to downsize. Now this stamp collection Jerry and I need to look at. Let's see what we have here."

She and Jerry leafed through page after page in the albums. When they reached the part of the collection with airmail stamps from 1930, Jerry pointed. "Look at this. Three stamps with the Graf Zeppelin."

"That must be what your father referred to. When you mentioned what he told you, I first thought of the Led Zeppelin music albums, but maybe he meant the Graf Zeppelin in his stamp album."

Karen bent over their shoulders, and they all stared at the page with the three mounted stamps—a green sixty-five cent, tan dollar-thirty and blue two-dollar-sixty.

"What do you suppose this all means?" Jerry asked.

"I don't know but let's take the stamps out of the plastic sleeves." They each slipped one out and peered at it. Millicent turned over the sixty-five cent one in her hand and flinched. "There's a tiny piece of paper connected to the back with an old-fashioned stamp mounting hinge." She gingerly removed the piece of paper and turned it over. It contained the word, "fish."

"That's your father's handwriting. What do you suppose he meant by fish?"

Jerry wrinkled his brow, and Karen looked blank.

"I'll have to noodle on this," Millicent said. "Nothing comes to mind immediately. In any case, I want you to take this stamp collection back with you, Jerry. I'll be cleaning everything out, and there's no sense having it kicking around in my way. Besides, as we discussed, it will be a good father-son project for you and Drew to work on."

"Okay, Mom."

*****

After her kids and their families caught flights home, Millicent began her new life. First, she deposited the huge, mysterious check in her checking account. Then she proceeded to the sales office of the Palindrome, a new condominium complex on the east side of Boulder. She received a tour of the facility and found a two-bedroom apartment on the second floor with a view of the Flatirons, the rock formation in the foothills west of town. Given the hefty price tag, this condo had not yet sold, but thanks to what she considered winning the lottery, she wrote two checks to pay for it outright.

"This first check covers the down payment from funds readily available in my account. The second check covers the rest of the payment and can be cashed as soon as my recent deposit clears. How soon can I move in?"

The astonished sales representative, stammered, "N—next week if you want."

"Fine. I'll start making the necessary arrangements."

The condo had built-in appliances so Millicent next went to Mattress World to order a new bed.

"I want it delivered next week to this address." Millicent gave the location of her new home.

Millicent walked out of the store, enjoying her new-found purchasing power. She couldn't press Katherine's hospitality too much longer, and she had decided that she could never sleep again in the bed where she and George had conceived their two children. That old bed had survived a lot of use over the years—many happy times entwined in each other arms. But it would be too painful a reminder to be sleeping in that bed by herself, consequently the decision for a new bed. As he aged, George would still get all hot and bothered once a week or so. But over the last few years Millicent didn't care that much about sex one way or the other. Sure, she had enjoyed their times of intimacy together, but it hadn't been at the top of her priority list as it was with George.

So with a new home and a new bed, the time had come to start cleaning out the house to sell. At her own pace she could begin moving things to her new condo, as she felt no pressure to do it in any rush. Only one part of the house needed immediate attention—George's den. She had mixed feelings. On one hand, she dreaded going though his things. On the other hand, maybe she would find some clue to his murder. At that thought, her stomach roiled. Whoever had killed George needed to be punished, but the police hadn't arrested anyone yet. And there also remained the matter of this mysterious government job. How strange that George never mentioned it. And the weird messages to Jerry and her that led to, of all things, the word "fish." How unlike George.

Chapter 6

Back at her old house, Millicent sauntered through the kitchen. Everything appeared in order. The cooking utensils were neatly stored in drawers, trivets decorated with straw flowers hung above the stove and a clean cutting board rested in the food preparation area. The cleaning service had restored the living room, all bedrooms had been vacuumed by the cleaning lady, and the bathrooms were sparkling white. No animal smells with the demise of their dog, Gladdy. Millicent grimaced. Maybe if they had had a watchdog, the intruder would never have killed George. With a sinking feeling she realized it was too late for considering that.

She pushed aside the ache in her chest and entered George's den. This would take all of her organizing skills and fortitude to complete. Bookshelves lined two walls, displaying George's haphazard collection of business books, motivational tomes and novels.

She shook her head. She'd tried for years to get George to cull his books, but he always insisted that they would come in handy. Right. As if he ever cracked them open again after he read them the first time. And a stack of books still remained that looked as if he had never even touched them. Millicent rolled up her sleeves, brought in half a dozen cardboard boxes from the garage and began sorting through books. One pile would be for those she would keep and another for items to go for a garage sale. She smiled to herself. It would be fun to conduct a garage sale when she finally cleared out the house. She would be significantly downsizing to fit into her condo. Things that she no longer needed would go up for sale and what didn't sell could then be donated to a local charity. She had her work cut out for her.

As she sorted through the shelves, she only found a few novels she wanted, and some books were in such bad condition that they went in a pitch pile, but the vast majority ended up in the sell category. Then she hauled the boxes out to the garage to store for the subsequent garage sale.

She dusted her hands together and returned to the den to tackle George's desk. This provided more of a challenge than the bookshelf. She loaded up a wastebasket with pens that didn't write anymore, pencils without erasers, bent paperclips, a ten-year-old Boulder phone directory, an eight-year-old listing of Boulder companies from the Chamber of Commerce, a badge from a tradeshow George had attended a year earlier, a broken ruler, pads with two or three sheets of paper left, reams of return address labels that had been sent by non-profit organizations, and a dried-up bottle of cologne.

Tears came to her eyes. She had given George this bottle for Christmas a number of years ago. She had wondered where it went, not being in the bathroom with his other toilet articles.

She wiped her eyes and finished cleaning out the desk. Fortunately, nothing made smoke or exploded.

After another trip to the trash bin, she returned to sort through the volumes of files George kept. He had always paid the family bills, so on the top of the desk she found the most recent ones requiring payment. She got her checkbook from her purse and took care of the CenturyLink, Xcel Energy, Comcast, Western Disposal and City of Boulder bills. She realized that she would have to go through the hassle of changing a number of these services to her new condo. Moving was never an easy process. She filled up the wastebasket again with unopened junk mail and flyers for management seminars and dumped these in the recycling bin.

Then on to the file cabinet. She tried the top drawer and found it locked. Great. Where would George have kept the key? She had not found any keys when sorting through the desk. Knowing George's penchant for security, he wouldn't have left it lying around in easy reach. *Think.* Putting herself in George's position, where would she have hidden the key? It would be somewhere that someone wouldn't casually find, but still convenient enough that he could use it every day when he needed to access his files. She knew he didn't carry it on his key chain. That only contained car keys and the house key. He wouldn't store it elsewhere in the house, so it had to be in his den. She had been through the complete two walls of bookshelves and found nothing there. That left the computer or the desk. She looked under the keyboard, mouse pad, lifted up the docking station for the laptop, and felt under the printer. Nothing.

Then she ran her hand along the inside top surface above each of the desk drawers. Nothing in the middle or right side drawers. But in the top drawer on the left side, her fingernail clicked on something metallic. She reached farther in and extracted a key wedged in a crevice on the underside of the desk surface. She tried it in the file cabinet lock, which clicked open.

Millicent smiled at what a good detective she had become.

The top drawer contained hand-labeled manila folders, which turned out to be tax, bill history, bank statements and other financial records. One folder contained the key for their joint lockbox at the bank. She'd eventually have to retrieve the documents stored there. They even had some silver dollars from long ago. She carefully placed this key in her purse.

She'd also have to acquaint herself with all these financial files at some time, but not today. They had an excellent tax accountant who would help her sort through everything. Fortunately, last year's taxes had all been filed on time in April. She would need assistance when it came time to take care of Uncle Sam for the current year. And how would she handle this "tax free" money from the strange government man?

The second drawer contained personal files, in alphabetical order starting with "Arthritis." George had suffered from arthritis in his left knee and had collected a file of articles on knee surgery, knee replacements and medication for arthritis pain. Since she didn't suffer from arthritis, she dumped this folder in the trash. Two folders contained sales slips from trips to Memphis and Indianapolis when they had last visited the kids. She scanned through the airline, rental car and hotel receipts and summarily dumped these into the trash.

Then she found a folder labeled, "Tickets." Inside she discovered contact information for some people who had sold George Bronco tickets. He rarely went to games, but one time when Jerry had visited, George had tracked down two tickets for father and son to go on an outing, unfortunately with a disappointing loss to the Oakland Raiders.

She didn't plan to attend any Bronco games, so this also ended up in the trash. The back half of this drawer contained files left over from George's business career. He had worked at four companies before retiring, and he had retained paperwork from two resignations and one layoff as well as information from when he started at each new company. She found a folder that had a picture of his retirement party from Research Tech. His colleagues had thrown quite a shindig at the Broker Inn with balloons, a huge spread of food, too much alcohol, and a Powerpoint slide show of George's life—she had surreptitiously contributed pictures for this event. She didn't empty this folder.

On to drawer three. This contained a box of miscellaneous stamp collecting material—tweezers, mounting material and an assortment of loose stamps. She decided to not even mess with anything in this drawer yet.

The bottom drawer contained filled manila folders, but not one of them had labels. Strange. The contents of the top two drawers had been meticulously labeled and alphabetized. She picked up the first folder and scanned through it. She found herself reading an agricultural report concerning central China. She leafed through more pages and found more of the same. Rice statistics for parts of the Asian continent.

George knew nothing about agriculture. He hadn't even been able to grow a vegetable garden with the kids when they were little.

The next folder had meteorological reports, again covering Asian countries. She wrinkled her brow. George didn't even watch the Weather Channel. Late day snowstorms always surprised him after he had headed off to work without a proper jacket. What was all this nonsense? She suppressed the urge to kick the wall.

The third folder she perused contained topographical maps. Also unexpected. Many men relished maps and prided themselves on their navigational skills. George always got lost, never even carried maps of Boulder, Denver and Colorado in his Acura, and had no male ego qualms about asking directions. None of this made any sense.

Finally, she found a folder with reports showing industrial production in a number of Asian countries. This was at least reasonable with George's business background. But why would he have kept all of these folders?

Millicent still didn't know what to do with this drawer full of useless reports. Nothing here appeared worth saving for the kids, and she didn't want to lug all this to her new condo. She considered immediately throwing it all away, but finally decided she would take care of that later. Instead, she relocked the file cabinet, put the key in her purse and lugged outside the most recent container of paper to recycle.

To relieve the frustration from looking through the strange reports, Millicent decided to take a trip to the grocery store for some cookie dough. She sauntered out to the garage, thinking how she needed to clean out all the old paint cans stored on the shelves. She clicked the remote on her key chain and reached for the door of her white Camry. A vice-like grip seized her wrist. She gasped and looked up to see an ugly man in a dark blue windbreaker with a black Rockies cap pulled down to eyelevel.

Chapter 7

"Where's the signet ring?" the ugly man holding her wrist growled.

"W—what signet ring?" Millicent stammered, fear hammering her as visions of being abducted or killed in her garage flashed through her mind.

"You know the one. I want it."

Millicent gasped but tried to compose herself. "I'd be happy to part with one if I had it, but I don't."

"Your husband's signet ring."

"He didn't wear one either."

"He has one somewhere, and I want it now." The man's gloved hand squeezed Millicent's wrist so hard she let out a cry. He continued to apply pressure. "I can snap your wrist if you don't give me that ring."

Tears filled Millicent's eyes from the pain and frustration of being helpless.

Suddenly she heard the sound of a car entering the driveway. The man looked wildly around, dropped Millicent's wrist, and whispered menacingly. "You find that ring for me or else." Then he ran across the lawn, hopped the fence and disappeared through the neighbor's yard.

A car door opened, then closed, footsteps approached, and Detective Buchanan materialized.

"Thank heaven you're here." She rubbed her wrist. "A man grabbed my arm and threatened me."

"Where'd he go?"

She pointed to the fence. "He ran through there, but he's gone now."

"Climb in my car, and we'll check out the neighborhood."

Once they were both in, Buchanan jammed his foot on the gas pedal as the car swerved in reverse along the driveway. He put the car in drive and accelerated down the block with the tires squealing.

Millicent's head slammed back against the headrest. She slipped to the side as they slid around the corner.

Buchanan tore down Darley. He braked into a right turn on Drexel. Circling the block, they could find no evidence of the intruder. After ten minutes of fruitless searching, they returned to Millicent's house.

"That man tried to hurt me."

Buchanan took her hand, inspected her wrist and whistled. "A nasty bruise."

"He was very strong. He must lift weights."

"Give me a complete description."

"Approximately five foot ten, stocky, dark menacing eyes, clean-shaven and a gold left earring."

"And what did he say to you?"

"He demanded a signet ring."

"A signet ring?"

Millicent rubbed her wrist. "Yes. It made no sense. I don't have one. Then he alluded to my husband's ring. George only wore a wedding band, no signet ring."

"Might that be something that your husband kept somewhere?"

"I've found no such object."

"Let's take another look around the house," Buchanan said.

She led him inside, and they went into the bedroom.

"George had this small container of jewelry." She pointed to an enamel box on the dresser. "It only contains two pairs of cuff links and an old tie tack."

Buchanan opened the container and verified the contents. "Any safe or other storage area?"

"No. I haven't had a chance yet to check the lock box at the bank, but other than that George only had a locked file cabinet in his den. I went through everything in his home office this morning and found no signet ring."

"Let me take another look."

Millicent retrieved the key from her purse, they entered the den, and she unlocked the file cabinet.

Buchanan leafed through the manila folders, inspected the stamp paraphernalia and relocked the cabinet.

"Now the reason for my visit, Mrs. Hargrove. I have a few more questions to ask you."

Millicent let out a resigned sigh. "I understand. I suppose this will continue for some time. Let's go sit down. Can I get you a cup of coffee?"

"No, ma'am."

They proceeded into the living room, and Millicent dropped onto the couch while Buchanan selected a chair facing her.

"In addition to this man threatening you today, has anyone else said or done anything to raise your suspicion?"

Then she remembered the conversation with the strange government man. "One other man inquired about a signet ring that George supposedly had." She recounted the incident at the funeral.

"And the man who approached you at the funeral gave no identification?"

Millicent shook her head. "And I was in such a state at that time that I didn't think to even ask his name. He did give me a card with an address to send the ring to if found." She reached in her purse and pulled it out. "Here. It's pretty cryptic."

He took the card, holding it on its edges. "I need to keep this for evidence."

"That's fine but I'd like to write down the address for future reference."

"I'll do that for you." Buchanan wrote the address down on his notepad, tore off the top sheet and handed it to Millicent. "I also want you to notify me immediately if you locate the signet ring."

Millicent shrugged. "If I find it."

Buchanan stared at her intently. "Now another thing. A neighbor of yours reported an argument between you and your husband the night he was murdered, and we found some of his blood on your pants."

Chapter 8

Millicent breathed deeply to compose herself after the latest accusations from Buchanan. "Yes, Detective, both of those topics have logical explanations. George and I did have a brief spat as I left the house to go play bridge. It wasn't a big deal. I only wanted him to clean up his den, and he told me to leave it alone. This was a recurring theme but nothing serious."

"Still, a neighbor reported the altercation," Buchanan said.

"I'm sure Mrs. Jensen overheard our argument. She keeps tabs on all the neighbors. I'm sure she can relate many heated exchanges from the Hendersons on the other side of her house as well."

Buchanan actually cracked a smile. "Yes, she did."

"There was nothing unusual in our little debate. If she had watched as well as listened in, she would have reported that our argument ended with a kiss before I left the back porch."

He regarded her with an unchanged expression. "How do you account for the blood on your pants?"

"George suffered a cut earlier that evening. I put a Band-Aid on his finger, and in the process a drop of blood fell on my pants. I'm sure your medical technicians noticed the Band-Aid on his left index finger. Afterwards, I wiped up as best I could. If I had been involved with more than that, there would have been signs of significant amounts of blood on my pants, not the miniscule amount your people found."

Buchanan smiled. "That all makes sense, Mrs. Hargrove."

"Good. Do you have any other questions?"

Buchanan put his notepad into his coat pocket. "That's it for now." He stood to leave and then commented, "Your house sure looks neat and orderly, Mrs. Hargrove."

"Why thank you, Detective. It's something I take pride in."

*****

Later that afternoon following a quick stop at Safeway, Millicent waited for Angie Redstone, the Realtor Katherine had recommended. When Angie arrived she blew into the house like a tropical hurricane. "Darling, I love what you've done with this place." She grabbed Millicent's shoulders and air kissed both sides of her face, released her and twirled around the room with her arms outstretched. "Lovely, lovely. We'll sell this in no time at all."

Millicent felt dizzy watching the whirling dervish.

Unfazed, Angie sniffed loudly. "Ah, you know the first secret of selling a house. Cookies baking."

Millicent smiled. "Yes. We must have a warm family environment for prospective buyers."

Angie grabbed Millicent's arm and dragged her toward the hall. "Now the cook's tour. Show me the rest of your wonderful house."

After Angie had stuck her head in every nook and cranny, they returned to the living room.

"Do you have recommendations for things I should change for the open house?"

"Darling, don't change a thing. You have this place in perfect condition. Bake your cookies Saturday morning, and we'll be set for the weekend. I wish my other clients had organized their homes this nicely." Angie put a finger to her cheek. "That's an idea. Would you like a job consulting with some of my messier home sellers on how to fix up their houses?"

Millicent's eyes widened. "I've never thought of doing that."

Angie patted her arm. "Well, consider it. Your sense of color, space and organization is a valuable commodity for someone selling a home. For a few hours of work you could increase the resale value of a cluttered home by thousands of dollars. Now I have to run. I'll meet you back here at eight on Saturday morning."

Before Millicent realized what had hit her, the whirlwind swirled out the door.

Millicent sank into her couch and gulped back tears. She couldn't rid her mind of the image of George dying here. She did need to move.

*****

That night Millicent again stayed at Katherine's. They had dinner together and Millicent excused herself early to get a good night's sleep. Unfortunately, as soon as she lay down on the bed in Katherine's guest bedroom, the tragedies of late fell in on her. She began to cry. She missed George. He had died in such an awful and violent fashion. She wanted things to be like they were before. Now he was gone, and she was alone. Finally, she cried herself out. As the images of the day gave way to semi-consciousness, she recalled that George would want her to pull herself together.

*****

On Saturday morning, Millicent put the cookies in the oven at seven and had the kitchen cleaned and ready by seven-forty-five.

Angie stormed in at precisely eight with a young couple and two children in tow. "Darlings, you're going to love this house. Four bedrooms like you need, three full baths, a basement for the kids to play in. Look at how spacious it is."

Millicent knew she should skedaddle, but she hung around in the background to listen to what the prospective buyers had to say.

"Henry, look at the living room," the young woman said. "Every other house we've been to, we'd have to repaint and add new curtains. We wouldn't have to change anything here."

"If you say so," the dazed husband replied.

The little girl, probably eight, went over and picked up a blue vase.

"Janet, put that back!" the mom shouted.

Janet dropped the vase and the water spilled out on the end table. "Oops."

Millicent grabbed a dish towel and raced into the living room to mop up the water. "No harm done," she said. "Only water."

In the meantime the little boy, probably no older than six, had gone into the hall and began kicking the metal baseboard covering the hot water heating pipe, making a clanging sound.

"Ralph, you stop that this minute!" the mother screamed.

Ralph smiled and kept kicking.

"Henry, take the kids outside while I finish looking around."

The husband seemed perfectly happy to drag the two monsters outside while the wife continued the tour.

Millicent followed safely at a distance and overheard "oohs" and "ahs" from the woman as she inspected each of the rooms. "Henry will love this den."

At the door the woman shook Angie's hand, and Millicent heard her say, "This is the best one we've found so far. I love how it's been organized."

Chapter 9

The house sold within three days, actually eliciting a bidding war between the couple with the two obnoxious kids and two other families. Millicent felt relieved when one of the calmer families won the bid so she wouldn't have nightmares of her house being torn to shreds. She would have a nice nest egg to put aside for any future emergencies.

Now began the process to fully clear out the house. Her bridge group offered to help, but Millicent politely declined, preferring to do it at her own pace the way she wanted with no well-meaning but interfering hands. She called Western Disposal to order a temporary dumpster delivered to her house. Then she sat down to plan out what she needed to do. First, she would group her possessions into categories; this would include things to keep for herself in her condo, to give to her kids, to set aside for a garage sale, to donate and to pitch. She selected items for her new condo and stored these in one bedroom. She decided to keep a minimum of furniture, only the best lamps, a few mementos and needed kitchen implements. She put sticky notes on the furniture items she would move to her condo. She carted the manageable sale items to the garage and packed up a number of boxes to send off to the kids.

When the dumpster arrived, she asked to have it put in front of the house.

"We can't do that, ma'am," the driver informed her. "City regulations state that it can only go in your driveway."

"I hadn't thought of that. Give me a minute to move my car." She parked in front, and then the trash service truck pushed the dumpster into her driveway.

Next, she began lugging disposal items out to the dumpster. She realized the advantage of having organized her house ahead of time. If she had kept all the clutter from over forty years of marriage, this would have been an impossible task.

Once again, the largest struggle became deciding what to do with the items in George's office. She steeled herself, realizing the sooner she got through this difficult task, the sooner she could be in a new residence. Still, tears flowed as she entered George's office. After two false starts, she wiped her eyes with a tissue and plunged in.

She decided to keep the computer but not the desk. Fortunately, she had already sorted out all the books, so the remaining unknown was what to do with the contents of the file cabinet. She decided to keep the tax records from the last seven years and the bills from the last year. The rest she set aside to be shredded. Most of George's personal files she reviewed to make sure they contained no financial information and then threw them in the dumpster.

But what to do with the drawer full of strange reports on Asia? Would some library want the information? Whatever George's mysterious government job had been, he had left no instructions to do anything with these reports, so she threw them away.

She needed assistance to move things to her condo and to stash some of the heavy furniture out in her garage for the sale. At her Tuesday night bridge game she inquired of her friends, "Do any of you know of a good moving service?"

"Two hearts and no," Katherine replied.

"Can't think of any," Allison said. "Two spades."

"Three hearts," Diane put in. "I know of one. A young man who helped Pete when he moved his office. Name of Ned Younger. You can check the Internet under Younger and Company."

"Thanks, Diane. I'll give him a call in the morning. Three spades."

After completing the hand, Diane served chocolate mousse.

"This looks better than my rhubarb pie," Katherine said, "but even taking one bite, I'd be in a heap of trouble. If I'm going to catch me a man again, I have to stay trim. And, Millicent, whether you like it or not, you now have the same predicament—stayin' attractive to other men now that George is gone."

Millicent gulped at the reminder of George dying. "That's the farthest thing from my mind right now."

Katherine shook her head. "No, you'll start payin' attention to some of those passin' britches now that George isn't around. Mark my word, within a month you'll be on the prowl for a boyfriend."

Millicent frowned. "I'm looking for moving assistance not a man."

"Give her some time, Katherine," Diane added.

"That's right," Allison said. "She's not thinking about men right now."

"I reckon that attitude will change," Katherine said. "Just wait."

*****

The next morning, Millicent located the number and called to set up an appointment for Ned Younger to stop by her house in the afternoon.

When he arrived, instead of the image she had expected of a slovenly moving guy, she was pleasantly surprised to find a handsome man in his mid-thirties, clean-shaven with a friendly smile. If her daughter weren't already married, this was a man she would consider setting up with Karen.

"Mrs. Hargrove, it's a pleasure to meet you," he reached out a scrubbed hand complete with trimmed fingernails. "I'm Ned."

She smiled. "You can call me Millicent. I have all the things I need moved in this one bedroom plus the furniture with sticky notes in the rest of the house."

"That will be easy. And all that stuff I saw in the garage and the other furniture?"

"I'm holding a garage sale this coming weekend. Whatever doesn't sell will go to Goodwill."

A grin came to his face. "Would you give me first crack at anything here?"

"Sure. Check it over and pick out what you want. I'll also need your assistance to move the remaining furniture into the garage and to carry heavy things like the mattresses into the dumpster."

Ned gave her a reasonable estimate. They agreed on the move for Friday, and Ned and Millicent ambled through the house and garage for Ned to peruse the things to be sold.

"I'd like to buy that," Ned pointed to George's desk.

"Make an offer and it's yours."

"I'll give you fifty dollars."

George had paid five hundred dollars for that desk, but she was happy to see it go to a nice person. "It's yours."

"Great. I'll pick it up on Friday when we do the move."

*****

On Friday morning, Millicent surveyed what she had accomplished. Again, she was glad she had the house so well-organized ahead of time or she never would have completed preparations for a move in a week. Then she assembled the final box of knickknacks she wanted to keep. She limited herself to several vases for flowers, a small Kachina doll and a mother-of-pearl fish that George had given her on their honeymoon in Acapulco forty-five years earlier. She looked at it, remembering the wonderful week on the beach, watching the cliff divers and eating delicious meals. She let out an audible sigh. She missed George.

As she picked it up, she had a thought. Did this souvenir have anything to do with George's cryptic message of "fish?" She examined it carefully but saw nothing that would be a further clue. Still, she would keep this in her condo.

Ned and another young man appeared and loaded all of Millicent's move items into their truck. Then under her direction, they carried the remaining furniture into the garage and the discarded mattresses into the dumpster. After calling to have the dumpster picked up that afternoon, she drove to the condo and waited as the movers schlepped things to the locations she indicated. They left her the boxes to unpack.

"That move was relatively painless," Millicent remarked.

"You made it easy," Ned replied. "You should see some of the things people put us through."

"Oh, such as?"

"Last week we had a woman who insisted that someone remain in the truck holding her prized lamp as we drove between Longmont and Boulder."

"Why didn't she take it herself?"

"That would have been too logical." Ned chuckled. "She told me her husband's company would pay for everything, so she didn't want to move anything herself. But she insisted on extra care for that one lamp. I told her we'd be happy to accommodate her request but it would add a hundred bucks to the charge. She spent half an hour haggling on that one extra charge until we agreed on seventy dollars. That after she raised no objections to the total move charge of over three thousand dollars. What a world."

"I suppose you meet all kinds in this business."

Ned's eyes sparkled. "The full spectrum. You're the type of client I enjoy working with. You know what you want, you're well-organized, and you make sense."

"Thank you. I worked for many years as a research administrator at the Boulder Medical Center. I, like you, encountered many interesting characters. I feel it's important to deal with people in a straight-forward and honest way. Everyone benefits."

"If others operated that way, this country would be much more efficient, and people would enjoy their jobs more." Ned gave a devilish smile. "Although, the weird ones have some entertainment value."

"I'm glad you're not putting me in the weird category."

"No, ma'am." He handed her the bill for the move less fifty dollars for the desk.

*****

By Friday evening, Millicent had her condo in some semblance of order. She left several unopened boxes in the second bedroom. She would get to those items next week. She organized her kitchen, living room and main bedroom to her satisfaction and then called it a day, since she would have to get up early for the garage sale the next morning.

*****

Saturday at six, Millicent drove through her old neighborhood placing garage sale signs on telephone and stop sign poles. Then she returned to her old house for the sale. She set up a bridge table with a cash box and moved some of the items out onto the driveway. She had put price tags on everything and labeled a cardboard box with a sign that indicated any book inside could be purchased for twenty-five cents or five for a dollar.

Those who attend garage sales on a regular basis arrived early and rummaged through the books, electronic equipment and CDs. By eight, the official starting time, she had cleared out a fourth of her items and already made over two hundred dollars.

At ten minutes after eight, Katherine arrived, having agreed to help, carrying two cups of Starbucks coffee in her hands. "Sweetie, I knew you'd need some caffeine by this time."

Millicent took a big swig, thankful to have such a thoughtful friend.

Families and neighbors arrived to peruse, sort through, debate over, select and ultimately purchase the key finds. One little girl spent more than an hour looking through some miniature animals that Millicent had decided she had no space for in the condo. The girl narrowed it down to a Dalmatian dog, a Persian cat and a brown horse and finally chose the horse. She excitedly dug a quarter from the pockets of her jeans and skipped down the driveway with her treasure in her hand.

Mid-morning when the rush of visitors thinned out, Millicent and

41

Katherine stepped into the garage to rearrange some of the items on a bench. As they worked, a half dozen more people arrived and began looking through items in the garage.

"What did you do with George's stamp collection?" Katherine asked.

"I gave it to my son and he took it back to Indianapolis. He and my grandson can continue collecting."

Millicent stood up and noticed two men right behind her, almost as if they had been eavesdropping. They immediately turned the other direction and started looking through a rack of George's clothes. They seemed out of place, wearing dark slacks amid the other people in jeans and shorts on this warm spring day.

Stepping over to them, she asked, "Is there something I can help you with?"

"Just checking out the suits," one man muttered.

"You have any desks?" the other man asked.

"No. None for sale."

He scowled.

A little boy tugged on her pants.

Millicent looked down to see he was holding a Curious George book. She had kept it for her grandkids, but they had now outgrown picture books.

"I want this book," the boy said.

"That's a good one. You'll enjoy it."

He beamed as he handed her a quarter.

When she looked back, the two men were gone.

*****

In the afternoon they experienced another flurry of activity. While things remained particularly chaotic, Millicent stood next to the cash box and took payments so Katherine could help people find what they needed. As she received money from a line of people, she saw Katherine talking to a tall, thin man in a dark sweat suit. He looked familiar, but she didn't have time to pay much attention as an impatient woman thrust a ten dollar bill in front of her to purchase a vase and get change.

When all the waiting customers had been helped, it finally struck Millicent who the skinny man was. She had seen him at George's funeral. She rose from the table to try to find him, but apparently he had left.

She approached Katherine. "Who was that tall, rail-thin man you were talking to?"

"He didn't give his name."

"Did he say why he came here?"

"Sugar, he asked if you had any stamps to sell."

Millicent furled her brow. "And what did you tell him?"

"That the stamps had gone to your son in Indianapolis."

Chapter 10

On Sunday night after the weekend garage sale, the weight of all that had happened fell in on Millicent again. Seeing her possessions of forty years disappear into the hands of strangers had been hard, but she enjoyed watching people find their own special gems, and she had made a few dollars on items that would otherwise be given away. Goodwill would be sending a truck on Monday to pick up everything left from the garage sale.

She felt a pain in her chest not from overdoing but from the loss of George. He had been her companion, confidante, friend, lover and general listener-to-complaints for all those years, and he was gone.

Pushing away a tear, she noticed the three family memory albums she had stacked in her bedroom. She wandered over and picked up one. She had assembled these for her two kids and herself two years ago. In one of her organizing moods, she had pulled out all the boxes of family pictures, old mementos from her and George's parents and assembled the albums. She scanned a picture of Karen as a baby, a trip with both kids to Disneyland, a vacation in Hawaii, Jerry parasailing behind a boat in Florida, a ration card from World War II and her parents' marriage certificate. She wiped another tear away. She'd send Jerry and Karen their albums and place her own on the bookshelf. Right now she held it to her breast. She missed George.

*****

The sunlight on Monday morning streaming through the opening between

44

the bedroom curtains of her new condo revived Millicent. She couldn't wallow in her misery. She had to get organized. After a cup of coffee and some scrambled eggs, she felt re-energized and turned into a whirling maniac, unpacking the remaining boxes and finding the appropriate location for each of her prized possessions. She did another round of culling, filling another container of items that she would drop off for Goodwill. She shook her head in displeasure. She should have eliminated these things before and not had Ned move them. Oh, well, live and learn. She was now extremely well-acquainted with the large Goodwill bin in the supermarket parking lot.

Next, she organized her closet, putting her shoes in the vertical shoe rack she had moved from her house. Then she organized all her clothes by type, season and color. Satisfied that she would be able to quickly find anything at a moment's notice, she went on to double-check all the drawers in her dresser. Finally, she unpacked cleaning materials which she distributed to the bathroom, kitchen and small laundry room.

Her errands that day included mailing the two albums to her kids, the stop at the Goodwill bin and a trip to the store to buy groceries and flowers. She had invited the girls over for a condo-warming bridge game the following evening. The afternoon flew by with the final redecorating of the living room, and she added a final touch by cutting and arranging the flowers.

*****

On Tuesday, she finished a final round of rearranging her condo, set up the bridge table and chairs, prepared the snacks and gave the place one last swipe with her cleaning cloth. Satisfied that everything appeared in immaculate order, she fixed herself a light meal of a Cobb salad and fruit plate, washed and dried the dishes and adjourned to the living room to read the latest Carolyn Hart mystery while waiting for her guests.

Katherine Pepper arrived first. "Looky here what you did with this place. If this don't beat all."

Millicent could feel the heat of a blush. "Thank you."

On Katherine's heels, Diane Cooney dashed in. "Wow, Millicent. Terrific digs."

They all went into the dining area to help themselves to snacks and drinks while waiting for Allison Petrov—always the last to arrive. Ten minutes late she rushed through the door. "Sorry. I had a last minute phone call from my Realtor."

"Realtor?" Katherine gave a start of surprise.

"Why yes. I've decided to follow Millicent's lead and sell my house and move into a condo."

"That will leave me as the last holdout with a house," Diane said.

"You're also the last one with a husband," Allison replied. "He helps keep the place up. I'm tired of taking care of a four-bedroom house when it's only me. To say nothing of the yard. At one time I liked puttering around with daffodils and irises, but that day is long gone. I don't enjoy the gardening that much any more."

"Same for me," Millicent said. "I no longer wanted to bother with the house and garden. And besides, I needed a place without all the reminders. It was time for me to move on."

"What you've done with this new place in such a short time!" Allison gushed as she circled the living room. "It's marvelous. Simply marvelous. I should hire you to help me organize for my move."

"That's a terrific idea," Diane said. "Millicent, you could start your own business. All kinds of people would hire you to organize their stuff."

"Goodness gracious, Millicent, you're the world's best organizer," Katherine chimed in.

Millicent gave a dismissive wave of her hand. "Posh. I merely like to make things look neat."

"That's exactly why you should start a personal organizing service," Katherine replied. "You have a needed skill and enjoy doing it . . . make some money from people who are all catawampus . . . and have a new focus now that . . . uh . . . George won't be around."

Millicent felt as if the blood drained from her face at the reminder.

"It's settled," Allison said, paying no attention to Millicent's reaction. "I'm hiring you to help me organize my house to sell and my new condo when I move in. I don't want to hear any argument, Millicent. I'm your first customer."

"And, hon, you can find plenty more," Katherine said. "Think of all the women our age who have to move into smaller places. The men disappear chasing young fillies or kick the bucket before we do, so we're left with big houses. I bet if you put up a flyer at the senior centers, people'd beat a path to your door."

"I go to a networking meeting once a month," Diane said. "People attend to offer various services to seniors throughout Boulder County. I'm there to make people aware of the financial planning services I provide. You'll have to come with me to the next meeting and pitch your personal organizing service."

"But I don't have a personal organizing service," Millicent said.

"Yes, you do," Allison replied. "I've already hired you. Now you need to put your organization skills to work at getting the business going. You'll have it rolling in no time. No more arguments. It's all decided."

"Don't you think that's my decision?" Millicent said, crossing her arms.

Her three friends descended on her for a group hug. "Of course it is, dear," Katherine replied. "And we've helped you make the decision."

Chapter 11

In spite of her protests, upon reflection, Millicent did think starting a personal organizing business made sense. As she drove home, the thought of helping people eliminate clutter appealed to her, and she did need something to take her mind off her loss. She couldn't mope around her new condo now that she had completed the move and unpacked. So if she started this business, what should she call it? Millicent tapped her fingers on the steering wheel as she looked at the tail lights ahead. Millicent's Personal Organizing? She stuck out her tongue. Too blah. Organize Your Things? Yuck.

What would she really do for people? She would help them organize and solve a major problem that most people faced. Just what she had been through. Too much stuff. Stuff that needed to be grouped, reduced and reallocated. Stuff, huh? What about Clean Up Your Stuff? She wrinkled her nose. That didn't have the right ring either. Then it struck her. She had the perfect name.

*****

Over the next two days, Millicent became like a tornado on steroids. She organized her spare bedroom into an office and cleared the table to be her work area. Then she logged into the home computer she had shared with George using the password of "stamp&bridge," and with software he had showed her how to use, designed a logo, business card, stationery and promotional flyer. Then she went to a printing service and had her business materials professionally produced. Finally, she called Allison and set up an appointment to begin organizing her house in preparation for selling it.

*****

When Millicent arrived at Allison's, she snapped out a business card.

Allison eyed it and chuckled. "Great name for your business. *Unstuff Your Stuff.* That says it all."

"Since you agreed to be my guinea pig, let's get started."

Allison led Millicent into the living room. "Okay, what's first?"

"Stand here with me for a moment." Millicent closed her eyes. She pictured in her mind organized space, a blend of harmonious colors, calmness and light. She took a deep breath and opened her eyes. The pile of magazines on a footstool broke the harmony. The mixture of grandkid pictures, a Greek urn and a pot with a wilted fern on the mantle above a dirty fireplace caused her to flinch. A shelf with a haphazard mix of CDs and falling books made her gasp. "We'll start in here. First a question. Do you want to hold a garage sale for unwanted items or give them away?"

"I don't want to bother with a sale. I'll donate everything to a worthy cause."

Millicent nodded her head. "Do you want to give anything to your kids?"

"Probably a few items."

"And how large a condo do you plan to buy?"

"Similar to what you just moved into. A place with a living room, dining area, two bedrooms and two bathrooms. I've given my Realtor those requirements."

"Good. Now do you have some cardboard boxes and garbage bags?"

Allison chuckled. "Boxes line one whole side of my garage. You can take your pick. Also you'll find several containers of black lawn bags just inside the garage on the left side."

They retrieved half a dozen boxes along with the trash bags and began the work.

"We'll go through everything in your living room first. The objective will be to group things by category, reduce what you have and then reorganize in your new place."

"I like that," Allison said. "You already have a mantra: group, reduce and reorganize. GRR."

Millicent smiled. "I hadn't thought of it that way."

"Yeah, like that advertisement with the dog. Take a bite out of grime. GRR."

Millicent laughed in spite of herself. "You can be my PR person. But back to the task at hand—the things to be eliminated. You can decide if they go to your kids or the pitch pile. We want this room to look neat, attractive and contain the items you want in your new place, nothing more."

Allison grimaced. "You're going to make me throw away a lot, I can tell."

Millicent put her hand on her friend's arm. "It won't be so bad once we get going. Think of it as peeling away the outside layer of rock to reveal a beautiful geode inside."

Within three hours, they had filled up six trash bags, five boxes of junk to give away, a box for each of her three kids and a recycle bin full of old magazines.

"We'll stage everything and then arrange for one of the services to pick up your donations," Millicent explained.

After moving all the garbage bags, boxes, two chairs and an end table into the garage, they returned to the living room. "What do you think?" Millicent asked.

Allison looked around with wide-eyed excitement. "The room seems twice as large. You've eliminated all the clutter. This looks like a place someone would want to buy."

"Exactly. It now has a comfortable, spacious, livable look to it. Ready for the dining room?"

Over the next two days, they completed the living room, den and guest bedroom before agreeing to resume the following morning with the kitchen.

They headed out into the garage to admire the collection of material stowed there. Suddenly, Millicent realized the mistake she had made. "Oh, dear. I didn't label anything. I can't tell what I set aside for donation and what to throw away."

Allison smacked her hands together. "Let's get with it, girl. You're the professional here."

Millicent's cheeks turned warm. "Yes, I guess I made a mistake."

Allison gave her a hug. "Live and learn, dear. Live and learn."

"Give me some masking tape and a black marker and I'll fix it all up," Millicent said.

When Allison returned with the requested material, Millicent spent half an hour opening bags and boxes, writing "Donation," "Trash," or "Kids" on the boxes or strips of tape which she then stuck to the bags. With that fixed, she made a mental note to always have a good system for grouping the stuff for disposition.

As Millicent drove back to her condo, she felt satisfied with the day's work. She could do this, and it certainly provided a needed service for Allison. She heard a horn honk and looked in her rearview mirror. She noticed someone in a parked Jeep waving to another person on the sidewalk. Behind her she spotted a gray BMW as she continued on her way and pulled into the Safeway parking lot on Arapahoe to buy some fresh fruit and vegetables for her dinner and to last her over the weekend. Afterwards as she exited the parking lot, she noticed the gray BMW behind her again. Was someone following her?

Rather than going right back to her condo, Millicent turned north on 28th Street and headed toward Target. She had nothing in mind to purchase but wanted to see if the gray BMW followed her. It did.

She parked and entered the store, watching to see if anyone got out of the BMW. No one did. A wave of shivers ran through her body. Inside the store she removed her smart phone and a slip of paper with Detective Buchanan's phone number from her purse.

He answered on the third ring.

"Detective, this is Millicent Hargrove. Someone's following me."

"Where are you right now?"

"I'm inside the door at Target. The car that's been tailing me is parked in the lot outside."

"Stay inside and don't go near that car."

She shivered. "Don't worry."

"Did you notice the license plate number?"

"I tried but it was covered with mud."

"I'll have someone there within ten minutes. When a patrol car pulls up in front, go outside to meet the officer and point out the car that's been following you."

Millicent looked at her watch and counted off the minutes. In exactly nine minutes and forty-five seconds a black and white police car came to a stop in front of the store.

Thank goodness, she said to herself. She exited the store and approached a young, husky man in uniform who had stepped out of the car. "Are you Mrs. Hargrove?" he asked.

Her eyes riveted on him. "Yes, I called Detective Buchanan."

"Please point out the car that followed you."

She turned back toward the parking lot. In the time she had focused on the police officer, the gray BMW had disappeared.

Chapter 12

"I'm so sorry for the false alarm and that you had to make an unnecessary trip here," Millicent apologized.

He smiled. "No problem, ma'am. Your safety is our primary concern."

She returned to her car and resumed the drive home, checking in her rearview mirror every block to assure that no gray BMW reappeared. She pulled into the garage at the condo and watched as the gate closed behind her, thankful that she lived in a restricted access facility. She unloaded her groceries and took the elevator up to her condo. Once inside she locked the door. She would have to be vigilant.

*****

The next day when returning to Allison's house, Millicent saw no gray BMW behind her. Hopefully, whoever it was had given up. Pushing aside the thought of a stranger stalking her, she jumped into the task of unstuffing Allison's stuff.

The kitchen proved a problem. Allison had enough cooking paraphernalia for a five star chef. Not only that, Millicent realized, but it would be like trying to pry a piece of candy away from a two-year-old.

"You never know when something special will be needed," Allison complained.

"Well, you can't take all this stuff with you. Remember what we discussed yesterday. Just the essentials."

Allison gave an expansive wave of her hand. "But everything here is essential."

Millicent clicked her tongue. "Allison, work with me here. You're going to have to reduce things. You'll have a smaller kitchen and can't keep all this stuff."

Allison let out a strained breath. "Okay, okay."

"First of all, you have two crock pots."

"One's for small meals and the other's for when I have company. Crock pots are essential for my cooking."

Millicent put her hands on her hips. "Choose one."

"You're right. The small one will suffice."

"Good. Now you have three frying pans, nearly the same size. One will do."

Through this process they filled another five boxes with the excess. Allison looked like she had just lost her best friend.

"No one will cherish my cooking implements as much as I do," Allison said with a pout.

"That may be the case, but you don't need all these things cluttering up your new kitchen. You still have everything necessary for making your fine meals."

Afterwards Millicent held one cupboard open for inspection. "You'll find everything visible and grouped by type. Even before you move, you'll be able to find things more easily. This will be a breeze to pack up for your move and will serve you well in your new condo."

Allison examined each cupboard and drawer. "Thanks, Millicent. I guess I've been too hung up on keeping things."

"That happens. You get used to having all the stuff, but you have a much more manageable kitchen now. Tomorrow we'll do the master bedroom."

*****

The bedroom provided another challenge. It became apparent to Millicent that Allison didn't want to rid herself of many clothes. Finally, smacking her lips in exasperation, she said, "Okay let's try this. Pull out all the outfits you haven't worn in the last year and put them on the bed."

Half the items on hangers moved to the bed.

"Pick two items out of these that you'd like to keep."

Allison sorted through and after hemming and hawing selected a sequined dress and a semi-formal skirt, blouse and jacket.

"All the rest go."

Allison looked at Millicent with large doe eyes. "All?"

"Go look in your closet and see the choices you still have."

Allison peered inside, and her shoulders slumped. "You're right. I have plenty of clothes left."

"Now on to the shoes."

With much arguing and cajoling, Millicent winnowed the shoes by half. The bookshelf and bedside tables proved an easier task and by mid-afternoon, a mound of donation material filled the garage.

"Now all that remains is the basement," Millicent said.

"That'll be easy," Allison said. "I got rid of pretty much everything down there after my divorce."

"Let's take a look."

Allison was right, Millicent realized upon looking around the basement. The place appeared eerily empty except for a dozen boxes stacked in one corner. "And all that?"

"That's my daughter's stuffed animal collection. I'll call her to see if she wants me to send them. If not, I'll donate everything."

They performed a walk-through of the house. "Notice how uncluttered all your rooms appear now?"

"Yes, I don't know how I let so much accumulate."

"It happens because we don't take the time to purge along the way. You're now in excellent shape to sell your house. We'll do another pass after you buy your condo and this place sells. At that time we'll know exactly how much space you'll have and what else will need to go."

Allison wrinkled her brow. "More to go after all of this?"

"Yes. You still have way too much stuff to fit into a two bedroom condo. But you have a very attractive house that should sell quickly. I also learned when I moved that I could save some time and expense by reducing to the bare minimum before the move. No sense moving stuff and then having to throw it away on the other end."

*****

On Wednesday, Millicent joined Diane for a morning meeting of the senior networking group. She pulled into the parking lot of the Actium Retirement Home. Inside, a meeting room had been set up with folding chairs, and a long table held fruit, sweet rolls, coffee and juice.

She exchanged business cards with a man who provided reverse mortgages, a woman who handled marketing for an assisted living facility in nearby Louisville and a woman who delivered a registered nurse service for traveling seniors. The meeting started with the moderator having all the people in the room introduce themselves. When Millicent's turn came, she stood and cleared her throat. "I'm Millicent Hargrove, and this is my first time here."

"Welcome, Millicent," a large woman on the other side of the room boomed out.

"Thank you. I've started a personal organizing business called 'Unstuff Your Stuff.' " This produced friendly chuckles. She handed a stack of her business cards to the person seated next to her. "I'll send around my business card, and I'd appreciate it if you'd pass anyone my way who needs assistance in organizing their home or apartment. In particular I can help people who need to downsize and move to a smaller residence."

The moderator jumped in. "For any of you new like Millicent, be sure to give your cards to Sandy over there. Sandy, wave your hand."

A stylishly dressed young woman in her twenties raised a hand.

"Sandy keeps the master list of people here. Once a month she emails the list out to everyone. It's a good way to keep in touch with others and you can send email notifications to the rest of the people in the group or contact someone to give a direct referral. With our objective to network among people providing services to seniors in the Boulder County area, we encourage helping each other."

After all the introductions, a woman in neat business attire announced an upcoming fundraiser for a seventy-eight-year-old woman who had been left homeless after a wildfire ravaged her home. Then the meeting closed with an invitation to the next meeting in a month at the west senior center in Boulder.

Millicent hung around, and Diane introduced her to a number of people. One woman, Rachel Kennedy, said she assisted elderly clients with legal issues when called in by social services. She had one client who had a messy home that needed attention and would recommend Millicent to help her organize. She gave Millicent a card and told her to call her that afternoon to set up an appointment.

Millicent left the meeting pleased at the friendly reception she had received and with one new prospect in the works.

Driving home, she passed a store that had a sign in the window advertising a special for cutlery. Her stomach sank at the lingering image of the knife in George's chest. She clenched the steering wheel. She needed to do something to find out more about what led to his untimely death but had no idea how to do so. She hoped that Detective Buchanan was making some progress in the investigation.

And the man who had grabbed her wrist in her garage. She ventured a look in her rearview mirror. At least no one seemed to be following her.

Chapter 13

Waiting to assure that she called after any extended lunch time, Millicent reached Rachel Kennedy at exactly one-thirty.

"I'm going to be meeting with my client in her home at three today," Rachel said. "Why don't you join me?"

Millicent looked at her watch. She had a few errands to run. "That works for me."

"And come in your work clothes. If my client agrees, you can start helping her this afternoon."

"Okay. I'll be there in my jeans. Give me the address."

So at exactly three, Millicent pulled up in front of the home of Gabriella Hutchinson in the Devil's Thumb residential area. The house needed a fresh coat of paint and the yard had turned into dried weeds. Millicent rang the doorbell and Rachel greeted her. They entered the living room where a woman in her late eighties sat, knitting.

"Welcome to my home," a clear voice said. "I don't move around as well as I used to or I'd offer you some coffee or tea."

"I'm fine," Millicent said. "How long have you lived here?"

"Over forty years. IBM transferred my husband James to Boulder, and we found this lovely house after three days of searching."

Millicent scanned around the living room. Magazines were strewn in the corner, nothing had been dusted recently, the pictures on the wall, all attractive landscapes, hung off kilter. The couch and chairs appeared in good condition although a coffee table had nicks and dings that needed to be touched up.

"Mrs. Hargrove is the woman I mentioned to you who specializes in helping people organize their homes," Rachel said.

"Yes, yes, I remember. Do you think you can assist me?"

Millicent smiled. "Absolutely. When would you like to start?"

"As long as you're here, why not now?"

"Let's walk through the house, and I can give you a bid."

Millicent received the quick tour, seeing that the work would involve the living room, one bedroom, kitchen, bathroom and garage. "All the other rooms in the house seem neatly organized," Millicent noted.

"Yes," Gabriella replied. "I don't use any of those rooms or the basement anymore."

When they returned to the living room, Millicent pulled out the one-page agreement she had put together and filled in the dollar amount with her pen. She handed it to Rachel. "Here's my quote. Since you're advising Mrs. Hutchinson, you might want to look at this and approve it before she signs."

Rachel gave it a cursory read and handed it to Gabriella. "This is fine and a very reasonable charge, I might add."

"Thank you, dear. It's nice to have someone looking after my best interests." Gabriella took the pen that Millicent proffered and signed.

"Now if you'll excuse me, I need to get back to my office," Rachel said. "I'll leave the two of you to start your work."

After Rachel left, Gabriella asked, "Where do we start?"

Millicent sat down. "First, let's discuss what you want to accomplish. This is your home, and I'm here to assist you. It's important for me to understand your wishes. That way we can be in complete agreement before we begin."

Gabriella groaned. "I can't manage my things anymore. There's too much, and I can't keep it organized and clean. I need to eliminate the clutter."

"Exactly. So you're going to have to give yourself permission to get rid of some of your things."

"Oh dear. That will be difficult. After James passed away, I really didn't want to go through everything. I know I've let things accumulate."

"That's why I'm here to help you. We'll be going through a simple process to group, reduce and reorganize. As a friend of mine likes to say it's the GRR process. You probably have presents from people that you no longer need, old mementos that you will be able to part with, duplicates and other items that you will never use again. Let's start right here in the living room. Now this stack of magazines in the corner."

"I've been meaning to get to those but haven't had the energy."

Millicent picked up the top one, a *Good Housekeeping*. She looked at the date. Six months old. "Why don't we eliminate any magazines more than a month old? You can still read the most current ones. Do you have trash bags or empty cardboard boxes?"

"Yes, they're trash bags in the cupboard under the kitchen sink."

"I'll supplement those with some boxes to be assembled that I have in the trunk of my car." Millicent retrieved the necessary material and brought it into the living room. She threw all but two magazines into a trash bag. Next, she tackled a pile of books.

"You have a number of old paperbacks with torn covers," Millicent said. "Any objections to giving these away?"

"I might want to read some of them again."

"You can always check books out of the library. Why not reduce the number of books and keep selected ones that remain in good condition?"

"I guess you're right."

"What do you enjoy reading?"

"Romance and mysteries."

Millicent stepped over and scanned a number of titles. "I notice you have quite a few historical novels and nonfiction books here."

"Those belonged to my husband."

"Will you read any of them?"

She wrinkled her nose. "No. I don't enjoy historical books."

"Then do I have your permission to give those away?"

"Yes."

Within half an hour Millicent had filled up six boxes. "We're making good progress here," Millicent said. "Now this shelf of phonograph records."

"I thought I might play those some day."

"Have you listened to them recently?"

"No, I don't even have a phonograph any more."

"In that case, give yourself permission to get rid of them. Would you like them to go to a relative, do you want to sell them or would you like to donate them to a charity?"

Gabriella concentrated her gaze on the floor. "My family won't be interested in those, and I don't want to hassle with selling them. I guess we can give them away."

Millicent packed them in a box and took a black marker out of her purse to write the word "Donation" on the box. "Good. Now you also have some old eight-track tapes here." As Millicent reached toward the tapes her arm grazed a vase on an end table, knocking it to the floor with a loud crash as it shattered into pieces. Millicent put her hand to her mouth, her face growing hot. "I'm so sorry."

Gabriella gave a surprising giggle. "I think you did me a favor. You've been telling me to eliminate things. My mother-in-law gave me that monstrosity as a present many years ago. I detested it, but always felt I should keep it. Now you've solved my problem."

Millicent let out a sigh of relief. "I promise to be more careful. I'm glad it wasn't an important keepsake."

They spent the next hour going through the living room, purging, sorting and labeling.

When they took a rest break, Millicent reached for her smart phone in her jeans' pocket to call for a donation pickup. It wasn't there. "Darn. Where did my phone go?" She looked over the items in the living room and then trudged out to the garage to check through the bags and boxes stored there. It took her fifteen minutes to go through everything, but she finally discovered her phone between two trash bags in the corner of the garage. Relieved that she had found it, she returned inside, having given up her break.

She called to schedule the donation pickup for Friday afternoon.

"We can't schedule anything else until next week," a polite young woman's voice informed her.

"Darn, I was hoping it could be done this week."

"Sorry. We have quite a backlog, but I'll put you down for next Tuesday afternoon."

Millicent stashed her phone, cursing herself for not anticipating that donation pickups couldn't necessarily be scheduled at a moment's notice. Another lesson in being a good organizer.

Gabriella shuffled out into the garage. "While you're out here, some boxes need to be removed from the rafters up there."

"Let's go take a look." Millicent found a stepladder and placed it beneath a plywood panel laid across the rafters that created a storage space under the roof. Climbing gingerly, she had to stand on the top of the ladder to reach the dusty boxes stored up there. As she extended her arm towards the nearest box, the ladder teetered. "Yikes!" Millicent shouted as the ladder fell away from beneath her feet. She grabbed for the rafter but missed. She found herself hovering in midair before falling. With a thump she landed in the middle of the trash bags full of magazines and newspapers.

Dazed, Millicent checked for any injuries and found that she had survived the fall unscathed.

Gabriella wrung her hands. "Do I need to call an ambulance?"

Millicent stood up and dusted herself off. "No, I'm okay. It's a good thing the trash bags cushioned my landing."

Gabriella smiled. "Another good reason that you insisted I get rid of all of those old things."

"I'm glad the bags weren't full of nails and knives."

Millicent picked up the ladder and positioned it again. This time she stopped short of the red warning on the ladder to not climb higher, watched her balance and managed to remove four boxes from the rafters. She opened them to find old camping equipment.

"I won't need that anymore," Gabriella said.

"We'll add it to the donation pile."

"I'm starting to get tired," Gabriella announced.

"In that case, we'll call it a day. What time would you like me to come back tomorrow?"

"I'm an early riser. We can begin at eight."

As Millicent left, she realized she had grossly underestimated her bid. She had thought they'd be a third of the way through the house already and in reality they had hardly made a dent. It was just as well that the donation pickup wouldn't be until next Tuesday. She'd need until then to finish. Oh well, she admitted to herself. Along with breaking a vase, losing her smart phone and falling off a ladder, all part of the learning process. As her first job with someone other than a friend, some minor glitches were to be expected.

*****

As Millicent started her car, she looked in the rearview mirror to check her hair. She looked like she had been through a tornado. She'd have to tie her hair back tomorrow, especially if attempting to fly from rafters. Then something caught her eye. She saw a gray BMW parked behind her. She squinted. A man sat in that car, watching her. She could see him clearly enough to recognize him. It was one of the men who had been pawing through George's clothes at the garage sale.

Chapter 14

Millicent carefully pulled out her smart phone, glad that it hadn't been lost. She now had Detective Buchanan's number in her directory. He picked up on the third ring.

"Detective, this is Millicent Hargrove. I'm being followed again."

"Where are you?"

"I'm parked on Wildwood in Devil's Thumb."

"Keep your doors locked and stay right there."

She looked in her rearview mirror and saw the man open his door. "I don't think that's a good idea." She started her car and took off.

"Mrs. Hargrove, what's happening?"

"He jumped out of his car, so I drove away."

"Did you get his license plate number?"

"No, the plate is still covered with mud, and I'm not about to go look at the rear plate."

"Is he following you?"

Millicent checked her rearview mirror. "I can't tell yet."

"Drive to the police station, pull into the visitors' lot on the north side, and I'll meet you there."

Every time Millicent came to a stop light, she clutched the steering wheel and craned her neck but didn't see the gray BMW behind her. Letting out a sigh of relief, she finally reached the police department and parked as instructed.

Detective Buchanan came right up to her window. "You still being followed, Mrs. Hargrove?"

"I don't think so. I didn't spot him behind me along the way."

"There's a patrol car out on the street, so let's wait a moment to see if anyone drives by."

With Buchanan standing guard, Millicent drummed her fingers on the steering wheel.

After five minutes when no gray BMW appeared, he said, "Let's go inside to talk." He escorted Millicent into the building and down a corridor, lined with pictures of past police chiefs. He took her to a small cubicle. After they both sat, he took out a notepad. "Describe the man you saw following you."

"Probably close to six feet tall, husky build, Caucasian with black hair."

"And you've seen him before."

"Yes. He and another man showed up at my garage sale."

Buchanan wrote a note on a pad. "And the type of vehicle he drove?"

"A gray BMW, fairly new."

"Any dents or distinguishing marks on the car?"

"Not that I noticed."

"I'll have a police officer stop by your apartment periodically to make sure everything is okay. Also if you see a black Crown Victoria following you, it will be one of our people keeping an eye on you. If you spot the gray BMW again, give me a call."

As Millicent drove home she took some consolation in the fact that Detective Buchanan took her seriously and appeared willing to protect her rather than lock her up.

In her condo, the light was flashing on her answering machine. She listened to a message from Allison and then punched in her number.

"You asked me to call, Allison?"

"Yes, I've decided to bite the bullet and buy a condo."

Millicent smiled at the thought of her friend selling her house and moving. "Where?"

"Actually, in the same complex you're in. After visiting you, I looked into it and found an adorable two bedroom apartment. I've put my earnest money down and expect to have my house sold immediately. You'll soon have to help me with some more organizing."

"I'd be delighted to."

*****

The first thing next morning, Millicent pulled the cords on her curtains and cautiously peeked outside. No gray BMW in sight. Letting out a sigh of relief, she fixed herself pancakes, bacon and coffee before heading off to Gabriella Hutchinson's to help her unclutter her life.

On the whole drive, she kept her eyes glued on the rearview mirror, willing no BMW to be in sight. Once at her destination, she dashed up to the front door, rang the door and ducked inside once Gabriella appeared.

"My living room does look nice after you helped me yesterday," Gabriella said. "I don't feel all cramped and overwhelmed with untidiness."

"That's our goal, and we're just beginning. Today we'll tackle your bedroom and closet."

"Oh dear. I hope you're not going to make me get rid of clothes and shoes."

Millicent chuckled. "That's exactly what we're going to do. Remember, our objective is to have no clutter and mess. Keep giving yourself permission to throw things away. You can feel satisfied that you've worn clothes in the past without having to keep them for the future."

Millicent assembled boxes labeled, "Give to family," "Donate" and "Trash."

"First thing, we're going to take all the clothes out of your closet and place them on the bed. Why don't you sit in that chair while I do that?" Millicent pointed to the one chair in the bedroom and Gabriella plopped down. Millicent proceeded to lug all the clothes on hangers out of the closet.

"Now comes the fun part." Millicent smiled and held up a dress with a wine stain on it. "This can go in the trash."

Gabriella looked up at Millicent with sad puppy dog eyes. "But I wore that to a baby shower for my last grandchild."

"And how long ago was that?"

"Only ten years ago."

"And have you worn it since?"

"No, but I might."

Millicent wagged her right index finger. "It's old, stained and out of style. Remember, we need to reduce clutter. It goes."

Gabriella stifled a sob. "I guess you're right."

"Now this wedding dress." Millicent lifted up the long gown in a clear plastic protective cover.

"Look at all the lace. And such a wonderful ceremony when I wore that dress. It's still in perfect condition. I saved it for one of my two daughters."

"And did they want it?"

Gabriella bit her lip. "No. They wanted something more modern."

"Exactly. This elegant gown served the purpose of complementing a beautiful bride. But you can keep your memories without the dress. Do you have a wedding album from your ceremony?"

"Yes, I've saved a number of pictures of me all in white."

"There you go. You can remember the event without having your closet filled with something you'll never use again."

"I guess that makes sense."

"That's the spirit. You'll have to show me the album when we get to it."

They worked through the pile, eliminating two-thirds of the contents, including many items that no longer fit. They took a break to have a cup of tea.

Millicent ventured a look out the front window, wondering if she would spot the gray BMW again. To her relief only an old Pontiac rested against the curb across the street.

After the refreshments, they resumed in the bedroom. Gabriella immediately went to the pile of giveaway clothes and picked out a blouse which she held up to her breast and looked at in the mirror.

"Ah, ah." Millicent wagged a finger. "No backsliding. You can always discard more but no going back to pull things out of what we've already eliminated."

"Oops." Gabriella's cheeks reddened, and she returned the blouse to the pile of clothes.

"Now shoes." Millicent hauled boxes and boxes of shoes out of the closet and placed them on the floor in front of Gabriella. She counted forty pair. "Which can you part with?"

Gabriella scanned the shoe menagerie in front of her and put a hand to her cheek. "I like all of them."

"Yes, you liked all of them when you purchased them, but that's not the question here. Remember, if you haven't used them in the last year, give them away."

"But I've only worn those tennis shoes, the black flats, the brown sandals, my bedroom slippers and the blue pumps."

"Good. We'll save those." Millicent placed them in the corner. "Select several others, and we'll get rid of the rest."

Gabriella's eyes widened as large as silver dollars. "I couldn't do that."

Millicent held a finger against her cheek. "Let's do this. Try the shoes on, and we'll see which ones fit."

A smile crept across Gabriella's face. "Yes, I'd like to see how they look on me anyway."

Millicent grabbed a pair of silver high heels with pointed toes and handed them to Gabriella.

Gabriella pushed her right foot in as far as the arch. "These seem to have shrunk."

"Exactly. They no longer fit." Millicent tossed them in the "Donate" box.

Most of the shoes quickly went the same way. Then they came to a pair of red spiked high heels. Gabriella smiled. "I wore these on our twenty-fifth wedding anniversary."

"And probably not since."

"No, I was saving them for our fiftieth." A tear formed in the corner of her eye. "But my James died two months before that anniversary."

Millicent handed her a tissue. "Well, try them on."

Gabriella dabbed her eyes, then put her right foot in the shoe, pushed and tugged. Millicent had the image of the wicked stepsisters in Cinderella trying to squeeze their feet into the glass slipper. Gabriella managed to get most of her foot in and tried to walk with her heel still protruding.

"These have to go."

Her client looked like a kid who had lost a lollipop.

Millicent snapped her fingers. "I have an idea. I'll photograph your shoes with my smart phone camera, print a picture from my computer, and we can put that in a scrapbook rather than keeping the shoes."

Gabriella gave a weak smile. "I guess that will work."

Millicent set the shoes aside.

Within an hour, they had filled up four cardboard boxes and five trash bags to donate.

Millicent had equal difficulty with Gabriella when sorting through items in the bathroom. One drawer overflowed with old sets of makeup—caked, crumbled, dried out and in bricks. The medicine cabinet had pill bottles with expiration dates five or more years ago.

"This all has to go," Millicent said.

"But I might need something from here."

Millicent put her hands on her hips. "Look, Gabriella. Most of this medicine isn't safe anymore, but I've saved your current prescriptions. And your makeup is unusable. We'll purge all of it, and you can treat yourself to a trip to Macy's to buy some new blush."

"I suppose."

"Good." Millicent quickly emptied everything into a large black trash bag and tied off the top before Gabriella had second thoughts.

Next, they went out into the garage. One whole side wall had a pegboard with tools, garden implements and a mounted cabinet containing nails and screws. A collection of yard equipment rested on the floor including an ancient push mower, a fertilizer spreader, rakes, hoes and shovels. On a workbench stood a power drill, sander, jigsaw and other woodworking tools. Millicent opened a large cardboard box and found a dozen radio-controlled cars.

"Any thoughts on all of this?" Millicent asked.

Gabriella gave a dismissive wave of the hand. "You can give everything here away. This all belonged to James."

Chapter 15

As Millicent drove home, she kept a wary gaze focused on her rearview mirror. No gray BMW. She did spot a black car that might have been an undercover police officer following her. At one stoplight she waved, and the man in the black car returned her wave. She turned on the radio to a classical station and felt much more at ease for the rest of the drive home.

Her voicemail had two messages, one from a woman named Paula Sutter who stated, "Gabriella Hutchinson gave me your name. She absolutely raved over how you're helping her fix up her house. I need some assistance as well. Please give me a call."

Millicent almost knocked the phone stand over in surprise. After all the hassle with Gabriella to hear that she had been pleased enough with the process to make a recommendation. You never could tell with some people.

The second message was from Allison. "I've signed a contract for the condo. They're so anxious to get people in that they're allowing me to move in right away. I need you to help me get ready for the move next week. Oh, and since you know moving services, I'd appreciate it if you could also arrange that. Kisses."

First she called Allison. "So you're ready to move. What about selling your house?"

"No problem. I've had a couple who have been after me for a year to buy my place. I didn't even have to list it. They made me an offer I can't refuse, requiring no inspection, and they want in as soon as possible. With the condo owner so anxious to get me in, I need you to take care of everything."

"I have an excellent person who can do the physical move. You know, Ned Younger, the guy Diane recommended. He's great. I'll give him a call."

"Good. Now what do we need to do first?"

"Let's start by looking at your new condo so we know how much room we'll have to work with. That will dictate what you can keep and what else you'll need to get rid of."

"Since it's in your building, I'll come by your apartment at nine in the morning."

"You're assuming I don't have another appointment."

"Hey, old friends have priority, don't they?"

Millicent clenched her teeth. "I'm working on another job tomorrow, but I guess I can start that one later in the morning."

"And how soon can you help me clean out my house?"

"I'm finishing up a job next Wednesday, so we could start Thursday."

"Fine. See you in the morning at your place."

Next, she called Paula Sutter, the new referral.

"This is Millicent Hargrove returning your call."

"Oh, thank you for getting back to me so quickly. I need your services to organize my home. My son and daughter-in-law visited me this last week and expressed concern that my house has become too messy. They're worried that I'll trip over something and hurt myself. They started making hints that I should move into a retirement home. I'm not ready for that. Do you think you can help me?"

"I'd be happy to. I'm still working with Gabriella and will be starting another job next week but I could meet with you the following Monday, say late afternoon, to size the job, if that's convenient."

"That will be fine."

Millicent quickly jotted down Paula's address and hung up the phone suddenly overwhelmed. She had started this business wondering if she would have any clients at all, and now she had more than she could handle.

While preparing to go to bed, her phone rang. She heard heavy breathing on the line and then the voice of her son, Jerry.

"We had a break-in at our house," Jerry gasped.

"Oh, no. What happened?"

"We went out to dinner, and when we returned home, someone had been in our house. It appeared to be a professional job, because we found nothing broken or damaged."

"Did they steal much?"

"That's the strange part. They only took Dad's stamp collection. Fortunately, I had it insured. Still, you can imagine Drew's disappointment as he was really getting into stamps."

"It's strange that they didn't steal other things from your house."

"I can't figure it out either."

*****

The next morning at exactly nine, Millicent's doorbell rang. She opened the door to see Allison standing there with her arms crossed.

"Chop, chop. Time to get cracking. My new apartment awaits us."

Millicent blinked. She'd never seen Allison arrive on time before. "Don't you even want a cup of coffee first?"

Allison tapped her toe. "No time to socialize. We have work to do."

After grabbing a tape measure, notepad and pencil, Millicent found herself being dragged out, practically pushed down the stairs and force-marched along the hallway to apartment 178.

"I don't have as good a view as you do," Allison said, "but I'm on the ground level when a thunderstorm knocks the elevator power out."

"That's not a problem. There's a backup generator for the complex."

"Right. As if those things really work in an emergency." Allison opened the door to her condo. "Now what do you think of my new place?"

Millicent looked around and then measured the living room. "Seems to be the same size as mine. Let's check the bedrooms."

They completed the survey with Millicent noting all the measurements.

"Now, how soon can you get me in here?"

Millicent held up a hand. "Whoa. First things first. I told you I have another job to complete. We also have a lot of work to do on the other end, and I need to line up the mover."

"What are you waiting for?" Allison slapped the back of her right hand into her left palm. "Make it happen."

Millicent realized that her friend might be a tougher client than Gabriella Hutchinson.

*****

Millicent drove off to Gabriella's house and strolled up to the door, taking in a deep breath of fresh air. After all her turmoil, she enjoyed the moment of sunshine on her bare arms. A neighbor's petunias were in full bloom and light sparkled off a rock containing mica. She rang the doorbell, and Gabriella ushered her in.

The laundry room became the first challenge. Millicent sorted through two shelves full of old bottles, cans and containers of dried up paint, caked laundry soap, empty bleach, and one unlabeled jar of what might have contained eye of newt for all she could tell. She filled two trash bags with materials to be hauled to the hazardous waste disposal site.

*****

After a frantic amount of activity through the weekend and into Wednesday, Millicent finally asked Gabriella to accompany her on a walk-through of the whole house.

"Look at all your open space, Gabriella."

"You've done a wonderful job of eliminating the clutter, dear."

"Now remember, you'll want to keep it looking this way. As you get new things, eliminate some of the old. With diligence you can have a comfortable and tidy house. Set purged items aside and periodically call a nonprofit organization for a pickup. Keep grouping, reducing and reorganizing and you'll be in great shape. And thank you for the referral. I received a call from your friend Paula Sutter."

"You'll enjoy working with her. She's a delight and really needs your assistance." Gabriella let out a satisfied sigh. "I feel freer already with all that you've done."

"All part of the service."

*****

In the early afternoon, Millicent spoke with Ned Younger. "I have a moving job for you."

"Great. I can always use the business."

"Can you stop by Allison Petrov's house near 55th and Baseline around 4:30 today?"

"That works for me."

"Good. You can meet her and get a feel for what we have to accomplish. I'll be spending several days with her prepping for the move." She gave him the address.

*****

At four Millicent pulled into Allison's driveway and was greeted by her friend all aflutter.

"You'll never guess what happened."

"No, I probably won't."

"I've signed you and me up for a duplicate bridge tournament this coming weekend."

Millicent came to a screeching halt. "Why'd you do that?"

"I know Diane and Katherine have a conflict this weekend, but you're around."

"But I hate duplicate bridge. I enjoy our low key social bridge. A tournament? What were you thinking?"

"You'll do fine. You're the best player of the four of us anyway. What do you have to lose?"

Millicent thought of saying her dignity but held her tongue. "Unfortunately, I have nothing scheduled this weekend."

"Then it's settled. We'll take the other bridge players by storm."

Millicent hoped she wouldn't get sunk by a typhoon. "Let's take a look at your furniture now that we know the size of your new condo." She regarded her watch. "And Ned Younger from the moving service will be stopping by to meet you shortly."

"Is he single?"

"He's too young for you, Allison. He's a nice young man so don't intimidate him."

Allison put her hand to her chest. "Moi?"

"You know what I mean. Now let's check to see how much you can keep."

They strolled into the living room, and Millicent took out her tape measure to check all the furniture. "I'd suggest keeping the couch, two chairs, one end table and your entertainment center."

"That's all?"

"Unless you want to have an overcrowded living room, that's all that will fit."

"I guess you're not going to let me install a pool table and indoor barbeque."

"Over my dead body."

"Well, we don't want any bloodshed, so I guess I'll go along with your recommendation."

In the master bedroom they selected the bed, two end tables, two lamps and the dresser. To make up the second bedroom in the condo, they chose the computer desk, one single bed and a dresser.

"This leaves a lot of furniture to dispose of," Allison said.

"Do you want to sell it or donate it?"

"I'll stick with the no hassle approach. Have someone cart it all away."

"We can stage the donations in the garage for pickup."

At that moment the doorbell rang.

Millicent accompanied Allison to the door and found Ned standing there with an older gentleman, a striking man with a full head of silver gray hair, matching mustache and still-broad shoulders.

"Allison, this is Ned Younger," Millicent said. "But I don't know his companion."

The older man gave a pearly-white smile. "I'm not only Ned's assistant, I'm his father." He shot out a hand. "Ray Younger."

Millicent took his hand and felt a warmth shoot through her body. She released his hand and turned toward Allison. "Meet our illustrious client, Allison Petrov."

Ray took her hand. "Charmed."

Millicent watched as Allison actually blushed.

"My dad insisted on coming along on this job," Ned explained.

"That's right. I've heard so much about Millicent that I just had to meet her."

Now it was Millicent's turn to feel blood rush through her cheeks.

"Well, come inside," Allison said, reaching to take Ray's arm. "Are you the muscle of the operation?" She batted her eyelashes at him.

"No, ma'am. Ned provides the brawn. I'm the brains."

Ned exhaled with exasperation. "Dad, you're only along for the ride today."

"That's right. Sightseeing." He turned and winked at Millicent.

Millicent didn't know what to make of Ray. He was handsome in a homey sort of way but acting a little too familiar. After her loss, she had no interest in a man paying attention to her. "Allison and I have been through the house and have selected the items that will need to be moved. Come this way."

They did a walk-through, and Ned took notes. Afterwards he said, "I can have an estimate for you in fifteen minutes, if you like."

"Can I offer both of you some coffee?" Allison said.

"That would be great," Ray replied.

"I'll pass," Ned said. "I need to go out to the truck, and I'll whip up the estimate."

Allison busied herself in the kitchen while Ray and Millicent waited in the living room.

"Ned tells me you recently started your organizing business," Ray said.

"That's right. My husband died, and I decided to do something different."

Ray lowered his gaze. "I'm sorry to hear of his death. Ned's mother passed two years ago. The time right afterwards can be very difficult. You have my sympathy."

"Thank you." Millicent choked down a tear. "It takes quite an adjustment after all those years together."

"On a happier note, Ned speaks very highly of your organizing skills, Millicent."

She gave a dismissive wave of her hand. "Something I've always done and now have turned into a business. I'll only be starting my third client job next week."

"And how long have you been doing this?"

"Three weeks."

Ray whistled. "Three weeks and three clients already. That's quite an accomplishment."

Millicent's eyes opened wide. "Do you really think so?"

"Sure, it took my young whippersnapper of a son over a month to gain that much business when he started out. But then there's a lot to be said for the wisdom of our generation versus the inexperience of the youngsters."

Allison reappeared with coffee for Ray and a plate of oatmeal cookies. "Please have something to eat, Ray." She placed the cookies in front of him.

Millicent noticed that Allison hadn't brought coffee for her.

Ray munched on cookies, and the phone rang.

Allison raced into the hallway to take the call.

Ray held up a half-eaten cookie. "Your friend is very obliging."

"Yes, she's quite the hostess . . . when she has something in mind."

"But I'd like to get to know you, Millicent. Could you join me for dinner tonight?"

Millicent was caught off guard. "Well, I'm . . . uh . . . not quite ready to go out on dates yet."

Ray smiled. "Don't think of it as a date. Just colleagues getting together. Consider it a consultation on future business prospects for the organizing and moving business."

"Will Ned be joining us as well?"

"Of course. I insist on it."

Millicent smiled. "In that case, yes."

"Good. Then it's all settled."

Ned returned and handed Millicent the estimate.

She looked at it. "This seems quite reasonable."

"Your customers get preferential pricing, Millicent."

Allison came stomping into the room. "The new owners want to start moving some of their furniture in here next Friday."

"We can get you moved on Wednesday if you want," Ned said.

Allison smiled. "That would be great. So what's the damage?" She pointed to the estimate in Millicent's hands.

"Very fair," Millicent said.

"And it also includes boxing up all your personal items," Ned said. "Clear out all your donations, and we'll take care of the rest, boxing, moving, unpacking on the other end."

"Is Ray going to be part of this?" Allison asked.

"No. He doesn't get his hands dirty with the actual work."

Ray wiped away the crumbs of another cookie. "As I said earlier, I'm the brains, not the brawn."

Remembering her lesson of allowing enough time for a donation pickup, Millicent pulled out her smart phone and contacted Goodwill to schedule a truck for next Thursday afternoon.

Ned tapped his watch. "We need to get going, Dad."

"These young kids. Always in such a rush." Ray stood. "Allison, a pleasure meeting you, and Millicent, we'll pick you up at seven tonight."

Millicent watched the two men amble toward to door to let themselves out. Ray turned one last time and flashed a smile in her direction. Her pulse quickened, but she dismissed it immediately as an extraneous reaction.

As the door closed, Allison asked. "What's that reference to seven tonight?"

"I'm going out to dinner with Ned and Ray."

"Not alone with that hunk Ray?"

"No. It's a business meeting with both of them."

Allison gave a Cheshire Cat grin. "He likes you. I'd go for him, but you have first dibs."

"I'm not in the market for anyone right now."

"You will be. Just give it time."

Chapter 16

Millicent made plans with Allison to begin work the next day. She called to have a dumpster delivered to the driveway and warned Allison to park in front of the house.

When Millicent returned home, she allowed herself some downtime with a nice soak in the tub. Luxuriating in her oriental blossom bath gel and lavender bubble bath, she thought over all that had transpired that day. As she lay back in the tub a bubble got up her nose and she sneezed. An image of George sneezing flashed through her mind. George. Tears came to her eyes. The loss of George always festered just below the surface. Who had killed him? Why did someone stoop so low as to murder him? She leaned over and convulsed with sobs. Eventually, she wiped away her tears with a soapy hand, and then stinging in her eyes gave her a physical reason to cry. The absurdity of this caused her to laugh, and she sat there with tears of sadness, pain and mirth all mingling with the soap bubbles.

Then came the surge of anger. The police needed to find the murderer. Why hadn't they arrested someone yet? After getting out of the tub, she dried herself with the soft terrycloth towel. She crushed it in her hands, wanting to hurt whoever had robbed her of her husband. Finally, she took two deep breaths to calm her emotions. She had to stay in control. She couldn't let this despicable person ruin what was left of her life.

She had her new condo and many new projects to occupy her time. The image of Ray Younger popped into her mind. After his aggressive introduction, he had been understanding. And he had suffered a loss of a spouse as well. Still, she didn't have time for a man, and it was certainly too soon after George's death to even consider such a thing. She would be content with business dinners for the time being.

After hanging up the towel, she dressed in a pair of black slacks and a gold blouse. At exactly seven the doorbell rang, and Ray stood there in a sport coat and open collar shirt. He handed her a rose.

"Your chariot and driver await you downstairs." His voice was low and comforting.

Forcing her lips into a faint smile, she set the rose on her entryway table, stepped out, closed the door and took Ray's arm as they walked to the elevator. "Why is Ned spending time with us rather than with a lady friend?"

"His fiancée's a lawyer and travels out of town on business a lot, so he has nothing better to do with himself than to accompany us. Besides, since I'm treating both of you, he always responds to a free meal. How about Italian tonight?"

"One of my favorites." This time her smile was genuine.

"Good. We'll go to Carelli's."

At the car, Ray and Millicent scooted into the backseat.

"You're making me feel like a chauffeur," Ned said.

"That's right, chauffeur and chaperone. Otherwise Millicent wouldn't have agreed to go out to dinner with me."

"That the case?" Ned asked, glancing at her in the rearview mirror.

"This is a business dinner among colleagues," she replied with a smile.

At the restaurant they were seated at a table near the fireplace. Ray rubbed his hands together. "Ah, the warmth of a fire and good company. Would you like Chianti with dinner, Millicent?"

"Only one glass."

"You're not a major tippler then?"

She smiled. "My one glass of red wine, for the heart of course."

Ray put his right hand over the left side of his chest. "For the heart."

He ordered calamari for hors d'oeuvres and selected the wine. Millicent decided on veal piccata and the house salad. As she reached for a piece of bread with her left hand, Ray said, "That's a nice setting you have for your engagement ring."

Millicent's jaw dropped. "You're the first man besides George who ever noticed it, and he paid attention because he selected it."

Ray took her hand. "Unique and lovely. The pattern of small diamonds around the main gem is very well-designed."

"You must know about jewelry."

Ned leaned forward. "Dad's a retired jeweler."

"Now I accompany my successful son around with his moving business," Ray added.

As Ray and Ned bantered back and forth, Millicent considered her engagement and wedding rings. She'd decided to keep wearing them and had no intention of giving off any vibes of being a single woman. She regarded Ray's left hand. He didn't have a wedding band but she could see a faint mark where it had been. He probably only recently took it off.

The conversation flowed, and Millicent felt comfortable in the company of the two generations of Younger men. They ordered tiramisu for dessert and then sat for awhile sipping coffee. Over Millicent's protests Ray grabbed the bill, saying he would treat it as a business expense.

"But you're retired," Millicent said.

"I know, but I invested in Ned's business. I'm Daddy Warbucks, and I have to check up on my investment periodically."

Ned threw his hands in the air. "Only because of you, Millicent. Before this, he hasn't accompanied me on a job for months."

"Hey, since I'd heard you singing her praise, I had to meet her. Reality exceeds expectations." Ray smiled at her.

She wiped her face with her napkin to hide her own smile.

Afterwards, he walked her to her apartment. "When can I see you again?" he asked.

"I'm going to be busy this weekend," she replied.

"So am I, but maybe next week we could get together for coffee."

"I have a full schedule of projects going on then."

"When Ned comes to move your client, maybe I'll tag along again and we can chat then. Have a good weekend." Ray bowed and headed down the hall.

Millicent appreciated that he hadn't pressed too hard. She twisted her wedding bands. No, she wasn't yet ready to be a single woman in the dating scene.

*****

Millicent spent all day Thursday helping Allison group, reduce and reorganize for her move, thankful that she had already spent the time eliminating the majority of Allison's clutter.

That evening after she zapped a frozen eggplant parmigiana in the microwave for dinner, Millicent decided to unpack the remaining boxes stored in the second bedroom. She sorted through the carton that contained tweezers, mounting material and loose stamps. She should have given this to Jerry, but it wouldn't do much good now that the stamp collection had been stolen. She'd probably donate this to George's stamp club. In the one last box she found her remaining knickknacks. She removed the mother-of-pearl fish. Tears came to her eyes as she relived George buying it for her in the shop in Acapulco. What a wonderful honeymoon, but now she only had memories. Would she ever stop having these moments of flashback? No, and she guessed she didn't want them to stop. She would take the sadness when it came for the memories of all their happy times together. She would continue to miss George. She snuffled, wiped her nose and took two deep breaths. She had now moved on to a new phase in her life—a businesswoman with her own apartment. She turned the fish over in her hand. George had left his strange clue, and she felt sure that his cryptic message referred to this fish. Maybe she now held something that would provide a clue to who had killed George and why it had happened. She inspected it again more carefully and noticed a nearly imperceptible crack in the mid-section of the fish. Probably damaged in the move. She should sue the movers. Covering her mouth, she suppressed a giggle. Given the proficiency of Ned and his crew, nothing would have been damaged in transit. The fish had probably reached the end of its useful life. Millicent tugged at it and it split neatly into two pieces. She peered into the larger of the two pieces. A folded piece of paper was glued inside.

Chapter 17

Millicent partially unfolded the piece of paper she had removed from the mother-of-pearl fish and found a small key inside. She squinted at it and determined it must be a lockbox key. She and George had the one lockbox at Gentry Savings and Loan. She rummaged through her purse to retrieve that key she had previously stashed in a side pocket. The two keys appeared to be the same size, but when she placed them together, she discovered they differed. George had never mentioned another lockbox. Then she finished unfolding the paper. In George's distinctive script appeared the one word, "desk."

Millicent put her hand to her chin and ruminated on this. George and his one word enigmatic messages. They only had one desk, the one she had sold to Ned Younger. Did some clue remain hidden in the desk that related to George's murder?

It was too late to contact Ned. She'd give him a call in the morning.

*****

After breakfast on Friday morning, the latest cryptic message from George still bounced around Millicent's brain, so she picked up the phone and punched in Ned's phone number. After it cut over to voicemail, she identified herself and asked Ned to call her back when convenient.

She slid the newly discovered key in an envelope to keep it separate from the known lockbox key and put it in her purse, before returning to the organizing job at Allison's house.

*****

On Saturday morning, Allison picked up Millicent at nine.

"Tell me again why I agreed to this?" she asked after jumping in the car.

"Because you're a good friend and I need a partner. Besides a lot of men our age play tournament bridge. You may meet someone interesting."

Millicent looked askance at her friend. "I don't need any men in my life right now."

"If the right one comes along, you'll change your tune."

"I'm not looking for Mr. Right. I'm happy to plug along by myself. Besides, I have my new business, and that's consuming my time."

Allison wagged a finger at her. "All work and no play—"

"Yeah, yeah, and then you drag me off for a weekend of serious bridge. That's no play either."

"Cheer up. You'll love it once you get started."

They arrived at the Jefferson County Fairgrounds and parked in a large lot, already half full.

"Look at all the cars here," Millicent said. "How many people play in these things?"

"Hundreds."

Millicent gulped. "I was expecting several dozen people or so."

"No way. This is big, big, big."

"Now you tell me."

They entered a barn-like building crammed full of bridge tables and folding chairs. Up on the stage stood a row of folding tables with four officials, a time clock and piles of plastic cardholders and forms.

"Wait here and I'll get us signed in," Allison said.

Millicent scanned the room. She'd never seen so many bridge tables in one place. What had she got herself into?

"We're in Section D at table twenty-three," Allison said as she pulled

Millicent toward the middle of the room.

"It's so intimate in here," Millicent said as a group of twenty people pushed past her, speaking loudly and waving their arms.

"Don't get smart. We have two days of bridge to play."

"But I haven't played very much duplicate."

"Just play like you always do. Bid, make your bids and set our opponents. Nothing to it."

Millicent gazed around the room. "But look at all these people. And they probably do this on a regular basis."

"You play bridge once a week. What's the big deal?"

"I don't know. I feel intimidated by the scope of this tournament."

They reached their table and met two men standing there who appeared to be approximately their age. Albert Peterson had a red, round face and shiny bald head. He smiled at Millicent and Allison. "My wife won't be happy to hear that I'm playing bridge with two such lovely ladies." He reached out and shook their hands. The other man who Albert introduced as Fred Langley only glowered and didn't put out a hand. "You'll have to forgive Fred. He divorced last year and isn't keen on women right now."

Fred glared at Albert.

Millicent regarded Fred, an average-sized man with a full head of gray hair and the hands of a pianist, long, thin, with an undertone of hidden strength. His raised, pointed chin radiated an aura of contempt and arrogance.

"Well, we're both single ladies," Allison announced. Millicent elbowed her in the ribs, but she ignored the signal. "I'm divorced and Millicent is a widow. Shall we get started?"

They sat down and each person removed a set of cards from the top one of the two plastic holders in the center of the table. Millicent felt uncomfortable without cards being dealt as in her party bridge games.

"Both teams are vulnerable, and Millicent has the deal," Albert announced.

Millicent arranged her cards, looked at her hand, counted the points and recounted. Satisfied that she had a five card heart suit and fourteen points, she announced, "One heart."

"Ah, ah, ah," Albert said, shaking a finger. "You need to show your bid."

"I don't understand," she replied.

Albert pointed to the yellow plastic container to the side of her. "Pull the bid marker for one heart from there."

She hadn't noticed this device sitting there. She reached over, took the correct marker and set it in front of her. "Sorry, I'm a little nervous."

Albert smiled. "You'll get used to it."

Fred gave her a dirty look.

Albert pulled out a pass marker and dropped it on the table. Allison pulled out a two-heart indicator to support her hearts, and after Fred showed a pass, Millicent pulled out the four hearts marker.

When the play began Albert led out the six of spades in front of him, and Allison put her dummy hand down. Millicent reached over and picked the ten of spades from the dummy and dropped it on top of Albert's six.

"Ah, ah, ah," Albert wagged a finger at her again. "You need to tell your partner what card to play from the dummy."

"Oops, I'm sorry." Millicent felt heat rise up her cheek and put the card back in Allison's dummy hand.

"That's a stupid thing to do," Fred said.

The heat on Millicent's face changed from embarrassment to anger. "I'm new to tournament play, so don't be such a jerk."

His mouth fell open.

She gave a satisfied nod of her head. "Okay Allison, play the ten of spades."

Allison pulled the card out and set it to the side, and then Fred showed the jack of spades and Millicent played her queen of spades to win the trick. She watched as the other three players turned their played card over, so she followed in doing the same.

Allison nodded toward Millicent and said, "Keep your winning cards vertical and losing ones horizontal. That way you can keep track of how many tricks you've won."

Millicent smiled at the needed advice from her friend. She reviewed her hand and pulled trumps before proceeding to make exactly four hearts.

"Well played," Allison said.

Albert smiled in agreement, but Fred only scowled.

On the next hand, Fred won the bid to play three no-trump. Millicent had the lead and thought a long time. She had always been taught to lead the fourth highest from her longest and strongest suit, but in this case Allison had thrown in a bid of two spades after Albert had responded two hearts to Fred's opening one no-trump bid. She decided to lead to Allison's strength which set up a finesse of the king of hearts on the board. They ended up setting Fred by one trick.

Fred gave Millicent an evil eye and muttered something that Millicent thought sounded like, "Women shouldn't play bridge."

She returned his stare with a pleasant smile. "Now what?"

"We only play two hands per round," Allison said. "We'll be moving around after tallying the score."

Albert entered the information into the Bridgemate handheld electronic device, and each of them wrote the scores on their score sheets.

As they stood to move, Millicent noticed a woman sitting in a folding chair watching one of the players at another table. "What's that woman doing?" she asked Allison.

"She's a kibitzer. A visitor can observe one player as long as the people at the table don't object. It's a good way to improve your game by watching some of the top players."

"I should have done that before you roped me into playing. Then I wouldn't have made the mistakes I did during the first round."

"No harm done. You figured it all out quickly."

In the morning session they played thirteen rounds of two hands each in three hours and then broke for lunch.

"You played well," Allison said.

"Once I overcame the jitters. That man Albert in the first round seemed understanding, but his partner Fred was sure obnoxious."

Allison shrugged. "You'll meet all kinds here. Some nice players and others who act very cutthroat. The top players willingly discuss what system they play and what their bids mean. Some people won't say anything, and others try to intimidate you." She pointed to a man drinking from a water bottle. "That guy over there is one of the top players in Colorado. He has over seventeen thousand master's points."

"Wow, how many do you have, Allison?"

"Thirty."

"That's thirty more than I have."

"That's only because you don't play in tournaments. You'd pick them up quickly with your level of play."

"I don't know. I'm still intimidated by this whole tournament scene."

Later in the afternoon session when switching tables while Allison went to the restroom, Millicent felt a tap on her shoulder. She turned to find Ray Younger with a huge grin on his face. "You said you'd be busy this weekend, but I didn't know you played tournament bridge."

Millicent smiled back. "I don't. Allison drafted me. And you said you'd be tied up this weekend. I didn't think it would be playing bridge."

"Yes, one of my main pastimes."

At that moment Fred Langley appeared out of the crowd. Without even smiling he stepped in front of Ray and said to Millicent, "Let's go out to dinner Tuesday night."

She stepped back in surprise. "I . . . I'm sorry Fred, I'm too busy with my social bridge to go out that night."

"Then why don't you be my bridge partner another evening?"

Millicent turned toward Ray and grabbed his arm. "Fred, this is Ray Younger. Ray and I would be happy to play bridge sometime against you and your partner."

"I know who he is." Fred glared at Ray and stomped away.

"What was that all about?" Ray asked.

"That obnoxious little toad was one of my opponents in the first round today. He treated me like dirt and then comes up and asks me out. What nerve."

Ray laughed. "I've known Fred for years. Snake is a more appropriate tag than toad. You're not one to mess with, Millicent Hargrove."

She shook her right index finger at him. "And you remember that."

Ray held up his hands as if he needed to fend off a karate attack. "Oh, I will. But I heard what you said to him. We will have to play bridge together . . . once your busy schedule lets up."

Her smile returned. "Just as long as it's social bridge and not a tournament."

*****

By the end of the weekend Millicent felt comfortable with the duplicate bridge format and found herself actually enjoying the games. To her befuddlement, she and Allison ended up placing within the top third of teams, not bad for a beginner. With the announcement of the winners, she received another jolt—Ray and his partner came in second. That man was full of surprises.

Chapter 18

On Monday morning, the ringing phone jerked Millicent's attention away from the cup of coffee she was nursing, and she found Ned on the line.

"Sorry I didn't get back to you, but I was out of town Friday and over the weekend," he informed her.

"I'd like to come over and look at the desk you bought."

"You having second thoughts?"

"No, the desk is yours. I merely want to search for something that might have been left in it."

"I didn't see anything when I put my files and supplies in it, but you're welcome to check it out."

Millicent peeked at her watch. "I'm going off to work with Allison, and I have a new client to meet with this afternoon. Can I come by your place some time later today?"

"You certainly have a busy schedule. I'm tied up most of the day myself but will be here from five on."

"I'll stop by at five."

Millicent headed over to Allison's house where the two of them finished storing all the easily luggable donations in the garage. It would fill most of a truck. They spent the early afternoon taking loads of junk out to the dumpster, which by one-thirty was half-filled.

"I think we're in good shape," Millicent said as she and Allison sauntered through the house. "Ned's team will be here on Wednesday to pack everything. They can also move the donation furniture into the garage. The Goodwill pickup is scheduled for Thursday, so your house will be cleared out for the new owners."

Allison gave her a hug. "I don't know how to thank you. I could never have done this by myself."

"I'll be over on Wednesday to check on the final move."

"Such service on top of filling in at the tournament."

Millicent found herself smiling. "That competitive type of bridge wasn't nearly as bad as I expected."

"You want to do another one?"

"No!"

"Okay. I thought I might have hooked you."

"I'll stick with our bridge group." She remembered that Ray had invited her to play and wondered how it would be to partner with someone as good as he must be. She figured she'd have a chance to find out when Ray asked her to join a game sometime.

*****

When Millicent arrived at the home of Paula Sutter at two, she immediately saw the problem. Paula must have been in her eighties and used a cane. Her small bungalow had turned into an obstacle course with magazines, books, old calendars and knickknacks strewn throughout her living room.

"Do you think you can help me with the clutter?" Paula asked with a trembling voice.

"Absolutely. You must follow one rule, though. You have to give yourself permission to throw out and give away stuff. Do you have some relatives who want things or a favorite charity?"

"My children told me to get rid of the mess but don't want anything themselves. I suppose I could have a garage sale or donate what I don't need."

"Garage sales can be a lot of work. Would you like to put one on?"

Paula grimaced. "Not particularly, but I might make some money."

"Most garage sales don't make that much," Millicent said. "You also have to consider how much your own time is worth. What value would you place on your own personal time on an hourly basis?"

A smile graced Paula's face. "I'd say I'm worth at least twenty-five."

"A typical garage sale will require at least twenty hours of your time. That means you'd need to take in five hundred dollars to make it worthwhile. I suspect you'd make two to three hundred dollars."

"I guess it's not really worth it then."

Millicent regarded Paula, who leaned heavily on her cane. "I think that's a wise decision. Let's take a look around your house."

They walked through the combined kitchen and dining nook and two bedrooms before ending up in another small room that was empty except for a stack of boxes in the corner. Millicent pointed. "What are those?"

"They contain my departed husband's stamp collection."

"That could be valuable. Has anyone given you an estimate for it?"

"No, I haven't even opened the boxes."

"My husband collected stamps too. I can have one of his club members meet with you to discuss what can be done with your collection."

"That would be wonderful. I wouldn't know where to start otherwise."

This reminded Millicent that George's collection had been stolen from Jerry's house. She frowned at the thought of the loss, since her grandson Drew had expressed interest in collecting stamps. She made a mental note to discuss the stamps with Detective Buchanan.

Surprisingly, the neatest room in the house was the bathroom. "You've kept this very tidy," Millicent said.

"Yes, this was the one place I cleaned out before I ran out of energy."

They next went into the garage, which also appeared well-organized, not like most of the house. "Things seem in good shape here."

"I have a gardener who comes once a week. He keeps everything where he can find it."

Millicent felt satisfied that she had what she needed. "I've seen the task at hand. We'll get your place in such good shape that you'll have a safe and comfortable house. Give me a few minutes to size the job." Millicent worked up an estimate and handed it to Paula.

Millicent's potential client put on her reading glasses and reviewed the quote. "This seems very reasonable. You're hired."

"Thank you." Millicent smiled and wondered if she should increase her rates.

"When can you start?" Paula stared at her with anxious eyes.

Millicent scanned the living room. "I can spend several hours with you right now to unclutter this living space. Then we can seriously get going tomorrow."

"I have a doctor's appointment tomorrow morning," Paula said. "I'll be back home by noon or so."

"Good. I'll be here around one. By the way, do you have a trash service that takes paper for recycling?"

"Yes. In fact tomorrow is trash day."

"With that in mind, I'm going to clear all these magazines first. That will give you some immediate results and make this room safer for you."

*****

Millicent parked on the street in front of Ned's house near the University of Colorado and proceeded up the walkway to the front porch. He lived in an old wooden one-story with a well-maintained yard. The neighborhood had signs advertising student rentals. The outside of the house didn't catch her attention, but once Ned let her in, she saw immediately that he had decorated it in simple good taste, not the messy bachelor's pad she had expected.

"May I offer you some coffee or tea?" he asked.

"Nothing right now. I'm anxious to take a look at the desk."

"Just missed it too much, huh?"

"No, I don't miss it in the least. But we have a mystery to solve." Millicent described the lockbox key and note she had found.

"Do you think George hid something in the desk?"

"Yes. I already found the key to the file cabinet hidden in the desk. I think he may have hidden something else there as well."

"Let's take a look."

They entered a room with a computer on a table and the desk forming an L-shaped work area. The view from the desk looked out the window toward the street. The only other furnishings in the room were a swivel chair and a file cabinet.

"This is my office."

"Very neat." Millicent smiled. "You won't need to hire me to organize this."

"No. I don't like a mess. I work best in an uncluttered environment."

"I know what you mean. Now the desk."

"Let me pull out all the drawers, and we can check all the inside surfaces." He stacked all the drawers on the floor, and Millicent held each up in turn and inspected the sides and bottoms, finding nothing.

Ned ran his hand along the inside wood paneling of the desk where the side drawers had been removed, searching for anything unusual. While he checked this, Millicent put her hand under the desktop where the center drawer had been removed. She patted the wood, finding nothing until her hand encountered a deformity. She felt an indentation in the wood. She poked at it with her fingernails and a piece of wood dropped away. Underneath she detected a small piece of paper wedged in. She carefully scraped at it, gained purchase on an edge and pulled it out.

"I found something here." She waved it toward Ned.

"Don't keep me in suspense. What is it?"

Millicent unfolded the paper, stared intently and found the words, "Boulder Union Bank - 352."

Ned looked over her shoulder. "Does this mean something to you?"

"It must be the location and number of the lockbox for the key I found in the mother-of-pearl fish. George went to a lot of trouble to set up clues. I don't know why he didn't just tell me he had a lockbox there and give me the key."

"Obviously he didn't want someone else to get their hands on it."

"I don't know about all this secrecy. It's like passwords for computers. They make it so difficult that the common person can't remember the password and ends up writing it down so that someone can find it anyway. If I figured this out, the people who have been following me could have found it too."

"But obviously they haven't, so George's scheme worked."

Millicent sighed. "I guess you're right. Now I'll have to go see if I can get into this lockbox at the Boulder Union Bank."

Chapter 19

When she entered her condo, Millicent found a message on her machine. She listened to hear that a woman named Hannah Judson wanted to hire her. Millicent returned the call and set up an appointment to stop by at eleven in the morning before her job at Paula Sutter's.

"Out of curiosity, how did you hear of me?" Millicent asked.

"Oh, darling, my friend Gabriella Hutchinson recommended you."

Millicent hung up, marveling at how word-of-mouth could produce new business. Gabriella had now provided two new clients for her.

*****

On Tuesday morning, Millicent awoke, remembering a strange dream with images of floating through a meadow that contained stamps growing on vines. She came to a hill with a large oak tree. Shiny keys hung from the branches. One fell into her hand. Then a field full of desks appeared, each locked. The key couldn't unlock any of them. Rain started to soak her when she awoke in frustration. Darn dream. All set off by the recent events. She still lacked any useful information or meaningful insight into what it all meant.

Then a drop of water hit her face. She looked up and saw a bubble of water forming on the ceiling. She groaned and scurried out of bed to call the maintenance number for the building. The man who answered said he would check the apartment above hers and come to her place within half an hour.

Millicent made the bed, placed a cooking pot on the cover to collect the drips and dressed. After her breakfast of fried eggs, sausage, juice and coffee, she sat down at the table to jot notes for her engagement at Paula Sutter's house. Periodically, she could hear a plunk of water hit the pot in the bedroom.

Finally, her doorbell rang, and a man in coveralls informed her, "I fixed a water leak in the condo above you. Let me see what damage has been done to your apartment." He entered, and Millicent led him to the bedroom. The water had stopped dripping but a wet patch could be seen on the ceiling. He took a rag out of his pocket, stood up on a chair and patted down the damp spot. "Let's give it a day to dry out. I'll have someone come patch and repaint the ceiling."

*****

At 9:05, Millicent entered the main branch of Boulder Union Bank. She marched up to a teller and asked to be allowed to view the contents of lockbox 352. The teller asked for her ID, pulled out a card and asked her to sign it.

Uh-oh. They wouldn't let her in the box if it had George's signature. She clenched her teeth and signed the card. The teller compared it to something under the counter and motioned to Millicent. "Please come with me."

Millicent didn't know what to make of this, but she followed the woman who led her into a vault. She inserted a key in one of the locks and had Millicent insert her key in the other lock. She removed a long narrow box. "Would you like to use one of the privacy rooms to view the contents?"

"Yes, please."

She handed Millicent the box and key and guided her out of the vault to a small side room. "Take as long as you want. Push the call button when you're ready to return the container."

Millicent locked the door, sat down on the small stool and stared at the box. What would she find inside?

Part of her wanted to forget this whole crazy adventure, but she knew her curiosity had to be sated. She lifted the lid and found only a folded piece of paper and a velvet-covered jewelry box. First she opened the box. Inside she found a gold signet ring with a red stone. Around the red stone were three Greek letters. It reminded her of a fraternity ring. But George hadn't been a fraternity man in college. He considered the Greek system a bunch of nonsense.

She unfolded the sheet of paper and found a letter addressed to her:

Millicent –

If you find this letter then something has happened to me. I set up this lockbox so that only you or I could get into it. You have probably forgotten, but one time I asked you to sign a card for our bank account. That was actually a signature for this lockbox.

Millicent thought back and remembered the event a year ago. She had been in a hurry and hadn't thought twice about the card that George had thrust in front of her to sign. She continued reading:

I'm sorry for all this secrecy, but it's necessary. I have to apologize for never telling you, but I was employed by a government agency and involved in some top secret activity that I could never divulge, even to you. If you're reading this now, then something has gone wrong and I need your assistance. Please take the ring and send it to the address below.

I have always loved you, George.

Millicent wiped away a tear from her cheek, before focusing on the address. She winced. It was a different address from the one given her by the government man who approached her at the funeral and asked about a signet ring.

Millicent inspected the signet ring again. She could find nothing unusual. It appeared to be merely a gold ring with a red stone. It didn't look valuable and didn't have any cryptic message other than the three Greek letters. She looked inside the band. No inscription. She placed it in her purse, reread the letter and committed the address to memory. Then she returned the letter and empty jewel case to the box and rang the bell for the teller to come return the container to the vault.

*****

As she drove home, her mind churned with questions. How could George have hidden all this from her? What agency had he worked for? What had he been doing all these years? He often took trips to Singapore, Hong Kong and England for his work. Had these really been guises for CIA or some other government spying? Why had she never picked up on this? Who was the government man who had approached her at the funeral? Who were the other people who had accosted her and been following her? Why did the address in George's letter differ from the one given her by the government man?

Finally, how did all this relate to his murder?

After almost running a red light, she pulled to the curb and sat there for several minutes, trying to get her thoughts under control. Then she took a deep breath and started up again.

What should she do with the signet ring? She didn't know which of the two locations to send it to. The government man had given her all that money and said that it resulted from some service George had performed. But why would George's note specify a different location?

Thinking it over, she decided she couldn't follow the government man's instructions if George had specified something different. But what had George been up to?

Chapter 20

Still in a muddle over how to dispose of the signet ring, Millicent let herself into her condo. She went into her kitchen and took down one of the two amaryllis plants from the window sill. She poked her finger into the rich dirt and dropped the ring in the hole. Then she covered it up. Should she put the plant back? She felt nervous leaving it in her apartment. Someone had invaded their house apparently looking for this ring and had killed George. Then she had an idea. After washing her hands, she called Katherine who answered.

"You going to be there for the next thirty minutes?"

"Shore nuff. No hot dates planned."

"I have something I want to drop off. I'll be right there." Then Millicent drove over with the amaryllis plant, constantly checking her mirror to make sure she wasn't followed. At Katherine's, she rang the doorbell and when the door opened, held out the plant. "Here's a present for you."

"If that don't beat all. I'll put it on my kitchen windowsill. What's the occasion?"

"Consider it a small thank you for letting me stay with you before I moved into my condo." As Katherine shut the door, Millicent dashed to her car, scrutinizing her surroundings to make sure no suspicious people were watching her. Satisfied, that she was not being observed, she drove off. The signet ring could remain safely in the pot in Katherine's apartment until Millicent decided what to do with it.

Millicent headed off to the home of Hannah Judson in North Boulder.

She pulled up in front of the address she had been given and spied a freshly mowed lawn and neatly painted white two-story house. Millicent rang the doorbell and was greeted by a woman in her seventies who looked like she had just left a séance—she wore a long gold silk robe decorated with stars and planets, and her head was covered with a purple turban. "Come in, come in. You must be Millicent."

"Ms. Judson, it's a pleasure to meet you."

She waved her hand. "It's Hannah, darling, and I know we're going to become wonderful friends. Enter my humble abode."

It appeared anything but humble. Rich marble adorned the entry way. On a table that could have come out of a mid-eighteenth century French court rested an elaborate array of gold balls. The living room had a deep purple shag rug with an ermine white couch and two matching white armchairs. A clear glass end table displayed a large book with a picture of an exploding nebula. Gold silk curtains hung from the windows. No other objects cluttered this immaculate room.

"Thank you for agreeing to help me organize."

"What do you want me to do for you?"

Hannah spun in a circle thrusting her arms out. "My house is a mess. I need you to help me with all the clutter."

Millicent realized that her new job gave her an interesting insight into the human psyche. She wondered how long Hannah Judson would have lasted in the old living room of Gabriella Hutchinson. Although Hannah had been recommended by Gabriella, Millicent had a hard time imagining the two of them sitting in the same room together. As she looked around Hannah's house, she saw no reason for being hired to do anything here.

But as Gabriella led her upstairs, she discovered the problem. One bedroom was crammed full of electronics equipment. Millicent gasped as she saw stacks of televisions, stereos, computers, boom boxes and every imaginable electronic gadget along all walls with only a small passageway to get into the room.

"What is all of this stuff?" Millicent had images of a snatch-and-grab gang using this room as their hideout.

"This is what I need you to organize for me. My son, Ronald, had a used electronics business. He closed it down two months ago and asked if he could store things here temporarily. Being an indulgent mother, I agreed, but then Ronald ran off to Prague with a floozy. He called last week. I told him I intended to get rid of all his stuff, and he said to go ahead since he didn't plan to come back to the States. So now you're here to help me."

"Do you want to sell or donate all of this?"

"Just take everything away as quickly as you can. I don't want to bother selling it."

"I'm tied up for the rest of the week, but I can definitely clear this out next Monday."

"That will be fine."

"Give me a few minutes and I'll put an estimate together."

"Take your time. I'll fix some coffee and meet you downstairs." Hannah sashayed out of the room leaving Millicent to plan her campaign.

First she called Ned Younger on her smart phone. When he answered she said, "I need to hire you or one of your strong assistants to help me move some electronic equipment next week."

"You give me the time and place, and I'll have someone there. Anything new on the lockbox key you found in the desk?"

"I was able to get into the lockbox." Millicent decided she didn't want to go into the details. "There are still more questions than answers."

"I'll look forward to the next installment of this mystery."

You and me both.

Next, to figure out who would take all this junk. Then one idea occurred to her, and she did a quick Google search on her smart phone. After being connected to the requested organization and suffering through several transfers, she finally found what she sought.

"We would be glad to pick up old electronic equipment, but we won't lug it out of a house. If you can have it in the garage or out on a porch we'll send a van to collect it."

"Perfect," Millicent replied. "I'll have everything ready by the end of the day next Monday."

"Give me the address, and I'll have a pickup scheduled for Tuesday."

She had guessed right. She had found a group of students at the University of Colorado who reconditioned old electronic equipment for resale. She prepared her bid and returned downstairs.

Over a cup of coffee, Hannah readily agreed to the estimate. "I'll look forward to your giving me back that room in my house next week." Hannah gave a majestic wave of her right hand.

*****

Millicent arrived at Paula Sutter's house after a quick lunch to continue the task of making the place safe. After the reminder speech about giving herself permission to give things up and reviewing the group, reduce and reorganize process, they dove in.

As opposed to Gabriella, Paula had no problem throwing or giving things away. "Whatever it takes to stay in my house. I understand I don't need all this stuff. I haven't had the energy to clear things out."

"We'll reduce the clutter, and you can show your kids how this will continue to be the best place for you to live. And when we're done, it will be easy for you to find and use your things."

Millicent spent the afternoon filling up bags for donations and trash, careful to mark everything appropriately. Once the recycling bin was picked up by the trash service, Millicent had that topped off again. By five she had completed the living room and Paula's bedroom with the garage stuffed full of bags and boxes. Millicent was amazed at how much progress she had made during the day. With the combination of it being such a small house and with no protests from Paula, it had gone quickly.

"I'll be back Thursday morning to continue, and once we're done, I can arrange for things to be picked up," Millicent said.

Tears formed in Paula's eyes. "The living room looks wonderful. Thank you for helping me take the steps to stay in my house."

As Millicent drove away, she felt a warmth in her chest at being able to provide a useful service to people in need.

*****

On Wednesday morning, Millicent hustled over to Allison's house to help with the final preparation for the move. Ned and two assistants were already there packing boxes and loading things into the moving van.

Allison stood with a cup of coffee in her hand. "Nice of you to finally show up."

"I'm sorry. With my busy schedule yesterday, I slept later than expected."

Allison grinned. "Just kidding. You've already whipped everything into such good shape that we only have to make sure these husky men don't break anything."

Ned looked up from a box he had sealed. "Hey, we're as careful as if moving our own stuff." He reached over and tossed a small vase, cup and dish into the air.

"What are you doing?" Allison shouted.

Ned smirked. "Nothing to it. I paid my way through college performing as a juggler."

"That may be the case, but don't give me a heart attack by doing that with my stuff."

Ned gave a pout. "Yes, ma'am."

Millicent grabbed Allison's arm. "Come on let's leave the packing to the professionals. You and I still have some bags of junk to lug to the dumpster."

They went out to where a dozen filled plastic bags rested on the floor of the garage. They grabbed one in each hand and headed out the driveway to the dumpster.

"I never realized I had accumulated so much junk," Allison said.

"It happens to all of us. That's why moving can be a cathartic process. Even if you don't move, you should go through your belongings every five years pretending that you're going to relocate. You can't let too much stuff accumulate."

Allison waved her hand. "I know—group, reduce and reorganize."

"Good. You've learned the mantra."

"Yeah, yeah. You organizing types. Now I'm converted."

At the dumpster, Millicent reached up and threw the lid back so they could toss the bags inside.

"This one is too heavy to heft up there," Allison said. "I'll get the stool that's still in the garage. She returned moments later, set the stool next to the dumpster and climbed up. "Now hand me the trash."

With Millicent hoisting the bag up, Allison started to toss it into the dumpster when she let out a blood-curdling screech. "A body," she blubbered, "A body, a body."

"What do you mean?" Millicent asked.

Allison gasped. "There's a man's body in the dumpster."

Chapter 21

After the 9-1-1 call, the paramedics arrived, followed by a police officer and then Detective Buchanan. Needless to say, the moving came to a halt as Buchanan interviewed Millicent, Allison, Ned, and his two assistants. Ned and his crew finally left with the agreement to return in the morning to complete the move.

"I have to be out of here by Friday," Allison wailed as she sat on the porch with her head in her hands.

Millicent patted her arm. "Ned will have everything done tomorrow. You'll be fine."

"But I've packed most of my stuff. And where am I going to stay tonight?"

"You can stay in my spare bedroom. Then tomorrow night you can sleep in your new condo."

Allison looked at Millicent with relief in her eyes. "Thanks. You're a good friend."

"Just don't sign me up for any more bridge tournaments."

"Come on. You eventually enjoyed yourself."

"Well, it was different, but I still prefer sticking with our little bridge group."

"Speaking of which, I'm hosting the event in my new place next week. Another reason I need to get moved in and organized."

Millicent swept her hand toward a stack of boxes. "We'll have you unpacked and in good shape with time to spare."

At that moment, Detective Buchanan strode over. "Mrs. Hargrove, I need you to accompany me to police headquarters."

Allison's head shot up in alarm. "Millicent isn't a suspect, is she?"

Buchanan gave an indulgent smile. "No, nothing like that. But I need to show her some pictures and a note we found."

"What kind of note?" Millicent asked.

"I think it would be better to cover that in the privacy of the station."

Millicent decided not to argue. "With the move delayed, I guess I don't have anything else I have to do right now."

"You're not going to leave me by myself, are you?" Allison pleaded.

"Why don't you go to my condo? Here." She handed Allison the door key. "I'll meet you back there after I'm done with Detective Buchanan."

*****

At the police station, an officer led Millicent to a small room and told her to wait for the detective. Feeling more like a criminal than a witness, Millicent nervously tapped the toe of her shoe on the floor.

In five minutes, Detective Buchanan arrived, closed the door and sat down across a worn table from Millicent.

"I want to see if you recognize the man in the dumpster," he said.

"Oh dear, I hope I don't have to go to the morgue."

"No. I want to make this easy for you. I have some pictures for you to look at. I've made sure they aren't too grisly."

Millicent swallowed, blinked and then stared at three photographs Buchanan placed in front of her. She pointed at the first picture. "That's . . . that's the man who showed up at my garage sale and later followed me."

Detective Buchanan regarded her thoughtfully. "That answers one question. Now two other things I want you to look at." He placed a ring and a piece of paper on the table. "Please look at that typed note."

Millicent read, "Mrs. Hargrove, you could be next." She gaped and gasped.

"I knew this would shock you. That's why I wanted you to see this in a safe and private place. Please look at that ring as well. The note was wrapped around it." He handed her a ring in a clear plastic bag.

Millicent carefully inspected it. It looked similar but not identical to the one she had found in George's lock box. "Were there any fingerprints on it?"

He shook his head. "It had been wiped clean. Does that ring mean anything to you?"

Millicent continued to stare at it. What should she do? She had instructions to send the signet ring she'd found to the address from the government man, a conflicting message from George and now this question from Detective Buchanan. Should she tell him? Should she send the ring to George's address? What should she do? She felt like she'd been plopped down in the middle of a messy room. She needed time to sort through and purge. But she didn't yet know what to throw away and what to keep. "I don't know what to make of this ring, Detective."

"You mentioned that the man who accosted you in your driveway asked about a signet ring."

"That's right."

"Now the dead man shows up with a signet ring."

"This is all very confusing," Millicent said, wiping away tears with her hand.

Buchanan handed her a tissue. "Let me know if any ideas occur to you."

Millicent dabbed her eyes and paused to let this all sink in. Then another thought popped into her mind. "Detective, there's something else you should know. My son Jerry, who lives in Indianapolis, reported a stamp collection being stolen. It had belonged to my husband. It may tie in somehow to my husband's death and this other body."

Buchanan jotted a note. "I'll check on that right away."

Millicent's phone chirped in her purse. She jumped and reached for it to answer.

"I just went to your condo," Allison said in a frantic voice. "Someone broke in and trashed your place."

Chapter 22

At Millicent's condo, a policeman stood in the hallway speaking with Allison, and in the background a woman dusted for fingerprints. Detective Buchanan pulled Millicent aside and said, "Once we check the scene, I want you to walk through your place with me to see if you notice anything missing."

Millicent slumped to the floor and rested against the hall wall. Too much was happening too quickly. All this had to do with the signet ring and George, but she couldn't put the pieces together. Although she had the desire to curl up in her bed and take a nap, she knew she had too much cleanup to do first. Finally, Buchanan reached out a hand and helped her up. "Let's go take a look inside."

She stumbled through the doorway, shocked to find everything in her living room tossed to the floor. She immediately dashed into the kitchen. The drawers had been emptied onto the floor, and the contents of the refrigerator were strewn everywhere. Her one remaining amaryllis plant lay smashed on the floor, dirt spread everywhere.

Then it struck her. If she had left the ring in her apartment, whoever had done this would have found it.

Then she noticed the door to her patio open.

"It looks like an intruder picked your lock to get in. He hadn't finished looking through your apartment. Mrs. Petrov must have surprised him, and he left by climbing down from the patio."

At that moment a police officer came up and whispered in Buchanan's ear.

Buchanan turned toward Millicent and cleared his throat. "Mrs. Hargrove, if you could please wait here, I need to speak with one of your neighbors."

Clenching her fists at her home being violated, Millicent sank into her ravaged couch as Buchanan strode out of the apartment. Someone had invaded her domain and destroyed her things. Tears welled in her eyes, but she willed them back. She wouldn't allow these people, whoever they might be, to intimidate her. She'd find out what was going on and get to the bottom of these awful events. She took a deep breath. She would move on with her life and not give up.

In half an hour Buchanan returned. "A neighbor saw someone drop to the ground and run away. The description she gave sounds like the man who confronted you in your driveway the day I came to your house."

"Who are these people, and what do they want?" Millicent snuffled.

"I don't know yet, but we'll find out."

"Did the dead man have any identification?" Millicent asked.

"No. But we'll check his fingerprints and DNA against known felons. Now let's finish checking your apartment."

They completed the walkthrough.

"Do you notice anything missing?" Buchanan asked.

"Everything seems to be here, but I have a lot of cleanup to do."

"I'd suggest having a deadbolt installed on your door. I'll also have a patrol officer check on you tonight."

"Thank you, Detective. This is all so disturbing."

After the police left, Allison gave Millicent a hug. "I guess I'm going to have to help you organize this time."

Millicent gave a wan smile. "Let's get to work. But first I have to call to have a deadbolt installed."

Using her smart phone, she Googled locksmiths in Boulder, called several numbers and found one eager for immediate work at a premium price. Then she and Allison set to cleaning and putting things away—the biggest problem being all the spilled food and broken jars. They filled up two trash bags with throwaways, mopped the floor and had things back to normal by the time the locksmith arrived to install the deadbolt.

While the locksmith worked on the door, another workman arrived to patch and repaint the ceiling in the bedroom.

"This place is like Grand Central Station," Allison commented. "I thought you were offering me a safe haven, but there's nothing but chaos here."

"Everything will soon be back in a semblance of order."

"And I'll be staying with you tonight to protect you," Allison said.

"Are you sure you want to risk it?"

"Of course. Besides there will be a policeman coming by to check on us. Maybe he'll be as handsome as that Detective Buchanan."

"Allison, I don't know what I'm going to do with you. You need to turn your attention to older men."

"Why? I can always look, can't I?"

*****

Millicent did feel more comfortable with Allison in the next room that night. Not that she slept well. She awoke with dreams of flying dumpsters, signet rings falling like rain and huge men jumping off balconies. She was glad when the morning light appeared and she had an excuse to get up. At least this morning no water was dripping in her face.

She salvaged enough coffee, bread and jam to make a continental breakfast. Allison dashed off to go to her house, and Millicent promised to follow in a few minutes. As she prepared to leave, her phone rang. She answered to hear Diane Cooney on the line. "Millicent, why don't you come here for dinner tonight?"

"Things have been pretty chaotic for me lately. Allison and I found a dead body in her dumpster, and someone trashed my apartment."

There was a pause on the line. "How awful. What's happening to you?"

"Too much."

"Now give me the details."

Millicent recounted the saga of the day before.

"Well, that settles it. You need a reprieve from fixing a meal for yourself. I won't take no for an answer. You show up here right at six-thirty."

Millicent suppressed her inclination to argue. "Okay. I'll be there."

*****

When Millicent reached Allison's house, Ned and crew were in full motion.

"Another half hour and we'll have the truck loaded," Ned informed her. "Provided you and Allison don't find any more corpses."

"I'm not going to look in that dumpster again," Allison said. "The trash service can just haul away any dead people, sight unseen."

At that moment Millicent remembered Paula Sutter. "Oh my goodness. I forgot I'm supposed to be at another client's house this morning."

"Now don't go getting senile on me, Millicent," Allison said.

"I have too much on my mind."

"Finding dead bodies will do that. You go ahead and take care of it. I'll do the final vacuuming and meet you at my condo this afternoon."

Millicent removed the canister vacuum from her car for Allison and drove away.

When she arrived at Paula's, she apologized profusely for being late.

"It's not a problem, dear. I didn't remember what time you planned to be here anyway."

Millicent worked furiously, and by two she had the small kitchen and eating area completed. Paula didn't have many cooking implements and stocked very little food.

"I've contacted a man who will call you about the stamps," Millicent said.

"Thank you. That will be a relief to get rid of those boxes."

"I'll be back tomorrow to finish the two remaining bedrooms."

*****

Millicent drove like a madwoman to get over to the condo and help Allison with unpacking. With their dedication and efficiency, Ned's crew had everything in the appointed places by three o'clock. Then Millicent helped Allison make a few changes to furniture placement to accommodate the sunlight streaming in through the curtains.

With everything completed, she adjourned to her own apartment to take a short power nap before her dinner engagement.

*****

Millicent arrived at exactly six-thirty, and Diane's husband, Pete, greeted her at the door. "Come on in. Meet a colleague of mine, Matthew Kramis."

Matthew held out a stiff hand. "How do you do?"

Millicent eyed him warily, seeing a man her age with a full head of wavy brown hair, a narrow face and serious, set lips.

"Matthew, Millicent is a longtime friend of Diane's. They're bridge buddies. She also recently started her own business."

Matthew focused a bored gaze a foot over Millicent's head and didn't respond.

Pete smiled at Millicent and slapped Matthew on the back. "This old guy retired from a thriving legal practice. We worked on some business projects a few years ago before he decided to take down his shingle."

"Yes, we negotiated quite an agreement on that Haskle deal," Matthew said without smiling. He stood stiffly, and Millicent almost broke out laughing. She imagined this guy with cardboard lining his chest, the proverbial stuffed shirt.

Pete poked Matthew in the ribs. "He only lost one case that I'm aware of. He tried representing himself in his own divorce proceedings. Patricia took him for a bundle."

Matthew glared at Pete but said nothing.

Diane entered the room and gave Millicent a peck on the cheek. "I'm so glad you could join us. You're having a really tough time, so you need a break from all your troubles. You've met Matthew, haven't you?"

"Yes, Pete did the introductions."

"Good. Good. What can I get you to drink?"

Millicent decided with all that had happened she needed to keep her wits about herself. "I'll have a glass of mineral water."

"That's all?" Diane eyed her warily.

Millicent smiled. "For now."

"What's your profession, Millie?" Matthew asked.

"It's Millicent. I worked at the Boulder Medical Center for years. I retired recently and now have a professional organizing business."

For the first time, Matthew showed some sign of life. He chuckled. "Helping people clean up their stuff?"

"Exactly. I call my business 'Unstuff Your Stuff.' "

"That's rich, Millie. Rich. 'Unstuff Your Stuff.' Very clever."

"It's Millicent," she said, realizing he didn't get it.

Diane served a delicious meal of salmon in a rich orange and ginger sauce accompanied by asparagus and mashed potatoes. Even if Matthew was a jerk, the meal lived up to her expectations.

"How's the new organizing business going?" Diane asked over fruit tarts.

"Four clients so far including Allison. No one's fired me yet."

Matthew stared at her without smiling. "That's important."

Millicent coughed into her napkin to keep from breaking out in laughter at how literally he took things.

"I bet when you move people you find all kinds of weird stuff in their houses," Pete said. "You have to clean out any porn yet?"

Millicent smiled. "I've been organizing for demure little old ladies so far. No porn."

"Don't let Allison hear you call her a little old lady," Diane said.

Millicent flicked her wrist. "You know what I mean."

"What do you do with all the junk people have stored away?" Pete asked.

"Some things go to relatives, quite a bit gets donated, and the rest ends up in the trash."

"How about garage sales?" Diane asked.

"I held a garage sale when I cleared out my house, but it's quite a bit of work for a small return. I wouldn't recommend it unless someone really enjoys standing around all day watching people pick through their belongings."

"If we ever decide to downsize, we'll have you come organize us," Pete said. "And you, Matthew. Do you need any help de-cluttering your stuff?"

"I can't image any woman who could do better than I do," he said and pursed his lips. "I keep my things immaculately organized."

Yeah, Millicent thought. Boxes with starched shirts lined up on a dresser, one for each day of the week. She looked at her watch. "It's been a wonderful evening, but I have to get home."

To her surprise Matthew walked her to the door. "Why don't you join me for dinner and a movie tomorrow night?" he asked.

"I'm sorry, but it's too soon after my husband's death for me to start dating, Matt."

"It's Matthew."

Chapter 23

As she walked to her car, Millicent chuckled to herself. Diane's effort to set her up with an eligible man had been a dismal failure. No wonder Matthew went through a divorce. She couldn't imagine anyone living with someone like him. She seemed to attract them somehow. Like the jerk at the bridge tournament. Now being a single woman, she had become a target for these weird bachelors. The only one with potential seemed to be Ray. He appeared interested in her, and she liked him, but as she had told Matthew, it was too soon after George's death to consider dating. She would contemplate that in the future but certainly not while the investigation into George's death was ongoing.

As she prepared to open her car door, a hand clamped over her wrist. She staggered and looked up to see a man in a ski mask.

"I want the signet ring!"

"W—what signet ring?" Millicent stammered.

"You know what signet ring. This is your last warning." He slapped her hard on her cheek, knocking her to the pavement.

With her ears ringing, she lay there, stunned. After gasping a deep breath, she pulled herself up on the side of the car. Her assailant had disappeared into the darkness.

Trembling, she held her stomach, afraid she would throw up. It took her another two deep breaths to stop shaking. Her first instinct was to run back to Diane's house to call the police, but the man was gone, and she had no desire to face Matthew again. As she locked herself in her car, she also realized a policeman coming to take a report wouldn't do much good. She needed to figure out the mystery of this strange signet ring and the events surrounding George's mysterious second career and murder before she joined her late husband at the hands of some psychopath. By the time she reached her condo, she made a decision. She went inside and turned on all the lights, making sure no intruder had invaded her domain. First she called Diane.

"Thanks for having me over for dinner," Millicent said.

"What did you think of Matthew?"

She paused for a moment. "Different. But I'm calling about something else. A man accosted me outside when I left your house."

"Are you all right?"

"Yes. But I want you to know that someone was lurking in your neighborhood."

"Should I call the police?"

"That isn't necessary."

"I won't go walking outside alone tonight, and I'll tell Matthew to be careful when he leaves."

After hanging up, she called Ray Younger.

"It's good to hear from you, Millicent."

"I have a favor to ask."

"You name it."

"I have something I'd like you to look at. Do you still have your magnifying glass thingy?"

He chuckled. "It's called a loupe, and I still have one I've used for over forty-five years. You need a jewelry appraisal?"

"Only inspected. Are you available tomorrow?"

"For you, I'll make time. When would you like to get together?"

"Would it be all right if I come to your place at nine in the morning?"

"I'll have coffee on and some of my world famous cinnamon buns ready."

Millicent sucked on her lip for a moment. "You don't have to go to any special effort."

"Hey, it's not often that I have an attractive young lady calling on me."

"This is strictly business, Ray."

He sighed. "I understand. Do you want me to invite Ned over to chaperone?"

"That won't be necessary. I trust you."

"I don't know if that's good or bad."

"I'll see you in the morning. Thanks, Ray."

Next she called Katherine and said she'd like to stop by at eight in the morning. With everything set up for the next day, she washed her face, momentarily regarding her cheek in the mirror. The skin shone red but wasn't cut. With a little makeup it would hardly be noticeable. She realized she wanted to look her best for Ray in the morning. Yes, when she was ready, Ray would be the one she'd like to spend time with. But in the future, not now.

*****

After another restless night, Millicent fixed herself a cup of high octane coffee and gulped it down. As she rinsed the cup, the phone rang.

A gruff male voice said, "I understand you help people organize."

"That's right."

"I'd like to meet with you to learn about your services. This afternoon."

"I could do it two o'clock or after. Where's your house?"

"Let's meet at the Continental View Church in Lafayette at two."

"And who shall I ask for?"

There was a pause on the line. "James Sanders. I'll meet you in the lobby."

She intended to ask who referred him to her, but before she could formulate the question, the line went dead. Strange call. She felt better meeting this James Sanders in a public place like a church rather than in his home.

*****

When she arrived at Katherine's apartment, she immediately explained, "I need to get something I hid in the amaryllis pot I gave you.

Katherine's stuttered, "W . . . well . . . er . . . there's a problem."

"What problem?"

"Yesterday, I accidently knocked the plant over and the pot broke."

"What did you do with the pieces of the pot and the dirt?"

"I swept everything up and put it in the trash."

Millicent smacked her forehead. "Is it still in your trash?"

Katherine looked downcast. "I hope I'm not in a heap of trouble. I took it out to the dumpster last night."

"I have to find it."

"You better hurry, sweetie. Today's trash pickup."

"What kind of bag would it be in?"

Katherine finally smiled. "I use pink trash bags, so you should be able to spot it near the top of the dumpster."

Muttering under her breath over her error in thinking she'd been clever to hide the ring in the plant given to Katherine, Millicent dashed out to the dumpster. She found some bricks to pile up and peered inside. She reeled back and had to grab the side of the dumpster as the stench of old garbage assailed her nose. She perused the contents and didn't see a pink bag. She picked up an old broomstick lying on the top of all the gunk and poked and stirred the witch's brew. She pushed aside the top layer of black trash bags. Still nothing pink. Then she heard the grinding sound of the trash truck. She looked up to see it at the other end of the alley, lifting a dumpster with the metal claws and dumping the contents into the gaping maw on the side of the truck.

She had to find that bag. She pushed aside another layer and spotted something pink. A momentary surge of hope passed through her chest until she saw only a pink, half-full bottle of Pepto-Bismol. She heard more grinding noises as the truck moved a building closer. She pushed at the trash with the broomstick, like a member of a crew team rowing through quicksand. She continued to struggle and managed to dislodge several large bags.

Finally, she spotted a pink bag. Leaning over as far as she could, she hefted the bag out, flicking a black banana peel aside.

At that moment the trash truck pulled up, and the driver waved out the window. "You done dumpster diving, lady?"

Millicent's cheeks grew warm. "Yes, I found what I needed."

She carted the bag off to the side. Dropping to her knees, she opened it to find rancid steak bones and some frozen dinner packaging. Holding her breath, she poked deeper into the bag and uncovered a withered amaryllis plant. Jackpot! Now she just needed to find the ring. Rooting around, she spotted a speck of gold. Eureka! With the ring in her hand, she resealed the trash bag and lobbed it back into the now empty dumpster.

She returned to Katherine's apartment for a thorough scrubbing of her hands before sealing the ring in a Baggie. Then she checked her watch—not too far off schedule.

*****

Next, she drove to Ray's house.

He ushered her in to the aroma of brewing coffee and cinnamon. "What took you so long?"

"I had a last minute emergency getting my hands on the signet ring I want you to look at." She inhaled deeply as Ray placed a steaming mug and a plate with a gigantic bun in front of her. This helped overcome the memory of the stench she had encountered in the dumpster.

"Eat and drink before we check out this ring of yours." Then he did a double take. "Something happen to your cheek?"

She put her hand to her face. "Yes, a man slapped me last night. It has to do with the ring."

"What?" He threw his hands in the air. "How dare someone do that to you?"

"I'm okay."

"You can tell me all about it after you've had something to eat."

She took a huge bite and savored the sweet, tangy taste. "Dis iz d'lishous," she said through a mouth crammed full of bun.

123

"Right out of the oven."

She swallowed and licked her lips. "In addition to cooking, what are your other talents?"

"The whole nine yards. Chief cook, bottle washer, and I even take out the trash. Either that or the place would end up looking like a dump, and I'd starve to death."

Millicent finished her coffee and bun, resisting the urge to ask for a second helping.

"Now this ring of yours. What's the background?"

"My husband had it in a lockbox. He left secret instructions that I tracked down. There must be something special concerning this ring. It may be the motive for George's murder since several thugs have been inquiring about it, including the one who attacked me last night."

"Let's go take a look at it in my den."

They ambled down the hall and entered a room where Ray had a desk with a bright lamp. He sat down and picked up his loupe. "Show me this secret decoder ring."

She reached in her purse and handed it to him.

He removed the ring from the Baggie and gave it a cursory inspection.

"Pretty standard fraternity signet ring."

"Do you see any unusual inscription that can't be seen by the naked eye?"

"I'll check again." He closely examined the ring. "Nope. Nothing."

"There has to be something. Too many people have been seeking it. Where on a ring could something be hidden?"

"It has a solid band. The only other spot could be under the artificial ruby."

"Can you remove it and look underneath?"

"Give me a minute."

She watched over his shoulder as he used a pick, then pliers to loosen the red stone and pry it out. He put the loupe to his eye and looked at the setting. "I don't see anything unusual here." He scraped with a pick. "No, all solid."

"And the back of the stone?"

Ray leaned forward into the light and inspected it. "Now here's something unusual."

Millicent bent over. "What?"

Using a pick, Ray extracted a small black object which he held up triumphantly. "I'd say your ring has a microdot that may contain coded information."

Millicent felt her heart race. "That must be what everyone's looking for."

Ray pulled out a small translucent envelope and dropped the dot inside. "What do you intend to do with this?"

Millicent thought over all the alternatives. The government man had given her an address to send the ring to, George had left instructions for a different address, and she also had the option of placing it in the hands of Detective Buchanan. But if George had been involved in a secret government agency, would the police know what to do? They might be well-meaning, but she couldn't let this fall into the wrong hands. She had to go with her instinct. She'd send it to the address George had requested. "Can you reassemble the ring without the microdot? It may come in handy later."

"Sure." He reinstalled the stone, tapped it down and then polished it with a cloth. "No one will be able to tell I've removed it."

"Until they look underneath."

"They'll probably figure they have the wrong ring anyway."

Millicent put the ring and separate envelope with the microdot carefully into her purse. Remembering the appointment she had set up for the afternoon, she said, "I have another favor to ask."

"You're becoming quite demanding. I didn't realize what a high-maintenance woman you are." He winked. "Really, I'll be happy to help you any way I can."

Her cheeks went warm. "Could you accompany me to a client meeting this afternoon at two?"

Ray raised an eyebrow. "And the reason you need company?"

Millicent bit her lip. "It's hard to explain, but I feel uncomfortable going alone."

"Do you want to notify the police?"

"I can't call the police every time I see a new client. No, this man's voice over the phone gave me a chill. It's not as if I'm going into an unknown home or anything. He wants to meet in a church. But I'd feel better if someone came with me."

"Tell, you what. Ned and I planned to sneak away for a golf game this afternoon. We'll go with you."

"Oh dear. I hate to disrupt your father-son outing."

"Hey, we can do that another time. There's a damsel in distress. The Youngers to the rescue."

"It's probably nothing, but I would appreciate the company."

Chapter 24

The rest of the morning Millicent spent finishing the organizing at Paula Sutter's house. The two bedrooms went quickly because Paula didn't use them at all.

As they conducted the final walkthrough, Paula said, "What a wonderful job you did for me. I'll have to invite you back periodically to help me reorganize."

"Now remember to not let things accumulate. Continue to give yourself permission to throw or give things away."

"I will, dear."

*****

On her way home Millicent stopped at a nursery and bought two amaryllis plants. Arriving home, she placed them on the windowsill of her kitchen. She punched a hole in the soil of one amaryllis plant and reburied the ring. She'd give the other one to Katherine the next time Katherine hosted bridge. Then she addressed a business envelope to the address in George's note and enclosed the smaller envelope with the microdot. She added a stamp and a return label with her new address. It amazed her—she had only been in her new condo a week and had already received one of those mailings with a request for donations and a packet of self-adhesive return address labels. How had the nonprofit organization, Save the Pit Vipers, found out her new address so soon?

Then she deposited the envelope in the mail pickup slot for the condo complex. She dusted her hands together. There. All taken care of.

*****

At one-thirty, Ray knocked on her door. "Ned's the chauffeur this afternoon. He's waiting outside."

Millicent grabbed her purse and a notepad. She now had what she needed to be ready for this new client.

As they sat down in Ned's Buick, he said, "We's got da muscle for ya, lady."

"And I appreciate it. There's probably no problem, but I'm grateful to have two strong men accompanying me."

"What made you suspicious about this guy?" Ned asked.

Millicent thought for a moment. "His tone of voice. He didn't sound like the typical person who would be contacting me for professional organizing. My intuition bells went off. I figured it best not to meet him alone."

"You want me to bring my lug wrench in for some additional protection?" Ned asked.

"That won't be necessary. Your presence will be all I need. I don't expect this initial consultation to last more than an hour. You can still get some golf in this afternoon."

"Dad's actually relieved that we don't have to play. I always win all his money."

Ray shrugged. "Hey, you get it now or inherit it later when I kick the bucket. Take your pick."

They pulled up in front of a box-like building with a huge cross by the doorway.

"This looks like a deserted warehouse, not a church," Ned said.

"It does say Continental View Church, but where are all the cars?" Ray asked, motioning toward the deserted parking lot.

They moseyed over to a series of glass doors. Ned tried the handle on one, but it didn't open. He went down the row but each door remained locked.

Millicent put her face to the glass and peered through, spotting a man approaching. He opened the door and she scooted in followed by Ray and Ned.

"I'm Sanders. What the . . . who are these guys?"

"They're my assistants, Mr. Sanders." She held out her hand and then noticed his face for the first time. He had a gold ring in his left ear. "You're the man who attacked me in my driveway!"

"Very observant." He pulled out a handgun from his pocket and waved it toward Ray and Ned. "You two get over here by the lady."

Millicent's heart raced. What had she got them into?

Ray and Ned followed the instructions.

Millicent took a deep breath to gain her composure. "Why did you have me come here?" She tried to make her voice sound indignant and brave but it came out as a squeak.

"I figure a little persuasion in an out-of-the-way place will help you remember where the signet ring is."

Millicent wondered if she should tell him where the ring was hidden, now that the microdot had been removed. Would he release them or shoot them? She decided to bide her time. "Why such an interest in a signet ring?"

"Let's just say I've been hired to get it."

"Who hired you?"

"Lady, you're not the one asking questions here. I am. Where's the ring?"

Out of the corner of her eye, Millicent saw two people entering through a side door. Steeling herself with all her nerve, she shouted, "Look out! There's a man here with a gun!"

The two people hesitated and then dashed back out the door.

Sanders fired two shots and Millicent saw spider webs grow in the glass where the two people had stood moments before.

"Damn!" Sanders roared. "There wasn't supposed to be anyone else here."

Millicent turned her head and saw some people coming to the front door where she had entered.

Sanders saw them at the same time, turned his gun and fired. The sound reverberated and another spider web appeared in the glass. People ducked and scattered.

Millicent could see cars driving into the parking lot. People were arriving for some event, but after the initial shots, the ones scared off must have been telling others to stay away from the doors.

"Up those stairs," Sanders waved his gun toward a stairwell and pushed Millicent, who bumped into Ray and Ned.

They stumbled up the stairs and found themselves in a small room that overlooked the lobby.

Sanders surveyed the room. "Crap. There's another stairwell leading up here. Okay, you three, close that back door, move a table over and turn it on the side to barricade that entrance."

Ray and Ned did as instructed.

"Put another table in front of the opening we came in."

Ray and Ned put another one in place.

"Now turn off the lights."

Millicent reached over and flipped the switch. The room fell into semi-darkness with a small amount of light coming in through the stairwell and the window overlooking the lobby.

"Okay, you pull over a chair and sit by the back barricade," Sanders pointed to Ned, who complied.

"The two of you set up chairs and sit by the front barricade."

Millicent and Ray pulled over chairs and sank down onto them.

"Good. If any cops try to storm this place, they'll have to get over the tables and through you. I'll sit in the back of the room with my gun ready. Don't move unless I tell you." He dropped onto a chair and waited.

Millicent looked around the room, her eyes now adjusting to the ambient light. This must be used for a children's craft area, she decided, noticing a flipchart easel, a blackboard, chalk, twine, watercolor paints, colored paper, crayons and poster boards.

Sanders seemed perfectly content to sit there and wait.

"I'm sorry I got you into this, Ray," Millicent whispered in his ear.

"Hey, you couldn't ask for a more romantic spot, sitting here in the dim light, just the two of us, my son and a crazed killer."

"What do you think will happen?"

"Those people outside will call 9-1-1 to report a shooter in the church. The SWAT team will respond. This place will be swarming with cops within thirty minutes."

"Will they get us out?"

"They'll move people away from the building, assess the situation, check out the rest of the church, determine where we're being held and try to establish communication with the shooter. Also when they find out that this guy has hostages, they'll have a negotiator talk to him."

"How do you know so much?"

Ray shrugged. "I attended a police citizens' academy a few years ago. We had a lecture on how the SWAT team operates. Do you know this man's name?"

"On the phone he said James Sanders. Probably not his real name."

"No, I would guess not."

"Shut up, you two," Sanders bellowed.

"I'm hungry," Ray said, winking at Millicent.

"I'm thirsty," Millicent added.

From across the room, Ned added his two bits, "I have to go to the bathroom."

"What do you think this is—a family car trip?" Sanders growled. "Just hold it."

"What can you accomplish by keeping us here, Mr. Sanders?" Millicent asked.

"It'll buy me some time to figure out how to get out of here."

"All this for a little ring," Millicent said. "Doesn't seem worth it."

"Don't keep mouthing off. I have enough bullets to finish the three of you as well as to take out any cops who show up."

They all remained silent for the next twenty minutes.

Finally, Sanders cleared his throat. "You, the old guy."

"I'm Ray."

"Ray, go look out the window into the lobby and tell me what you see."

Ray stood up, stretched and ducked over toward the window to peek out. "I can see some guys in camouflage outfits sneaking around the sides of the lobby."

"Damn. SWAT."

"Wouldn't it be best to give up before anyone gets hurt?" Millicent asked.

"No. I'm in control here. You're my hostages, so they aren't going to storm this place or do anything stupid that will get you killed."

"That's reassuring," Millicent said.

"But if you don't follow my every command, you'll all die."

"That's not very reassuring." Millicent inspected her feet, finding nothing but her old blue pumps. She sat in silence, only venturing a glance over at Ray. He looked straight ahead but reached over, took Millicent's left hand and gave it a gentle squeeze. She found his touch reassuring.

Her mind reviewed all that had happened. George's murder had set off this whole sequence of bizarre events. But the root cause was buried in the past with the secret life he had lived. She tapped her lower lip with her right index finger. There must have been signs all along but somehow she had missed them. George must have been very proficient at whatever he did in order to hide it even from her. She considered herself a good judge of human character and thought she could read George like a book. Apparently she had missed a few chapters. She prided herself on being able to tell when he had a work issue on his mind. But she hadn't been able to discern when he had a secret work issue on his mind. Now all these people trying to get their hands on the signet ring. First, the government man who had paid her all the money. Then this man who confronted her in her driveway and now was holding her hostage. Who did he work for? Who were the two goons who showed up at the garage sale, one of whom ended up dead in Allison's dumpster? How did they fit in? To say nothing of the masked man who slapped her outside Diane's house. Had that been the same man now holding her hostage? Then she faced the discrepancy between the addresses given to her by the government man and George's instructions. All very mystifying.

A voice called up the stairwell, interrupting her thoughts. "Hello, up there."

Millicent looked toward their captor.

He raised the gun, stood up and snarled, "I'll do the talking. The rest of you shut up unless I tell you otherwise." He paced over toward Millicent and Ray and shouted, "What do you want?"

"I'm here to talk to you. How many of you are up there?"

"That's none of your business."

A moment of silence followed and then, "Who am I talking with?"

"You can call me James. Who the hell are you?"

"I'm Dave. Is everyone okay up there?"

"Yeah. Nobody's dead yet. If you try to storm the stairs, though, Dave, everyone in here dies!"

"And how many would that be?"

"Dave, you're not listening. Now if you keep acting stupid, I'll start shooting hostages. You play it smart, and no one gets hurt, understand?"

"I understand, James. You need any water or food up there?"

"Yeah. You can send up some beer and pizza."

"I'll be happy to do that if you release a hostage."

"No deal. We'll get by without anything."

Several minutes of silence ensued, and then the voice shouted up the stairs again, "James, I do have something for you."

"What's that?"

"I can send a phone extension up so you can talk directly without shouting. I can have someone take it up the stairs."

"No way, Dave. No one comes up here. Give me a minute."

James paced around and then pointed to Millicent. "Lady, you go to the top of the stairs with your hands up. I'll tell them you're coming down to pick up the phone. If you take too long or don't come back, I'll kill one of the other hostages. You got that?"

"Yes," Millicent said through tight lips.

"Now, nothing stupid or one of your companions gets a bullet in the brain." He cleared his throat. "Dave, are you listening to me?"

"I'm here, James."

"I'm sending a hostage out onto the landing at the top of the stairs. I'll have her in sight. She'll then walk down the stairs to get the phone. If she doesn't return within fifteen seconds, I'll shoot one of the other hostages. You got that, Dave?"

"Yeah. Hold on a minute. I'm adding enough phone cord to reach upstairs."

Millicent heard some rustling and thumping at the bottom of the stairs.

James shouted, "You screw up on this, Dave, and so help me I'll leave a room full of blood. If anyone else comes on those stairs, people will start dying. And no talking to the hostage I send out or I'll kill someone up here."

"I understand, James. I'm almost finished hooking up the extra cord. Give me another minute here."

After what seemed to Millicent to be an hour, Dave shouted, "All set, James. You can have the hostage come out to get the phone."

James waved his gun at Ray. "Pull the table aside, old man."

"Watch who you're calling old," Ray muttered.

"What did you say?" James tapped the gun on the back of Ray's head. He winced. "Nothing."

"You keep your yap shut." Then he motioned to Millicent. "You go out on the landing and stand there with your hands up. You wait until I instruct you and then go down the stairs to get the phone. And don't say anything to anyone."

Millicent felt her heart beating at an unsafe level. She gulped and stood up from the chair, her legs shaking.

Ray slid back the table, and Millicent shuffled around it and stumbled out onto the landing with her hands reaching toward heaven.

"Stop right there," James instructed.

Millicent halted and looked down the stairwell.

"What do you see down there?"

Millicent craned her neck. "Just an empty stairwell at the moment."

"Dave, are you ready with the phone?"

"Yes, James."

"Okay, the hostage will come down to pick it up." He pointed his gun at Millicent. "Remember, lady, no talking. Now move."

Hesitantly, Millicent took two steps down with her arms still over her head. A man in camouflage gear came into her view holding a sign which read, "How many people including you? Signal with fingers."

As Millicent passed out of sight of James she closed her left hand and curled her right thumb into her palm, leaving four fingers sticking up.

The man at the bottom of the stairs held up four fingers to confirm, and she gave a slight nod. As she reached the bottom of the stairs, he handed her a phone and some coiled cord. She lowered her hands to take the phone, turned and scampered up the stairs, not wanting to take too long and antagonize James. She reached the landing and staggered back into the room with the phone in her hand.

As soon as she passed the table, James signaled to Ray. "Push the blockade back in place, put the chairs next to it and sit down."

Ray did exactly as instructed.

James grabbed the phone from Millicent. "Go back to your chair."

She sat down as James uncoiled the cord and took the phone with him to the back of the room. Shortly afterwards the phone rang, and James picked up the receiver. "Yeah?"

He listened for a moment. "This is James. Who are you? . . . Okay, Carol, you pay attention. I want a helicopter flown into the parking lot to take me and one hostage away . . . I know it takes time to get a helicopter . . . I've seen the parking lot. There's plenty of room to land a chopper out there unless you have the place packed with SWAT vehicles. You clear them out and bring a helicopter . . . I'll release the rest of the hostages when you make the arrangements . . . okay, you look into it and call me back." He slammed down the phone.

"Damn hostage negotiator. Trying to game me."

"Thank you for not shooting anyone while I went to get the phone," Millicent said.

James looked up, a surprised expression showing in the dim light. "I keep my word. You do the same and no one gets hurt."

"I will. I don't want anyone hurt either. What's so important about the signet ring you're looking for?"

James seemed to slump. "Damn. I never should have taken this job. I was paid a lot of money to find that ring, for all the good it will do me now."

"Why is it so valuable to your employer?"

"Hell if I know. I'm just the hired gun."

"But you and your cohorts have been harassing me for weeks now."

"Yeah, I thought we'd have convinced you to give up the ring by now. That's why I took the more direct approach today. Now it's all gone to hell." He waved his gun at Millicent. "I'll tell you this. I'm either escaping this place or dying in the process. I'm not giving myself up and going back to prison."

Millicent flinched and clenched her fist. "Did you go into my house and stab my husband?"

"He wouldn't tell me where he hid the ring. I threatened him and he attacked me. I had to defend myself."

Millicent's hand went to her mouth. "You *were* the one who killed George."

"And remember that. I have no qualms about stabbing or shooting people. Any of you mess up in here and you're dead. Got that?"

Millicent crumpled back into the chair. "Yes." Then she straightened up. "But you searched through our house. Obviously you didn't find the signet ring or you never would have asked me to come here."

"You got it, lady. You came home while I was searching. I had to leave. I couldn't chance you spotting me, and I needed to keep you alive to find the ring for me. Now, no more yakking. I need quiet to figure things out."

They sat in silence for fifteen minutes. Then the phone rang. James picked it up. "You got my helicopter? . . . Carol, weren't you listening? Do I have to start shooting hostages? . . . all right then. Let me be very clear. I'm not going to release a hostage for food and water. I don't care crap about that. I want a helicopter, at which time I'll release the other hostages once I'm assured of safe passage with one hostage . . . I'm not kidding. You forget the diversionary tactics. Call me back when you have a helicopter arranged." He slammed the phone down again.

"Stupid bitch," he muttered. "Thought I'd release a hostage in exchange for food and water. I'm fine and I don't care if the rest of you die of thirst or starve to death. I hope she got the message through her thick skull this time."

Millicent checked her watch. They had been in this building for two hours now. It was a good thing that she hadn't drunk too much coffee that morning. She didn't think James would let anyone have a restroom break.

Finally, the phone rang again and James picked it up. "Whatcha got for me, Carol?"

"Helicopter being arranged? . . . hell, if you were serious about this, you'd have it here by now . . . I know you don't have choppers just lying around . . . well, you get one here ASAP if you want your precious hostages to live . . . okay, and when it gets here I want you to have it hover over the building for one minute. I'll be timing. Once I hear it, I'll know you're serious. I'll call you when I hear the helicopter." This time he didn't slam down the phone.

He chuckled out loud. "She's getting the message. Now we wait to see if she can be trusted."

By Millicent's watch it took another hour before she heard the sound of a helicopter's blades over the building.

"Hot damn!" James shouted. He picked up the phone. "Carol, I hear the chopper. You kept your word. Now I'll keep mine. Have the helicopter land in the front parking lot, and I'll call you back shortly." He placed the phone in the cradle. "Show time. Now, here's what we're going to do, lady and gentlemen. Since they probably have some description of my clothes from the people I shot at in the lobby, I'm going to change clothes with you." He pointed his gun at Ray. "Get over here and take off your pants and shirt."

Ray stood and stumbled over to the back of the room. They switched clothes and Millicent couldn't help but sneak a peak at Ray's muscled legs and tight butt. James struggled into Ray's smaller pants and had difficulty zipping them up. Then he picked up a ball of twine from the craft area and handed it to Ray. "Now, you tie up the young guy. Come over here." He signaled Ned to join them.

Ray followed James's directions and bound Ned's hands behind his back and his feet. "Now, you sit down with your hands behind your back." He pushed Ray to the floor. "And you stay right where you are, lady. No funny business."

Millicent nodded her head. "I'll wait right here."

James bound Ray's hands behind him and then wrapped twine around his ankles. Then he stepped over to Millicent and whispered to her. "You go over to the back door and move that table out of the way and wait there."

She did as instructed.

Then James picked up the phone. "Carol, you took care of your part as promised, so I'm going to release two hostages. They'll come out with their hands in the air. Later, we'll make final arrangements for me and another hostage to come to the helicopter." He hung up the phone and marched over to where Millicent stood. He bent over and whispered in her ear again. "You and I are going down the back stairs. You'll be my shield. Keep your hands in the air and don't say a word."

"Won't they see your gun and figure out who you are?" Millicent whispered back.

James chuckled. "I'll have it tucked under my armpit with my arms partially raised. I'll come down behind you. They'll think I'm a hostage. But remember I can reach for that gun at any time and shoot you. So don't try any dumb stunt."

Pained to be polite to the creep who had killer her husband, she spit out, "Yes, sir."

James cracked the door and checked. Then he thrust it open and pushed Millicent forward. "Hands up."

Millicent's arms shot skyward.

"Move." He pushed her through a short hallway and down the stairs.

Chapter 25

As Millicent reached a bend in the stairs two men in camouflage gear and helmets appeared with automatic rifles. "Get down!" the first one shouted.

Eyes squeezed shut, Millicent dropped to the stairs, sliding down as shots reverberated in the tight space. She screamed as she thrust her hands over her ears while adrenaline surged through her body and her mouth turned to cotton. Finally, she was dragged down the rest of the stairs.

"Hands behind your back!" someone commanded.

Millicent put her hands behind her and felt handcuffs being snapped on her wrist as the bands of steel cut into her skin. Then large, rough hands patted their way down and around her body.

Her heart raced as she wondered what she could do to convince the man she had been a hostage.

"She's clear," a deep voice reported as the hands stopped frisking her.

"Ma'am, I'm going to remove the cuffs." The voice had turned cordial, so different than moments before.

"Thank goodness. I was just a hostage."

"We check everyone—standard procedure. You never know when someone is pretending to be a hostage and is really the perpetrator."

"The man behind me took us hostage."

"We know. He pulled a gun. We shot him."

"Is he dead?"

He helped her to her feet. "I'm afraid so. I'm sorry to have scared you."

"There are two hostages tied up in the room upstairs."

"They've been searched and identified. We've accounted for the four people you said were up there. We're still checking all the side areas upstairs to make sure there's no one else."

"You've found everyone."

"If you'll come with me, a detective will want to take a statement from you."

The SWAT team member led Millicent to a Sunday school room on the first floor where a man in a suit waited for her. He waved her to an adult chair rather than the tiny ones under tables containing cartons of crayons. "I'm Detective Rodriguez. May I offer you a water bottle?"

"That would be wonderful."

He handed her an Evian, which she uncapped and chugged like a college beer-guzzler.

"Ah, that's better." She smacked her lips.

"Now please give me your name, place of residence and recount exactly what happened this afternoon."

Millicent took a deep breath. "My name is Millicent Hargrove." She gave her address and described being a personal organizer who had an appointment to meet a prospective client at the church.

"Were you suspicious of the arrangement to meet here?" He looked at her from the corner of his eyes, as if sizing her up.

"The tone of the man's voice on the phone disturbed me. That's why I asked my friends to accompany me."

"And when you reached the church?"

Millicent went through the litany of going into the building, the man pulling a gun on them, the shots fired and then being taken hostage.

"Do you know the name of the hostage-taker?"

"He identified himself as James Sanders, but I suspect it's a false name. I recognized him by sight as a man who accosted me previously. I think this all relates to a homicide case. My husband was recently murdered. You can check with the investigator, Detective Buchanan, of the Boulder Police

Department. This James Sanders admitted that he killed my husband. Ray and Ned Younger, the other two hostages, also heard his statement."

Detective Rodriguez's brow furrowed as he madly scribbled notes on his pad.

It took an hour before she completed the interrogation. As she stood to leave the room, he asked her, "We have a victim's advocate program. Would you like to speak to a counselor?"

Millicent paused for a moment. "I don't think that's necessary right now. I have my two friends. If we can talk things over, I think I'll be fine."

"They should be able to rejoin you shortly." The detective handed her a card. "If you think of anything else or want to speak with a counselor, call this number." He stood and led her out of the room. She noticed Ned and Ray seated ten feet apart on the other side of the lobby.

Rodriquez left her on her own in the lobby with instructions not to speak to Ned, and then he led Ray toward the adjoining room. Ray smiled at Millicent and gave her a thumbs up sign.

Millicent paced around in a circle, gulped from the bottle of water she had been given and then slumped into a folding chair as she waited for Ned and Ray to complete their statements.

Finally, the three of them received permission to leave.

"I'm so relieved neither of you was hurt," Millicent said.

"And I was worried about you," Ray replied. "That madman taking you down the stairs. Then we heard gun shots. The next thing we knew, SWAT guys were frisking us."

"Whew. Quite a different experience than a game of golf, eh Dad?"

"If you hang out with the older generation like Millicent and me, you'll have all kinds of interesting experiences."

"Older generation?" Millicent crossed her arms.

"Maybe wiser generation?" Ray smiled.

"Let's grab something to eat," Ned said. "I'm starved."

"You up for a dinner date, Millicent?" Ray winked at her.

She scowled back.

"With you here, Ned, Millicent will feel comfortable having a chaperone again."

They stopped at a Subway, and Millicent had a foot long roast beef sandwich, which she finished quickly.

As she relaxed with a full stomach, all the energy drained from her body. "I never thought the professional organizing business would be this enervating."

Chapter 26

Ned pulled up in front of Millicent's building, and Ray hopped out to walk her to her apartment. "Pretty exciting date, huh?" he said with a twinkle in his eyes.

She groaned. "That wasn't a date."

"Well, maybe sometime we can go on a real one—dinner or movie with only the two of us. You let me know when you're ready."

She patted him on the arm. "Thanks, Ray. You'll be the first to know."

"I'll hold you to that. Now, get a good night's sleep."

"I'm bone tired. I hope the image of that awful man holding us hostage doesn't keep me awake."

"If you have any trouble sleeping, give me a call and we can talk over the phone for a while. I promise to put you to sleep."

She flashed him a smile. "You couldn't be boring if you tried, but thanks for the offer." She closed the door and slumped against it, the exhaustion and tension causing her muscles to go weak. Yes, she was ready to get some sleep.

But it wasn't to be. She got as far as washing her face when the doorbell rang.

She threw on a robe and peered through the peephole. Detective Buchanan. She exhaled loudly and opened the door.

"I'm sorry to bother you after your trying day, Mrs. Hargrove, but I need to ask you some further questions." His voice was polite but the skin around his eyes sagged as if he'd been without sleep for several nights.

She led him into her living room and after they sat down asked, "Have you spoken with Detective Rodriguez?"

"Yes. He filled me in on the hostage situation. I'm sorry you had to go through such a terrifying event."

"Has that awful man been identified?"

"Not yet. He had no identification on him. We'll be checking his fingerprints and DNA against various databases. I understand he confessed to killing your husband."

"That's correct. Both Ray and Ned Younger heard it as well."

Buchanan tapped a finger on the arm of the chair. "Yes, there's no question regarding what he said, but I'm interested in the motive. Have you learned anything more to indicate why he wanted this signet ring?"

"He said someone hired him to find it. I couldn't get any information as to why or by whom."

"That's still the unresolved part," Detective Buchanan said. "With this James Sanders now dead and the other body found in the dumpster, this case centers around the missing signet ring and who wants it enough to kill for it. We need to find the person behind all of this."

Millicent looked toward her kitchen and thought of the signet ring buried in the dirt of her amaryllis plant. Should she come clean with the detective? She felt embarrassed that she had withheld that information but was too tired to go into it tonight.

"Have you spoken with the federal authorities?" she asked.

"I've made inquiries, but have found no one who admits knowing about your husband or his activities."

"For the life of me I can't figure out what George was involved in."

"I'll get to the bottom of it. If you think of anything else, please call me."

After Buchanan left, Millicent dropped onto her bed. She ached from falling down the stairs, and her wrists still stung from the handcuffs. Then the tension of the day cascaded through her. Her chest heaved from the loss of George, and tears welled in her eyes. After a good cry, she wiped her face. Then the recollection of the man in the dumpster popped into her mind followed by the memory of James Sanders pushing her down the stairs and the shots being fired. She shuddered. Her heart raced. She thrashed in bed, trying to push aside all these images. Finally, she calmed down and sank into a fitful sleep.

Unfortunately, she shot up in bed, wide awake at four in the morning. She thought of Ray's offer to call him if she couldn't sleep, but instead read a romance novel until sleep finally overtook her at dawn.

*****

After cocooning all weekend, on Monday morning Millicent dragged herself out of bed at nine, ready to get back to work. After a breakfast of French toast, orange juice, and coffee, she checked email. To her delight she found a message from someone she had met at the networking meeting, a woman who had three referrals for her.

Millicent immediately followed up and gained three new prospects. This would help her forget the recent events.

She called the first number and spoke with Ruth Haven, a woman with a voice so shaky Millicent had to ask her to repeat much of what she said.

"Do you think you could come to my house today?" Ruth asked.

"I could be there in the afternoon, three or later."

"Let's make it right at four. My children will be coming back at that time. I'm in such a muddle."

"Oh?"

"They're arguing over the things I want to give them. I don't know what to do."

Millicent made a quick decision. "Mrs. Haven, let me come over at three today. You and I can confer for an hour before your children arrive."

"All right. Maybe you'll have some helpful ideas."

Next, Millicent reached Keith Noble.

"Mr. Noble, I was referred to you. I provide organizing services."

"Thanks for calling. I do need some help. I can't see very well and have a lot of old stuff to clean out of my house."

"I could come over tomorrow morning, if that's acceptable."

They agreed on nine, and Millicent added the address to her calendar.

Finally, she called a man named Ashton Beaumont whose deep resonating voice greeted her over the phone.

"And the nature of the organizing assistance you require, Mr. Beaumont?"

"I'm movin' into a retirement home. I need to figure out what to take and what to get rid of. Lots of decisions to make."

"I could meet with you tomorrow afternoon."

With that appointment set, Millicent had her next two days well-planned. As she prepared to go to Hannah Judson's, she heard a knock on the door. She looked through the peephole to see Allison standing there holding a tray with two cups on it.

"I thought now that we're practically neighbors, I'd stop by to offer you a cup of my freshly brewed Columbian coffee."

"I can't resist an offer like that." Millicent smiled, thankful for whatever company she could get that didn't come with a badge or a gun. "Come in."

Millicent heated up two cinnamon raisin bagels in the microwave, and they sat down at the dining room table.

Allison spoke up before Millicent had a chance to say anything. "I want to remind you that I'm hosting bridge tomorrow night. That way Diane and Katherine will have a chance to see my new place and how you helped me organize it. By the way, I looked for you Friday afternoon before I went out of town for the weekend. I stopped by twice but you weren't here."

Millicent suddenly worried that living in the same complex with Allison might lead to too many visits. "I was kind of tied up, or rather handcuffed."

Allison choked on her bagel. "You getting into that kinky sex stuff?"

"No, but I was taken hostage."

"You're into bondage?"

Millicent breathed out with exasperation. "I was involved in the hostage situation that's been in the news." "Allison, get your mind out of the gutter.

A man who approached me as a prospective client turned out to be the man who murdered George, and he took me hostage."

Allison put her hand to her cheek. "That's awful. What you must have gone through."

"This thug locked up Ray, Ned and me in a room with him at the Continental View Church, and the SWAT team rescued us."

Allison's jaw dropped open, and her hand holding the coffee cup froze halfway to her mouth. Then a smile appeared on her lips. "You and three men locked up together and husky brutes running around to rescue you. Sounds exciting."

"Allison, you've been watching too many R-rated movies."

"Now tell me the whole story, uncensored of course."

Millicent recounted her experience on Friday, and Allison listened with wide eyes. "In any case, you didn't end up like Patty Hearst, posing for a picture with an automatic rifle."

"No, but I've seen enough guns for a while. I'm ready for a few days of nothing more threatening than old boxes of hand-me-downs." Millicent looked at her watch. "I hate to cut this short, but I have a client waiting."

"I know, you busy career woman. Let me know the next time you're meeting with the SWAT team."

Millicent forced a smile. "That was a once-in-a-lifetime experience. Things will be quiet from now on."

Chapter 27

Hannah Judson escorted Millicent inside the house. This time Hannah was wearing a silver turban. Maybe she had tuned in to the spirits of orphan electronics equipment.

Millicent went out to the garage to assure she had adequate space to stage everything, and by the time she returned inside, a burly young man had appeared, sent by Ned.

Millicent and her assistant spent the rest of the morning and early afternoon lugging electronic equipment from the upstairs bedroom into the garage at Hannah's house. It took both of them to carry several large televisions down the stairs. Millicent concentrated on moving the smaller devices. She couldn't believe the number of printers, monitors and computer workstations in the stack of stuff in the bedroom. She wondered when she would get too old for this much exertion. Fortunately, she had kept herself in shape and had a strong helper. Besides, this type of work would keep her slim and trim without the expense of attending aerobics classes.

*****

At three o'clock, Millicent pulled up in front of Ruth Haven's house along the foothills in west Boulder. She noted the good repair of the small, older house. A miniature white fence surrounded a small rose garden adorned with ceramic rabbits and squirrels.

Ruth, a short woman in her seventies with her silver hair pinned back in a bun, met her at the door. In a quavering voice she said, "Thank you for making time for me so quickly. Come inside."

They sat down in a neatly-appointed living room, complete with white doilies on most of the surfaces. Millicent scanned the room. "You have things well-organized, Mrs. Haven."

"Yes. This room contains things that I'll be keeping. I don't need your services to eliminate clutter, but I do have a dilemma."

"It sounds like you have a family emergency to deal with. Tell me what's happening."

"I've decided to downsize and have three grown children. I plan to give them most of the possessions I no longer need. I thought it would be a simple process. I estimated the value of everything and divided the total equally. I put things in three groups in the spare bedroom. When the three of them arrived yesterday, they began haggling over what I had set aside for them. Rather than a pleasant family event, it turned into a disaster. Andrea wanted the doll collection I thought Bernice would like, and Harry felt I planned to give too many things to the girls."

"Let's take a look at what you have."

As they walked into the spare bedroom, Millicent flinched when she saw the stuff—clothes, collectibles, china and furniture resting in stacks in three corners of the room.

"And you're ready to get rid of all these things?" Millicent asked.

"Yes. I read a book about organizing, and it emphasized purge, purge, purge. I spent weeks dividing everything up very fairly. I thought my children would be delighted, but it didn't work out." She frowned again.

Millicent found herself empathizing with this new client. "Fairness exists in the eye of the beholder. Obviously your children have different ideas of value."

"Apparently so. What should I do?"

Millicent surveyed the stacks of stuff for a moment and had an idea. "Since they don't like your suggestions, let them select what they want.

When I was a child, we had games on playgrounds. We'd take turns picking people to be on teams."

"Yes, we did similar things during my childhood." She chuckled. "I always got picked first for games of jacks but didn't play stickball very well so usually ended up selected last."

"We can try using that same strategy with your things. Let your kids take turns choosing what they want to keep. If they see something of value or importance to them, they can select it. That way you're not trying to dictate priorities."

"That might work."

Millicent checked her watch. "We have forty-five minutes before they arrive. Give me a hand and we'll reorganize everything here so things become more visible." Millicent entered whirlwind mode, quickly directing Ruth and moving things to form a more visible display of the goodies. Then she went into the dining room and placed a quarter, dime and nickel under overturned cups.

"Why did you do that?" Ruth asked.

"Just wait. You'll see."

Shortly, the front door banged open, and Ruth's kids entered all together. The three of them glared at Millicent during introductions, but she paid no heed to their reaction.

"This afternoon I'm here to help divide up Ruth's bequests to all of you." Millicent gave her most professional smile.

"Just as long as I get the doll collection," whined Andrea, a woman in her fifties wearing a dark business suit.

"You're always trying to boss everyone around, just because you're the oldest." Bernice in a bright yellow dress wrinkled her nose at her sister.

"You two are impossible," Harry said, flicking a piece of lint off his Brooks Brothers shirt.

"This can all be worked out to everyone's satisfaction." Millicent raised her voice and her hands to gain their attention. "I understand you aren't pleased with Ruth's choices for each of you. Therefore, we're going to let you select what you want." She checked and validated that she had their undivided attention. "We'll take turns, and you each can pick something that you want to keep. Now who wants to go first?"

All three hands shot up.

Millicent smiled. "Okay, in that case let's step into the dining room." When everyone had assembled there, she pointed to the three cups. "Each of you put a hand on a cup."

When they had charged over and done that, Millicent said, "Under the cups I've put a quarter, dime and nickel. Whoever has the quarter gets to select first, followed by who has the dime and then who has the nickel. We'll proceed in that order until you select everything you want. Anything left will be donated. Understood?"

Three heads nodded. They uncovered the cups and found that the order would be Bernice, Andrea and Harry.

"One final ground rule," Millicent said. "Once everything is allocated, we'll stack everything in three groups in the garage. You have a week to take everything away. Anything still here a week from now will also be donated."

They returned to the spare bedroom, and Bernice immediately went over and selected a box with a collection of ceramic dogs. Andrea picked the doll collection in a cardboard box and Harry lifted up a wicker chair which he moved to his part of the room. Within an hour, the majority of stuff had been moved into three corners, jealously guarded by the three offspring.

A pile of clothes still remained.

"Last chance," Millicent said, feeling like an auctioneer. She pointed to the loose items. "Going once . . . going twice . . . gone to Goodwill. Now let's get everything into the garage."

After moving all the stuff and the three kids had left, smiling rather than grousing, Millicent sat down with Ruth.

"I don't know how to thank you," Ruth said. "I thought I'd have my children fighting forever."

"You have to remember, they may be grownups in age, but in some ways they still act like little kids. They each found things that appealed to them

152

emotionally from their past. Different people gravitate to different things. It isn't the inherent value but the perceived value that's important. You can't predict how anyone will react. Each person will have his or her own selection criteria."

Millicent presented her invoice for the afternoon's work. She had jacked up her normal rate, figuring it should be closer to what a psychiatrist would charge.

Ruth didn't express any concerns, whipped out her checkbook and wrote a check for Millicent's requested amount.

Millicent gave Ruth the number of a local charity to call for the pickup of unclaimed items. "Remember, if your kids don't get their things, have those picked up as well. You're not responsible for long-term storage."

Satisfied that she had done her part to unclutter the universe, Millicent returned home.

*****

Upon entering her condo, Millicent found the message light blinking on her machine. It was Detective Buchanan asking her to call him. She returned the call and he asked to immediately come over to speak with her.

"I'll be here," she said.

Twenty minutes later her doorbell rang. She let the detective in. "May I offer you some coffee or tea?"

"No, ma'am. May we sit down?"

She led him to her living room. Buchanan looked around the room. "You sure have a way of making things look neat and tidy."

Millicent smiled. "That's what I now do for a living. But I don't think you're here to discuss organizing."

"No. I want to tell you we've identified the man who held you hostage as well as the man found dead in the dumpster last week. Do the names Justin Magnuson and Ralph Alden sound familiar to you?"

Millicent shook her head. "Never heard them before."

"I was afraid of that. We're still trying to learn more regarding these two. Apparently they were mercenaries—crime-for-hire types. Records on both of them. They worked together on jobs and teamed up with a third man named Reed Eggleston. That name ring a bell?"

"No."

Buchanan reached into his inside coat pocket and pulled out a picture. "Here's Eggleston. Look familiar?"

Millicent picked up the picture and squinted at it. "Yes, detective. I saw him at my garage sale."

Buchanan took back the picture from Millicent. "That confirms his link to the two dead men. We have a bulletin out on him, and we'll see if we can find him. But we still have no clue who these guys worked for."

Chapter 28

After the detective left, Millicent sat in her living room contemplating all that had happened. Two of these men were now dead with a third still out there somewhere. That didn't give her a comfortable feeling. What if he burst into her condo or tried to attack her on the street? She fidgeted, ventured a nervous glance around her apartment, then stood up and went to the door to set the deadbolt. She would have to be careful.

The phone rang, and she jumped, her heart beating double time. She picked up the receiver, willing herself to stay calm.

"This is Matthew Kramis. We met at the Cooney's house."

"Yes?"

"Diane mentioned the unfortunate incident you had after you left their house the other evening."

Millicent thought that maybe Matthew wasn't such a jerk after all if he called to express concern for her. "Yes, it frightened me to be attacked by a man in a ski mask."

"You shouldn't go walking around alone," Matthew continued. "That's not a smart thing to do."

Millicent bristled. He was still a jerk. "I've been going out on my own for over fifty years, and no one has ever accosted me before."

"You're getting older now and need to be more careful."

Millicent almost gagged. "Why are you calling?"

"Checking up on you. I've seen too many cases of people who have run into problems like you did. I thought I'd warn you."

"Okay, I've been warned."

"How'd you like to go to a concert tomorrow night at Chautauqua? I have two free tickets."

With an offer like that how could she resist? "No, thanks. I have a bridge game tomorrow night."

"Aw, you can't keep turning me down. Wouldn't you like to go on a little date sometime, Millie?"

"No, I'm not ready to start dating."

"When will you be, Millie?"

"In five years, Matt."

*****

The next morning Millicent began her busy day by driving to Keith Noble's house in south Boulder. The sun was shining, and Millicent felt the warmth on her skin as she strode up the walkway. She thought of how difficult her job would be if she had reached the age and condition of not being able to drive. Independence remained important to her, and she planned to stay fit both physically and mentally as she grew older. Her new job helped with both categories—lots of exercise and mental challenge such as solving problems with feuding heirs.

A man holding a thin white cane met her at the door.

"Mr. Noble, I'm Millicent Hargrove."

"Come in. Come in." He led her into the house, his cane clacking on the tile floor.

Millicent did a double take at all the signs of disorder. A table in the entry way stood misaligned and stacked with unopened mail, some scattered on the floor. Clumps of dust collected along the baseboard. She scrunched up her nose, seeing some small pellets she swore were mouse droppings.

The living room could only be called a disaster. Broken glass littered one corner of the room, yellowing newspapers teetered in a stack up to her belly button, a lampshade tilted at a forty-five degree angle, the couch had torn places where stuffing showed through and the piece de resistance—a vase of dead flowers lay on its side in a dried-up puddle of gray muck on a coffee table.

"Mr. Noble, you said over the phone that you have poor eyesight."

"Yes. I'm legally blind."

"Do you ever have anyone come in to clean your house?"

He grimaced. "I use to, but she quit and moved to Phoenix. I haven't found a replacement yet."

"How long ago was that?"

He paused. "She moved last year."

"It shows. Your house needs a major cleaning."

"I suppose it does. I can't see much to do it myself."

"What would you like me to do for you?"

"I need to organize everything. My son and his family will be visiting. I want the place to look nice and neat when they get here."

"And they haven't been here recently?"

"No, my son's had a work assignment in Germany for the last two years. They're returning to the States." A smile crossed his face. "I'm hoping they'll settle back in Boulder, so I can see my grandchildren regularly." The smile disappeared like a cloud covering the sun. "Or hear them actually, since I can't really see them anymore. They're my only family with my wife dead these three years."

"Let's take a look at the rest of the house," Millicent suggested.

She checked out the master bedroom with a poorly-made bed, clothes strewn everywhere and a closet that could contain unspecified flora and fauna. Due to not having been entered recently, the two other bedrooms seemed in relatively good shape other than needing dusting and a good scrubbing. Then she stuck her head into a bathroom that would need a flamethrower to clean.

The kitchen could have been a centerfold for *Mold and Bacteria Monthly*. Millicent couldn't believe Keith Noble survived after eating food from this place. This would definitely be one of the first priorities when she started this job, if she wanted her client to survive long enough to pay her.

Finally, she inspected the small basement and proceeded into the garage to find cans and bottles covering the whole cement floor. "What's all this?" Millicent asked.

"Old paint and solvents as well as chemicals from my darkroom. My hobby used to be photography, but I haven't been able to pursue it since I lost my sight."

They returned to the living room and Millicent sat down. "It seems to me that your house needs significant cleaning and organizing. I'd also suggest that we could take some steps to make your life easier. It must be difficult for you to find clothes and food. I think with the proper organization you'll be much happier."

"Yes. I spend considerable time searching for things. Particularly, in the kitchen, I have trouble finding the right pots and pans and then I often open bottles and cans to smell them to know what I have."

"We can eliminate a lot of duplicate cooking implements, and I can group similar things together so it will be easier for you to find what you need. Give me a moment, and I'll put together a quote for you, if you'd like."

He nodded his head. "I need to do something right away. My family arrives in two weeks."

The cleaning and uncluttering of this house would require major surgery. Millicent needed to subcontract a cleaning service for the serious scrubbing. After a call on her smart phone to check on cleaning rates, she took out her notebook and did some quick calculations. This project would take her the rest of the week.

When she told him the amount, he smiled broadly. "You're hired. When can you begin?"

"I have another appointment this afternoon but I can start as early as you like tomorrow morning."

"I'm up by seven, so any time after eight will work."

"We'll start at nine. I'll need you here to discuss what we do with things, since the decision ultimately is yours. Once we're done, you'll be ready to welcome your family into your neatly organized home, and you'll have a much easier time getting by on your own once they leave."

*****

In the afternoon, Millicent pulled up in front of the home of Ashton Beaumont. Ashton, a man in his seventies with a weather-worn face, stood at the door, looming over her at more than six feet tall, and welcomed her with an expansive wave of his hand. "Come on in. Feast your eyes on the Beaumont estate." After the mess she had seen that morning, this house presented a refreshing change. Everything appeared neat and tidy. But there still remained lots of stuff—railroad gear neatly arranged everywhere.

"You're a train enthusiast, Mr. Beaumont?"

"I shore am. Call me Ashton, little lady." He pulled an engineer's hat out of his pocket and put it on over his thinning hair. "You a railroad fan yourself?"

"My husband and I enjoyed several trips on the California Zephyr. I never did anything with model trains, though."

"Oh, you don't know what you missed. Railroads are my life."

"Tell me what you want to accomplish with the organizing, Ashton."

A frown crossed his face. "Unfortunately, I have to give up this place. I'll be moving into the Louisville Retirement Village in a month and I need to clear this house out for sale."

"How much space will you have in your new residence?"

"A living room, kitchenette and two bedrooms—one bedroom for me and one for my model trains. Let me give you the grand tour."

Millicent surveyed the house, Ashton pointing out railroad paraphernalia on every shelf and surface. One side of the basement contained a table with an HO gauge model railroad, replete with a mountain, tunnels, railroad station, several engines, lines of railroad cars and miniature people.

"Quite a setup," Millicent said. "Will this fit in the room at the retirement home?"

"Yes indeed, ma'am. I measured it. I'll even have space to get into the closet. No room for an extra bed though. My guests will have to share my bed or sleep in the living room." He winked at her.

She ignored him and stepped over to the other part of the basement, covered with thick tan carpet and containing a well-used brown leather couch and a large entertainment center with television, DVD and stereo. On the sides rested four-foot high speakers.

He followed her over. "You should hear the sound I get out of those woofers."

"Too large for a retirement home. Also, you won't be able to play things very loud with neighbors."

"I love those big speakers."

"I'm sure you do, but you're going to have to be practical regarding how much room you have in your new apartment. You'll have to settle for smaller, more compact equipment."

"I've always been one for large equipment." He winked at her again.

Millicent refrained from rolling her eyes. How much of a problem would this guy be? "You'll have a lot to do to prepare for your move."

"That's why you're here, little lady. Help me squeeze all my stuff in."

"Yes, but we'll also have to eliminate quite a bit as well. Let's go look at your garage and yard."

Tools, gardening equipment and model train gear filled the garage. The yard held a large wooden railroad crossing mounted in one corner, a crumbling picnic table, the headlight from a railroad engine mounted on a post and a cowcatcher with daisies growing around it.

"What do you plan to do with that cowcatcher?" she asked.

He chuckled. "That's the old term. Actually they're called pilots but same use whether a cow or other obstacle needs to be knocked off the tracks. To answer your question, though, the Realtor wants me to clear everything out of my yard. I thought I'd donate all the railroad items to the museum in Golden. I'll keep a few small items for my new apartment and the other stuff will have to be pitched."

"I can arrange for a dumpster to be brought to your driveway."

"That would block my car. Can you have it put on the street?"

"The city won't allow that. You'll need to park your car on the street during the cleanup period with the dumpster in the driveway."

"If you say so, little lady. You're the expert."

Millicent took the smart phone out of her purse. "This backyard will require a lot of hauling of material. I'll have to hire some assistants to carry things to the dumpster. I'll take a few pictures to help with finalizing an estimate for you." She snapped the pictures and looked at the display to make sure she had captured everything.

"What's all this going to cost me?"

"I'll have an estimate to you tomorrow."

"When can you start and how long will the whole process take?"

"I can start Monday and dedicate all of next week to this."

"Good. That will give me plenty of time before I move into the new place. Now, little lady, would you care to join me for a late afternoon meal? There's a great steak place around the corner."

Millicent looked at her watch. "I'm sorry, but I have a bridge game tonight. I need to head home to change clothes. I also have to get cracking on your estimate."

His face fell. "Maybe another time?"

"We'll see. Now I must be on my way."

*****

As Millicent drove home, she wondered what caused all these men to make passes at her. This had never happened before George died. Did she have a sign around her neck that read, "Pathetic widow, hit on me," or what?

A tear trickled down her cheek. She missed George. And she was still feeling all the stress from people seeking the signet ring and from being taken hostage. Things had been anything but normal lately. At least she had her organizing business, so she could bury herself in someone else's mess.

*****

At home, she took a shower and changed for bridge. She zapped herself a panini and fixed a garden salad. A light meal before the snacks that Allison would serve for bridge was the best policy. She always tried, unsuccessfully, to restrain herself from gobbling the bridge mix. Tuesday night was the time for her chocolate fix.

She was cleaning dishes after her meal when her doorbell rang. She seemed to be having a lot of visitors these days. Peeking through the peephole, she saw Ray and Ned standing there. The sight of them brought a smile to her face. Her fellow hostage survivors.

"Gentlemen, what brings you here?"

"We wanted to stop by to make sure you're okay after the harrowing events last week," Ned said. He turned toward Ray. "Actually, Dad insisted on it but wanted me to come with him."

Ray smiled at Millicent. "Have to do these things aboveboard with my chaperone present at all times."

She put her hands on her hips. "I don't know what I'm going to do with you two."

"Well, you might invite us in so we don't have to stand in the hallway," Ray replied.

"Come in. Come in. I can't chat too long since I have a bridge game starting in half an hour."

"That's fine," Ray said. "Seeing your smiling face and that you're fine will keep my old heart beating for another day."

Millicent turned to Ned. "Is your father always this way with the ladies?"

"No, it appears to be something with you. Usually he couldn't care less about women."

Millicent arched an eyebrow. "I find that hard to believe. Ray seems to me to be a died-in-the-wool flirt."

"It's that you bring out the best in me, Millicent."

"Or the worst."

162

"Have the police been checking up to make sure no one is harassing you?" Ned asked.

"Detective Buchanan called on me, but I haven't seen anyone else."

"There's a police car parked out in front," Ned said. "We saw an officer sitting there. It's good to know that they're taking the threat to you seriously."

"All kidding aside, we're both worried about you, Millicent," Ray said. "We like you, and, besides, your customers are apt to bring all kinds of new business to Ned so he'll be able to afford to take care of me in my old age. I view it as my long-term care insurance policy." He winked at her.

She exhaled with exasperation. "Can't you be serious at all, Ray?"

"Nope, that's for young people like Ned. Old guys like me have to always play to an audience."

Millicent turned toward Ned. "I have another job where I need to subcontract your services."

"Good. I can always use more business."

"This will entail some heavy lifting. My prospective client, Ashton Beaumont, has a yard full of railroad equipment and other stuff that will need to be carted out to a dumpster. It's too heavy for me to carry, so I need your strong arms."

"This woman is after your body, Ned. Why can't she be after mine?"

Ned glared at his dad. "This sounds like something I can handle. Put me in your bid at my normal rates."

"Good. I'll get it worked up after bridge tonight and deliver it in the morning."

At that moment Millicent heard a pounding on her door. Being cautious, she looked first through the peephole and then opened the door to find Allison standing there, wringing her hands.

"What's the matter, Allison?"

"We have a major catastrophe."

Chapter 29

"Catastrophe?" Millicent wrinkled her forehead at her friend's obvious consternation.

Allison peeked around Millicent. "I'm sorry. I didn't know you had company."

"Come on in. Ned and Ray are here. You can tell us all what happened."

Allison staggered into the room.

Ned and Ray waved to her.

"I don't know what I'm going to do," Allison said. "Diane called five minutes ago. She was under the weather this afternoon but waited until the last minute hoping she'd feel better. Now she's sick to her stomach. We'll never find a substitute at this late date." Then her eyes lit up. "Do either of you gentlemen want to play bridge tonight?"

"Nope," Ned said. "I never play the game. I stick to golf and poker once in a while."

Ray beamed at her. "I play a little bridge."

"Oh, don't let him fool you," Millicent said. "He's a championship level bridge player."

Allison batted her eyes at Ray. "Would you be willing to fill in for the sick member of our group?" She looked at her watch. "We start in ten minutes."

"I would be delighted to, under one condition."

"Oh?"

"Ned drove me over and has an engagement this evening. If Millicent

164

is willing to give me a ride home afterwards, I'll be happy to stay for a bridge game."

"Done," Allison said. "The game is on."

"Wait a minute," Millicent said. "I haven't agreed to that yet."

"Yes, you have," Allison replied, patting Millicent's arm. "She would be happy to give you a lift home afterwards. It's all decided. I'll see the two of you at my place." She spun on her heels and pranced out of the room.

"Looks like I'm signed up for an evening of bridge." Ray chuckled. "I hope I remember how to bid."

"Don't give me that," Millicent said. "Your problem will be dropping down to our level. Our style of play differs from the tournament bridge you're used to. We do a lot of gossiping along the way."

"Good. Maybe I can learn some interesting tidbits about you, Millicent."

"My friends are sworn to secrecy."

"If I ply them with bridge mix and sparkling conversation, I'm sure to learn your deep dark secrets."

"I think you already have. My biggest secret is having been a hostage, and you know all the details."

Ray wagged his right index finger at her. "Ah, there's always more. Maybe George didn't work alone. Maybe this signet ring only presents a diversion to cover for your being a secret double or triple agent. Millicent Mata Hari."

Millicent's eyes rolled upward. "You read too many spy novels, Ray."

"I'll let you get on with your bridge game," Ned said. "Is it safe for me to leave you two alone together?"

"You can walk with us to the elevator," Millicent said. "It's time to go to Allison's anyway."

As they strolled down the hall, Ray asked, "Is there anything special I should know ahead of time regarding this bridge game?"

"Yes. Don't eat all the chocolate mints. Those are Allison's favorites."

When they entered Allison's apartment, Katherine had already arrived so everyone loaded up paper plates with fruit, vegetables and dip, grabbed a beverage and sat down at the bridge table set up in the middle of the living room.

"I'd like to partner with Millicent for the first round," Ray said.

"Since you've been kind enough to fill in at the last minute, that can be accommodated." Allison gave him her best hostess smile.

Ray and Millicent each grabbed a deck of cards to shuffle.

"Do you ladies play Stayman?" Ray asked.

"No," Allison answered. "We play WCTM."

Ray looked puzzled. "I'm not familiar with that convention."

"Whatever Comes To Mind. Now pick a card so we can see who deals first."

Katherine had the highest card with a jack of spades and dealt the first hand. She rearranged her hand for a minute and looked thoughtfully at it. "Pass."

Millicent looked across the table at Ray. "When Katherine takes that long arranging her hand and then passes, it means she has eleven to twelve points."

"Ah," Ray replied. "Part of the WCTM convention."

"Exactly."

Ray and Millicent won the bid at four hearts with Millicent playing the hand. She finessed the king of diamonds to make the bid.

"Well played," Ray said, gently clapping his hands together. "That finesse was the only way you could have made it. If you had tried to develop the clubs, you would have gone down a trick."

"Lordy, lordy," Katherine said as she batted her eyes at Ray, "You must have played a bit of bridge before, sir."

"I get out now and then." He turned toward Millicent and winked.

"Don't let him fool you with his innocent farm-boy pose," Millicent added. "He's an expert."

Ray gave an "aw shucks" smile. "Since I have the pleasure of the company of you lovely ladies tonight, this would be a good time to learn all of Millicent's deep dark secrets from her best friends."

Allison grinned. "Ooh, ooh, I'll tell first. She pretends to not like chocolate, but when you're not looking, she'll eat all the dark chocolate chips in my special bridge mix."

"And she's quite the tippler," Katherine said. "She's been known to have half a glass of red wine on occasion."

Ray gave a conspiratorial smile. "Do tell."

"And don't get her started on school reform. She's a fanatic on the subject of class size. She can go on for hours about how we're spending too much on school administration and not enough on teachers and students."

"Enough." Millicent smacked her hand on the table. "Allison, hand me the cards, it's my deal."

Katherine gave a fake pout and leaned toward Ray. "Spoil sport. I'm going to wait until Millicent has to visit the ladies room and tell you some really interesting things about her."

"I guess I'll stay at the table the whole night then," Millicent replied.

"Keep drinking lots, Millicent," Allison said. "Think waterfalls, dripping faucets, flowing streams. Then you'll have to go."

"I like this group," Ray said. "When I play with men, they're so serious with the play of the game that you never learn anything interesting."

"Stick with us and you'll hear all kinds of good tales," Katherine said.

*****

Ray and Millicent won the rubber, and they changed partners. During the break Ray excused himself to use the restroom.

"Down the hall, first door on the left," Allison called after him.

Once he disappeared, Katherine said, "He's quite a catch, Millicent."

"Just a friend."

Allison looked thoughtfully at Millicent. "I think he's interested in more than friendship. It's time that you had a little romance anyway. You can't be a grieving widow forever."

"It's too soon after George's death for me to even consider another man."

"That's an old wives' tale," Katherine said. "You need to get on with your life, girl. Get back in the saddle. Enter the dating scene. Don't be a hermit. And why not start seeing Ray? He's handsome, polite, plays bridge and obviously thinks the world of you. If you ignore him too much, someone else will make a play for him. Maybe me. I'll give you two weeks and then it's my turn."

Millicent couldn't tell if Katherine was kidding or not. She experienced a surprising twinge of jealousy. Then she admonished herself. She wasn't even ready to date yet, much less pursue a serious romance. Still, she felt good about the attention Ray gave her. "I'll let you know if there's open season."

"Hah," Allison said. "Katherine, you have her thinking now."

"Good. That man shouldn't go to waste."

*****

At the end of the evening, Allison tallied up the score. "Ray has high point with Millicent close behind. I came in third and Katherine gets the booby prize." She turned to Ray. "The hostess always gives something to the winner and loser. Everyone wait here." She disappeared into the kitchen and reappeared with an amaryllis plant in one hand and a small box in the other. "Ray, you get the grand prize." She handed him the plant.

Millicent noticed that it looked similar to the plant in her kitchen with the hidden ring, only in a black plastic pot rather than her ceramic pot.

"And Katherine, here's your booby prize."

Katherine took the box, opened it and pulled out a small object. "Lord a mercy, a lucky penny, so I'll win top prize next time."

"That's right," Allison said. "When Diane is back playing, you'll have a better chance of winning it all. Now I have something for Millicent, too." She handed her a baggy full of chocolate chips. "The leftover dark chocolate. The Mayans considered chocolate an aphrodisiac."

Millicent took the bag, and her cheeks grew warm.

"You be careful of her, Ray," Allison. "She's now a woman with chocolate."

168

Ray bowed. "I'll be very careful. Thank you for including me in your game. I had a wonderful evening."

As they left Millicent said, "I need to stop by my apartment to get a sweater before I give you a ride home."

At her condo, she unlocked both the regular lock and the deadbolt and preceded Ray in. "I need to use the restroom. You can look through my bookshelf in the spare bedroom while you're waiting." She dashed off so that she wouldn't have an accident after sticking to her decision to not leave Ray alone in the clutches of Allison and Katherine.

After using the bathroom, Millicent grabbed the gray sweater from her closet and returned, finding Ray leafing through a book of Baudelaire poems.

"Do you enjoy poetry?" Millicent asked.

"Yes. My wife hooked me on Baudelaire. I still read poems to myself when I have a chance."

Millicent's eyes lit up. "George used to read out loud from that book. It was our favorite. The English translation, of course."

"Same with us. I never learned French." Ray leafed through several pages and read, "*So in the forest of my heart's exile, an old memory sounds its clear encore!*"

"That's from *The Swan*."

"Very good." He turned a few more pages. "Millicent, look at this."

"What did you find?" She approached Ray and looked over his shoulder.

"There's a stamp in here." Ray turned it over, held it up to his eyes and gasped. "With a microdot stuck to the back!"

Chapter 30

Millicent stared at the little black dot on the back of the stamp. "Can you remove it?"

"I think so. Do you have tweezers?"

"In the bathroom." She dashed out of the room, returned and handed the tweezers to Ray.

He gently removed the dot. "Do you have a plastic sandwich bag that I can put it in?"

Millicent grabbed one out of a drawer in the kitchen and brought it to him.

He deposited the dot inside and returned the bag to Millicent. "Here you go."

"I wonder what I should do with this."

"It's up to you to decide."

"Yes. I guess it is. I'll take care of it in the morning. For now I'm going to put it in a mailing envelope and leave it on the dresser here. Now let's get you home." She pushed Ray out of the room, put the plastic bag in an envelope, dropped it on the dresser, glanced back once and turned off the light.

As they drove along Arapahoe, Ray said, "Another microdot like the one we found in the signet ring. Are you sure you had no idea your husband was involved in espionage?"

"That's the strange part. I never picked up any signs. I guess he must have been very good at whatever he did."

"You're a very perceptive person, so I'm surprised that he could have hidden it from you all those years. I'd never be able to do that. I'd give it away in nothing flat."

Millicent smiled. "You mean you don't have any deep, dark secrets?"

"Nah. I don't even cheat at bridge. Although, I did catch a team I played against in a tournament once, using illegal signals. That spoils the whole game. The challenge with bridge is using known techniques to communicate and then relying on superb play to make a contract. You're good at bridge, Millicent. If you worked at it, you could be a solid tournament player."

She clicked her fingernails on the steering wheel. "I'm not interested in that, Ray. I enjoy my social games once a week."

"Just consider it. I'd be happy to enter tournaments with you."

"But you have your regular partner."

"We each play with other people as well. Sid enters more tournaments than I do, so he often partners with others. He wouldn't mind."

Millicent scrunched her forehead. "Maybe sometime."

"Good. At least you didn't say no."

They pulled up in front of Ray's house.

"You want to come in for a moment?" Ray asked. "That occasional half-glass of red wine or some chocolate or something?"

"Thanks, Ray, but I have to get back. I still need to complete an estimate and get a good night's sleep before some major cleanup work tomorrow."

"Ah, you busy business types. Maybe another time." He stepped out and blew her a kiss.

*****

Millicent drove home, her emotions in a jumble. She liked Ray. He wasn't like the other jerks who had hit on her lately. Still, she didn't want to get involved. She had enough complications in her life right now. She needed to stay organized in her personal life in order to sort through this mystery of what George had been doing. Besides, she now ran a business with a needed service to provide to people who suffered from too much stuff. That was the appropriate focus for her energy.

She unlocked her door and stepped inside. She thought of her luck, having her friend Allison living in the same building, Ray and Ned coming by periodically and the police checking on her. She stepped over to the patio door to make sure it remained securely fastened. All appeared in order.

She retrieved her notebook and sat down at the dining room table to put together an estimate for Ashton Beaumont. She could drop if off in the morning on her way to Keith Noble's. She completed the bid, having tacked on a surcharge for potential unwanted romantic advances.

On the way to her bedroom, she stuck her head in the spare bedroom and turned on the light. Her gaze settled on the dresser. The envelope with the microdot was gone.

Chapter 31

Millicent shivered. Someone had been in her apartment. Everything was locked, and she saw no signs of an intruder. How did someone know of the envelope and then get in? Like a jab with a needle, the answer struck her.

She grabbed her purse, raced out, took the stairs down one floor rather than waiting for the elevator and pounded on Allison's door.

Allison opened it, standing there in a nightgown and robe. "Millicent? What are you doing here?"

"I need a place to stay tonight. Can I sleep in your spare bedroom?"

"Sure. Did something bad happen with Ray?"

"No. He's a gentleman. But there's been an intruder in my apartment."

Allison's eyes widened. "Have you called the police?"

"No, but that's the next thing. I'll contact Detective Buchanan." Millicent called his number and reached his voicemail. After leaving him an explanation of the events that had transpired, she asked him to call her mobile phone in the morning.

*****

After another fitful night of sleep, Millicent awoke to the aroma of cinnamon and coffee. Allison had prepared her a large mug and two sweet rolls.

"Thanks for being such a gracious hostess," Millicent said, rubbing her eyes.

173

"Hey, you're welcome to come for a sleepover anytime someone breaks into your apartment."

Millicent scowled. "Don't remind me."

She had just finished her breakfast when her smart phone rang. She answered it to hear Buchanan.

"Detective, someone broke into my apartment last night and took something. And I think they must have bugged my place somehow. They overheard I would be gone and knew exactly where I left the missing object."

"I'll be over in an hour with someone who can check for electronic surveillance devices."

Millicent agreed to meet him in her apartment. She looked at her watch. That should give her enough time to change, let the police in and then get to her nine o'clock appointment.

"Do you want me to go up to your apartment with you?" Allison asked.

"Thanks, but that shouldn't be necessary. The people who came in last night already took what they wanted. I don't expect them back."

But when she opened her door five minutes later, she steeled herself, afraid someone might be there. She turned on all the lights, picked up a knife from the kitchen drawer and gingerly peeked inside each room. With no sign of an intruder, she let out a sigh of relief.

Later when her doorbell rang and she saw Detective Buchanan through the peephole, she stepped into the hall. With him stood a rotund man wearing a sweat suit and holding a black bag with an antenna poking out.

She leaned toward Buchanan and whispered, "Since I think someone is bugging my condo, I don't want to say anything inside."

"Mack will check everything first, and then we can talk more." He signaled with his hand. Mack took a magnetic leakage probe out of his bag, pushed a button and began scanning through the house. In the living room he reached up and retrieved a small black object from the top of Millicent's picture of a California seascape. In her bedroom he opened the handset of her phone but found nothing. In the spare bedroom, he found a device behind the dresser, and in the kitchen he removed another small object from the leaves of the amaryllis plant where the ring remained hidden. Millicent almost laughed at the irony.

Mack put all the devices he had collected in a pouch of his bag and left the apartment.

"We can talk now with no one overhearing us," Buchanan said.

"What's Mack going to do with those, smash them?" Millicent asked.

"No, he's going to see if he can determine where a receiver might be."

"Come with me into my spare bedroom," Millicent said.

They entered the room. "Yes, this may sound like a spy novel, but my friend Ray discovered a microdot on the back of a stamp hidden in a book on the shelf. We placed it in an envelope which I left right here." She pointed to the dresser.

"Could your friend have taken it with him?"

Millicent shook her head. "No, he went out of the room before I did, and I consciously checked the location of the envelope before I turned off the light and followed him. We left immediately, so I know for sure the envelope was still on the dresser when I went out. When I came back later, it was gone, so an intruder entered in the meantime. And I could find no sign of a break-in. Someone obviously picked my lock."

"Let me do a walk-through of the whole apartment now that the recording devices have been eliminated. Wait in the living room."

Millicent sat down, twiddling her thumbs and wondering what her life had come to. Her husband murdered and involved in some kind of secret spy work, people bugging her condo, being taken hostage. Her calm, normal life had sure changed in the last month. She took a deep breath to calm her nerves, consoled herself that she had her organizing business now and looked at her watch. When Buchanan reappeared, she said, "Detective, you're welcome to stay here longer, but I need to go to an appointment."

"Fine. I'll check a few more things. If I need to speak with you, I'll give you a call on your cell phone."

Millicent dashed off, jumped in her car and drove to Ashton Beaumont's. He greeted her at the door and invited her in, but she explained that she had another appointment and handed him the estimate. He scanned through it and agreed to the bid. Before he could make any unwanted advances, she thanked him and headed back to her car, arriving at Keith Nobel's house with two minutes to spare.

Keith greeted her at the door with a smile. His unfocused gaze seemed to be aimed somewhere above her left shoulder. "You're really going to get me organized?"

"That's why I'm here. First, we need to color code what we're doing. I've brought black trash bags for the throwaways and white for donations."

"I can still distinguish black from white, so I can help," Keith said.

"I'll need your assistance for consultation as we sort everything. We'll eliminate things that get in the way of you living comfortably here. And remember, we'll get rid of anything you haven't used in the last year."

"Got it. Where do we start?"

"Let's begin in your living room. That will give you a comfortable place to relax during breaks as we work through the rest of the house. First of all, we have all these old newspapers and magazines."

Keith bit his lip. "I might want to refer back to something in one of them."

Millicent put her hands on her hips. "Keith, be realistic here. Can you even read a newspaper or magazine any more?"

He hung his head. "No."

"What good does it do having them clutter up your living room?"

He exhaled loudly. "You're right. I guess I'm still holding onto the hope that my vision might return some day, but I know the odds of that are remote."

"If that happens, then you can have the enjoyment of buying new magazines. In the meantime, we're going to pitch all of these." Millicent proceeded to fill up three black bags and lugged them out to the garage.

"Next, you have a lot of ceramic pots on surfaces in your living room. Several of these have been knocked over and broken. They don't serve you well."

"Those belonged to my wife. I hate to get rid of them."

"Is there any family member who wants them?"

He chuckled. "No. No one except my wife, Geraldine. She loved them."

"Be honest here, Keith. Do you enjoy having them here?"

"I hate to admit it, but not particularly."

"You're the one living here now, so you need to have a home that contains things that you like and can use. We'll add these to the donation bag." In fifteen minutes, Millicent had filled a white trash bag. After lugging it outside, she turned toward Keith. "Good. We're making progress. Now the furniture. We want to make sure you have the furniture you'll actually use, a minimal amount to allow space for your mobility. Walk with me through the room."

As Keith followed her, his cane banged against a chair and a coffee table.

"You should be able to navigate through here without hitting furniture. Which chairs do you actually sit in?"

"Only the easy chair when I'm listening to music or audio books."

"All right. That's a keeper. You should have a couch and a maximum of two other chairs in here—sufficient for when you have visitors. The coffee table isn't practical because it gets in your way. I'll tell you the items I suggest you eliminate."

Half an hour later, Millicent had moved two chairs, the coffee table, a pole lamp and an end table out to the garage, thanking her lucky stars she had stayed in shape.

"Now walk around your living room."

Keith circled the room without whacking anything with his cane.

"What do you think?" she asked.

A smile lit up his face. "This is much better."

"Now on to your music and audio books." Millicent pulled out all the CDs from the cabinet and piled them on the floor. "I'm going to read the labels to you and you tell me if you've listened to this music in the last year." She scanned through the collection. "I see you have quite a number of jazz recordings."

"I love those. But I have trouble finding the ones I want."

"I can see why. They're not in any particular order. You have jazz mixed in with pop tunes and classical music. I'll help you organize these in a way that will make it much easier for you to find what you want. Now you also have quite a few Broadway musicals. Do you listen to them often?"

"No, not at all. Only Geraldine played those CDs. I feel like I should keep them in her memory."

"We've been over this before. You have no obligation to save anything of your wife's you don't use. Your memories of her are in your head, not in things. Since you're not going to listen to these, we'll put them in the donation pile."

She soon filled another white bag. When she lugged this one outside, she noticed that she was running out of storage space in the garage with all of the material on the floor. She went back inside and led Keith out. "We have the living room in good shape but need to work in the garage now because we're running out of storage space. First order of business—clear out all these cans and jars. You told me before that you had chemicals from your photography. Since you won't be using them again, I'll need to take everything to the hazardous waste disposal site."

"But I might use those again some day."

"Keith, remember what we discussed before. There's dust all over these containers, and they're probably a fire hazard. I'm sure some have dried up or are no longer even useable. Let's go through and figure out what we have here."

Keith put a hand on a large glass jug and twisted off the lid. He sniffed it.

"What are you doing?" Millicent shouted.

Keith reeled backwards, and Millicent caught him, preventing him from toppling over. He coughed. "Developer."

"Don't inhale these things. Do you want to get sick?"

"That's how I can tell what's in them. By the aroma."

"We're not going to use that system. I'll check any that have labels, but I see no reason not to throw everything out." She navigated through the collection of stuff. "There's paint and all these chemicals. For safety reasons, I'll take all of these away this afternoon."

"I guess you're right."

"Next, you have a lot of gardening equipment—rakes, hoes and spades. Any reason to keep any of this?"

"Only the rake. I hire a neighbor boy to clean up periodically."

"Now along the inside of the garage you have quite a tool collection."

"There should be a toolbox up on a shelf."

"I see it," Millicent said.

"That has all the standard screw drivers, pliers, wrenches and a hammer. Everything else can be given away."

Millicent smiled. "Good, Keith. You're getting in the swing of things. Now, this old push mower?"

"That can go as well."

By the end of the day, Millicent had filled up her trunk with hazardous waste to dispose of and had organized the things in the garage for various donations. She wiped her forehead in exhaustion as she left Keith to rest while she took all the toxic material away. Driving off, she felt like the engineer of a chemical train weaving its way through a city. She had this awful image of her car exploding in a huge fireball. Fortunately, she successfully deposited all the crud at the local waste disposal facility for a minor fee which she would add to Keith's charges.

*****

The next day, Millicent was back on the job to tackle Keith's kitchen. This proved to be an interesting challenge because she discovered many of his cooking implements covered in filth. In addition to organizing things so he could find them and purging the unnecessary items, she gave the "keepers" a good washing. It took her an hour to clean out and organize the refrigerator. She didn't even need to resort to Keith's sniff test because she spotted moldy luncheon meat and yogurt with expiration dates of six months ago. She figured Keith must have a cast-iron stomach if he ate any of the stuff in there.

179

*****

During the rest of the week even with the cleaning service handling the dirtiest part of the job at Keith's, Millicent continued to work harder than she had in her life, knowing that she had a commitment at Ashton Beaumont's on Monday. She also received a call for another project and set up an appointment for the following Wednesday to visit and make an estimate. Her retired life had turned into a firestorm.

While organizing Keith's bedroom, Millicent discovered a cardboard box in the closet full of mementos. She asked him to join her as she went through them. She opened one box to find a Purple Heart bearing the name Alexander Noble. When she described this to Keith, tears came to his eyes.

"My brother Alexander died in World War II."

Millicent gave Keith a hug. "I'm sure you miss him."

Keith wiped his tears away. "Yeah, he was one year older, and we played baseball together all the time as kids."

Millicent found a small Bible with a metal cover. Inside she read a message to the troops from Franklin Roosevelt. When she described this item to Keith, he said the Bible had been found on Alexander's body when it was recovered.

As she rummaged through the box, she winced at finding a plastic bag filled with teeth. After her recent experiences, images of dead bodies swirled through her mind.

"Wh—what are these teeth?" Millicent asked.

Keith grimaced. "I had those removed before I got my false teeth."

"Why did you keep them?"

Keith shrugged. "I guess as a memory of a painful experience."

Millicent also found an old plaster cast that Keith explained had been from the time he broke his arm. She realized that personal organizing gave her new insights into the human psyche on each job she did.

Chapter 32

By the end of day on Saturday, Millicent had completed the remaining bedrooms and part of the basement at Keith's. Once again recognizing that this job had taken longer than she had expected, she returned on Sunday to finish up the basement and to walk through the house with Keith so that he would be able to find everything he needed. Furthermore, she promised never to over-schedule her assignments so she wouldn't have to give up her weekends in the future.

At five, Millicent left Keith relaxing in his living room and listening to *Coltrane Plays the Blues*. She felt like she had taken a bite out of clutter and prevented Keith from dying of toxic chemical inhalation or food poisoning. Now if she could only figure out the events and people involved in George's secret second career.

*****

That evening Millicent had a long talk on the phone with her daughter Karen.

"Mom, do you want me to come spend some time with you?"

"That's all right, dear. You need to be with your husband. I'm doing fine."

"But I've been worried that you're living alone."

"I have my friends, I play bridge every Tuesday night, and I'm keeping extremely busy with my organizing business. You should see all the people I'm meeting. In addition, I feel like I'm really helping my customers who struggle with clutter."

"I'm sure you're doing well with it. You always managed to organize Jerry and me."

"Yes, raising a family provided good practice. I've run into people now even messier than you two were as kids."

"But you straightened us out. I'm a neat freak now."

"It's a female thing. We're responsible for keeping order in the universe. If we left it to the men, all the old cars, tools and electronic equipment would be stacked in huge mounds in every yard."

Karen chuckled. "I know what you mean. It's a constant battle of organization versus chaos. So far we're staying slightly ahead."

"That's why I enjoy my new work so much. I go into a house in complete disarray, and within a few days it's livable again. My last client was so delighted that he gave me a hug and a hundred dollar tip."

"I'm sure a lot of men would like to give you hugs, Mother."

"Oh, posh. I'm too busy for that."

"I know you miss Dad, but there's nothing wrong with a little male companionship."

"You sound like all my friends. Diane tried to set me up, but the guy turned out to be a real jerk. And I have this client I'm starting with on Monday who has already made advances."

"Sounds interesting."

"Not really. He's a good old boy who keeps calling me 'little lady.' If he weren't the customer I'd show him a good right from the 'little lady.' "

"Oh, Mom. I'm sure he's just flirting with you."

"Which reminds me, I have to confirm that a young man is coming over on Monday to help. He can also serve another purpose—as my bodyguard."

"Mother, what have you gotten yourself into?"

"Everything is under control, but it's been interesting around here lately."

"Boulder—the center of intrigue."

Millicent flinched, thinking of signet rings and microdots. "More so than you realize."

After getting off the phone with Karen, Millicent called Ned to reconfirm their meeting at Ashton Beaumont's at nine on Monday. "I had a dumpster delivered to his driveway, and we have some major crud to move out of his yard."

"I'll be there with one assistant."

"Good. Some things will require two people to move, and I'm not strong enough for that." She now felt prepared for whatever Ashton Beaumont would throw at her.

*****

Monday morning, Millicent stood on Ashton Beaumont's front porch with Ned and his assistant, a young man with shoulder-length brown hair.

Ashton came through the door with outstretched hands, like a bear ready to squeeze Millicent to death. She ducked under his grasp and said, "Ashton, meet Ned and his crew member."

Ned immediately rescued Millicent by grabbing Aston's hand and giving it a vigorous shake.

Millicent did a quick once-over of the living room and said, "Let's go out in the yard and get started there. The young muscles can begin hauling things to the dumpster while, Ashton, you and I continue with the garage."

"Do you need me out in the yard first?" Ashton asked.

"Absolutely. We have to separate what you plan to donate from what will be thrown away. We'll stage all the donations on the floor of the garage."

They walked through the yard, and Ashton pointed out which railroad items he would be donating. This still left a considerable number of heavy objects to move to the dumpster including the crumbling picnic table, torn lawn chairs, and a haphazard pile of railroad ties.

Then Millicent led Ashton into the garage where they sorted through the shelves lined with tools and model train gear. Soon the shelves were clear, and piles of boxes, garbage bags and yard items covered the floor.

"Looks like even if the dumpster didn't block the driveway, I wouldn't be able to get my pickup in here, little lady."

"There's a lot to do here, but we'll get everything cleaned out this week. Now this collection of old, worn tires."

"I guess I don't need those anymore. You going to put them in the dumpster?"

"No, we have to dispose of these separately."

"I'm glad you know the rules and regulations, little lady."

"That's what you're paying me the big bucks for. Onto the inside of the house."

They sorted through a guest bedroom. There were signs of a female presence from some time in the past. Millicent figured Ashton would not have selected a flower print for the bedspread.

"I think I'll donate that mattress," Ashton said.

Millicent shook her head. "No, we'll have to put it in the dumpster."

"It's practically new."

"Doesn't matter."

Ashton scratched his head. "Shucks. All these good things going to waste."

"Some things are accepted as donations, and some are refused. No one wants old mattresses."

"If you say so, little lady."

By the end of the day, Millicent had cleared out the guest bedroom, living room and dining room. Ned and his assistant had completed their work in the yard and garage.

Ashton took off his cowboy hat and wiped his forehead. "Woo wee, little lady. We did a lot of work today."

Millicent eyed him skeptically since he had spent most of the day sitting, drinking lemonade and watching all the work. "Yes, we made good progress. We'll pick up again in the morning."

"You interested this time in a nice steak dinner, little lady?"

Millicent smiled. "Are you offering to take Ned's team and me all out for dinner?"

His face fell. "Maybe another time."

Chapter 33

At the Tuesday night bridge game, Millicent was back with her regular foursome at Diane's house.

Katherine said to Diane," We missed you, but we had quite a substitute last week."

"Oh?" Diane blinked with surprise.

"Yes. An excellent bridge player and down right handsome too. Millicent's new boyfriend."

Now Diane really looked flummoxed. "Millicent has a boyfriend?"

"He's just a friend," Millicent said, glaring at Katherine.

"Don't believe a word of it," Allison said. "The rumor grapevine indicates signs of a hot-and-heavy romance."

Millicent stomped her foot loud enough that the others jumped. "Please, let's keep to the facts. Besides we have some bridge to play."

"See how she conveniently changes the subject," Katherine whispered in Diane's ear.

"I heard that," Millicent said.

"She's always eavesdropping," Allison added. "Millicent, how's your organizing business? Any new clients?"

Millicent picked up the deck that had been cut and began dealing. "I completed another job last week, and I'm in the middle of one right now, with another prospect to meet with tomorrow."

"Sounds like you're keeping the local economy humming."

Millicent picked up her cards and arranged them by suit. "I've been very fortunate to get some good referrals. I also have become an expert on model railroads."

"I didn't know you had an interest in trains," Allison said.

"I don't, but my current client has a huge supply of railroad paraphernalia that I've been cleaning out. I now know about switches, siding, transformers and how to construct a papier-mâché mountain."

"I gather this client is a man," Allison said.

Millicent moved a five of diamonds that she had accidently place with her hearts. "That's right. Not too many women get their jollies from model trains."

"Millicent is collecting boyfriends left and right," Katherine interjected as Diane and Allison smirked.

"One spade." Millicent tapped her cards. "I'd be happy to introduce any of you to Ashton Beaumont. He's quite a catch if you like good old boys and their model trains."

*****

On Wednesday morning before continuing at Ashton Beaumont's, Millicent drove to a house east of town.

Jean Vanley, a young woman with a no-nonsense demeanor that matched her business suit greeted Millicent with a firm handshake. She wore dark stockings and utilitarian dark blue pumps.

"What do you need done here?" Millicent asked.

"I'm executor for the woman who owned this house. She died a month ago."

"I'm sorry. Was she a relative of yours?"

"No, but I had known her in the community for some time. Her family members live on the East Coast and have asked me to settle her affairs. I'll hold an estate sale for furniture, paintings and a large doll collection, and sell the house once it's cleared out."

"And what would you like me to help with?"

"The garage. There have been no cars parked in it for years, and it became the repository for all the unused stuff in the house. I need you to clean it out, donate what's salvageable and pitch the rest."

"Nothing you want saved for the estate sale?"

"No. Let me give you a tour, and you'll understand why."

Jean unlocked the house, and they entered the living room.

Millicent did a double take. Dolls of every imaginable size and shape, from miniatures to four feet in height, covered every chair, couch, table and corner. One wore a wedding gown, another a peasant outfit, a third a sequined party dress.

Millicent gasped. "This is incredible."

"You've only seen the beginning. Follow me. Every room in the house contains more of the same."

In the dining room, dolls covered the table, every chair, a side counter and the floor. Each of the bedrooms had dolls all over the beds, dressers and bookshelves. Outside of a small walk space in each room, hundreds of dolls occupied every surface.

"How much are all of these worth?" Millicent asked.

"That's the sad part. The owner must have paid hundreds of thousands of dollars for all of these, but some have been damaged, and with the current market for this type of collectible, the estate sale will probably bring in ten percent of what she paid, if we're lucky. There's nice furniture and a reasonable art collection to sell as well. Again, we won't recoup anywhere near what was paid, but we'll do the best we can."

Millicent admired a painting of a European village with people promenading through streets, lined by houses with steeply sloping roofs. She ran her hand over an antique china cabinet and shook her head. All this stuff and now it needed to be sold.

"I can handle the interior of the house, but let me show you the garage," Jean said.

Through the kitchen they entered the back of the garage, and Jean turned on the light.

Millicent recoiled. In the middle of the garage stood a five-foot-high mound of furniture, old rugs, mattresses, toys, and stacks of cardboard boxes. Along the wall old brooms, mops, rakes and sticks poked out as if a medieval army had tossed their weapons in random directions. Then she looked up. In the rafters rested boxes, old chairs, a red wagon and a bicycle clamped to a beam.

She put her hands on her hips, considering for the first time walking away from a job. Then she took a deep breath. No, she would step up to the challenge.

At the back of the garage against the wall stood several folding tables. She could use these for staging. She also spotted a stepladder which would come in handy to reach the junk up in the rafters. Upon closer inspection of the pile in the middle of the garage, Millicent saw layers of dust on everything. She'd definitely have to wear her grubbies for this job.

"Do you think you could clear this all out?"

Millicent nodded her head. "I can arrange for a dumpster to be delivered to the driveway and sort out everything salvageable for donation."

"Good. Give me a proposal."

"I'll need fifteen minutes to look through the garage, and then I can write up an estimate for you immediately. If it's acceptable, I should be able to schedule this as a one day job next Monday or Tuesday. I'll have a dumpster delivered and also arrange for the donation pickup. A number of items here can't be put in a dumpster, such as paint cans. I'll have to dispose of those separately."

"Whatever it takes, clear this garage out. Everything goes one way or another. But one question, how will you document the donations for tax purposes?"

Millicent smiled. "I'll photograph them with my smart phone to provide you with visual evidence that can be used for your valuation."

"Good. Take a look around and I'll wait for you in the living room."

Millicent inspected the garage, lifting pieces of carpet, peeking in boxes and scanning the rafters. Once satisfied with what she saw, she extracted her smart phone and called Ned.

"You available for part of the day next Monday or Tuesday to help me do some heavy lifting on a job east of Boulder?" she asked.

"I have a job on Tuesday, but I'm available Monday."

"Fine. I'll give you a call back if my proposal is accepted." Millicent pulled her estimate form and a calculator out of her purse and sat down to put the bid together. She priced out her time and Ned's, the cost of the dumpster and tacked on two hazardous waste trips. Then she added a premium for the risk of climbing around in rafters. With this completed, she returned inside to give the proposal to Jean.

"Looks fair. I'll sign it. When can you do the job?"

"Monday. We'll have the garage cleaned out by the end of the day. I'll have the dumpster delivered first thing Monday morning and picked up on Tuesday. I can schedule a donation pickup for Monday afternoon, and what they don't accept will go in the dumpster. Finally, I'll dispose of the hazardous material. I'll need to have someone here to let me in and to pay for the dumpster."

"That will work. I'll be here Monday morning working with the auction people on the dolls, furniture and paintings. What time would you like to begin?"

"Given what's here, let's make it eight."

Millicent returned to her car and started making calls. First, she let Ned know that they had a job. She wanted an hour on her own to get things laid out so he agreed to arrive at nine. Next, she arranged for the dumpster to be delivered between eight and nine on Monday. Finally, she called Goodwill and was pleased to hear that they had a truck available for a pickup between two and three Monday afternoon.

Satisfied with the preparations, Millicent started the engine for her drive to continue the job at Ashton Beaumont's. She had only gone a quarter mile on South Boulder Road when she noticed a dark blue Toyota Prius in her rearview mirror. The erratic driving, swerving from side to side, had caught her attention. Kind of early in the day for a drunk driver. She turned onto

189

Foothill Parkway and the Prius remained behind her. *Uh-oh.* Was someone else tailing her? She made a quick right turn onto Baseline and took a side street to see if the Prius disappeared, but it stayed with her. She reached for her smart phone and called Detective Buchanan.

"There's another car following me," she panted into the phone.

"Same drill as last time," he replied. "Head toward the police station. I'll have someone out in front watching for you."

Millicent wiped a drop of perspiration from her forehead. Why did she keep finding herself in these predicaments? Why couldn't she have a calm life and be left alone to her personal organizing business without these creeps following her? As she drove along Arapahoe, the Prius still remained behind her. When she turned onto 33rd, she scanned quickly in her mirror. The Prius had disappeared. She felt a sense of relief and let out a breath she'd been holding. Then a sinking feeling of despair overtook her. The police wouldn't be able to catch whoever had been following her. She pulled into the parking lot of the police station and called Buchanan again.

"When I neared the police station, it took off," she explained. "I'm in your parking lot right now."

"I'll be right out to get a statement from you."

In five minutes, Buchanan strode out of the building, came up to her passenger side and waited for her to lower the window. "Tell me exactly what happened, Mrs. Hargrove."

"Like the time before. I noticed a car following me and tried to shake it. It kept with me until close to the police station. Then it disappeared."

"Give me a full description of the vehicle."

"I noticed a dark blue Prius that seemed to be new and in good condition."

"Could you see the driver?"

Millicent shook her head. "No. I never had a good look."

"Did you get a glimpse of the license plate?"

Millicent let out a sigh. "Sorry. It didn't have a front plate."

"Where did you first notice the car following you?"

"After I left a meeting with a prospective client in Paragon Estates off

South Boulder Road. The Prius followed me all the way into Boulder until I turned on 33rd."

"Let me know if you spot the car again."

*****

Millicent drove away from the police station, shaking. Why wouldn't these people leave her alone? She drove aimlessly for half an hour, constantly peering in her rearview mirror, willing the Prius not to reappear. Satisfied that she wasn't being followed, she continued on to the house of the good old boy, Ashton Beaumont.

*****

That evening upon returning to her condo and parking in the underground garage, she pulled out her smart phone and called Allison, who fortunately answered.

"Can you meet me in the lobby?" Millicent asked.

"Yeah, but why?"

"I've been followed. I'm a little frightened right now and could use company going up to my apartment."

"You want me to bring my gun?"

"Heavens no. Do you even own a gun?"

"No, but I thought I'd ask."

"Meet me there in five minutes."

Millicent locked her car and dashed out of the parking garage as though someone was after her, which might have been the case. She arrived in the lobby breathless.

Allison stood there with her arms folded, clenching a rolling pin in one fist. "I thought this would be the next best thing to a gun." She unfurled her arms and waved the rolling pin over her head in a circle. "Let's go check your place."

When they arrived in front of the door, Millicent unlocked her two locks and threw the door open like the knob was a hot coal. She peeked inside with Allison leaning over her shoulder, rolling pin held at the ready above her head.

"Seems deserted," Allison whispered in her ear.

"And no one has trashed it," Millicent whispered back. "Let's take a look."

The two of them tiptoed inside and divided up to check each of the rooms. They reconvened in the living room. "All clear," Allison said, dropping the rolling pin to hip level.

"Thanks so much for coming with me," Millicent said, giving Allison a hug.

"Any time. Do you want to keep my weapon?"

"No, thanks. I have one of my own in the kitchen."

Allison tapped her rolling pin. "I'll keep it within easy reach for whenever you need me."

Chapter 34

A fter dinner, Millicent received a phone call.

"Mrs. Hargrove, this is Arnie Talbert. We've never met, but I was a stamp collecting friend of your husband. I'm deeply sorry for your loss."

Millicent once again felt the twinge in her chest. "Thank you."

"I'm calling to invite you to a tribute we're giving in memory of George at the stamp club next Wednesday. I'm hoping you can join us."

Millicent checked her calendar. "Yes, I can be there."

*****

The rest of the week proved to be uneventful other than making sure Ashton Beaumont didn't try anything funny. She completed the job late Friday, congratulating herself on keeping within the hours she had estimated. Ashton leering at her had provided the necessary motivation to wrap it up quickly.

*****

After tossing and turning all night with dream snippets of cars following her through a field, on Monday morning, Millicent dressed in old work boots, jeans and a stained, plaid long-sleeve shirt. As she drove to the job, she noticed the overcast sky which the Weather Channel had predicted would give way to a sunny summer morning. She experienced the mixture of excitement over what she was going to accomplish and dread at the hard work she'd have to put in for the day. Oh well, all part of her new life.

At least she had spent a quiet weekend relaxing, reading and doing no organizing. She arrived at five minutes before eight and found Jean Vanley already there. Millicent unpacked her supplies, located the automatic garage door switch and opened the mess for business. First, she set up a folding table on one side of the driveway, allowing enough room for the dumpster. Under the table she stashed her toolkit, a bottle of water and a granola bar for a snack.

Then the fun began. She removed items from a shelf lining the side of the garage, including an old globe showing East Pakistan instead of Bangladesh, two small plug-in room fans, a box of Christmas lights, and another box full of Easter baskets. These she set on the folding table and took a picture with her smart phone. Then she moved them onto the side of the driveway to begin the donation pile. The process continued with skis, snowshoes, old vinyl records, a rocking chair, two Christmas tree bases, bicycle helmets, golf clubs and jumper cables.

With the sound of rumbling and clanking, the dumpster arrived and was positioned in the driveway. Millicent opened the swinging door so that she could walk things into it easily. She flinched as images of the dead body in the other dumpster flashed through her brain. *Get a hold of yourself.* After her heartbeat slowed, she returned to the task at hand.

She immediately unloaded a bunch of mildewed carpet from the pile in the middle of the garage and carted it into the back of the dumpster, dropping it with a loud thump.

When Ned appeared, his first task was to carry a heavy, scarred desk and some broken chairs into the dumpster. Within two hours the huge stack of junk in the center of the garage had been distributed, the majority into the dumpster and the few good items set aside to be donated.

Millicent found six manhole covers piled in a corner, and Ned lugged them into the trash. Other items that needed to be thrown out included an old children's swing, pieces of a bed frame, two stained mattresses, rotted bicycle tubes, broken pieces of bamboo and a stroller with a wheel missing.

She also began another pile that included an aged studded snow tire, several plastic containers of motor oil, paint cans, and a number of unlabeled jars of toxic-looking liquids. These would require special handling and transportation to the toxic waste disposal site.

Ned took apart several broken tables and carried the pieces into the dumpster. On a shelf Millicent removed an old stereo, a videotape player, and a box with miscellaneous remote controls. She photographed these and added them to the donation material.

Taking a break, Millicent ate her granola bar and took a long swig of water. "Now comes the challenge of bringing things down from the rafters. I'll climb up and hand them down to you, Ned."

He winked at her. "Yeah, that way I get to catch all the dirt."

"We'll both be inhaling our fair share of dust, I'm afraid."

At that moment, a car pulled up in front of the house, and Ray hopped out. He ambled into the garage. "Ned said you'd be here, so I thought I'd come lend a hand."

"If you don't mind getting dirty, all hands are welcome," Millicent said.

"That's why I wore grungy clothes. I'm ready to do whatever's required. Send me in, Coach."

Millicent eyed Ray warily and noticed that his definition of work clothes included clean new jeans, a long-sleeved tan T-shirt with a picture of a mountain goat, marmot and snow-covered peaks on the back, and solid hiking boots.

Lining up a stepladder, she climbed to the top to begin handing boxes down to Ned and Ray. She tugged at one and it crumbled. "Look out below," she cried, as dirt cascaded down on Ned and Ray's heads, and old plastic baby bottles careening off the garage floor.

Ray shook the dirt out of his hair. "I didn't know I had signed up for the dust bunny shampoo special."

"Just be glad that nothing heavy fell on you."

"Yeah, I don't think Workers' Compensation will cover my volunteer assistance."

The next box contained old blankets and dead bugs. Millicent gingerly lowered it to Ned who carted it off for disposal. She removed a bunch of egg cartons, expecting to find plastic Easter eggs inside. When she opened one container, her eyes grew wide. It held the colored shells of real eggs. The insides had been blown out, but the shells had been kept for probably thirty years. Amazing what people would store away in a garage. She lowered down a bassinette, three broken chairs, a parakeet cage and a red wagon full of dirt and what looked like chipped paint and crumbling crayons.

After Ray handed up a broom, she tugged one last box within reach. She started to lift it out when a spider crawled onto her hand. "Ack," she squealed, dropping the box, which sailed off and missed Ray by inches, spewing baby clothes all over the garage floor.

Ray jumped to the side. "You trying to get rid of me?"

"Sorry, a spider scared me."

"I didn't think anything scared you, Millicent," Ray said, dusting himself off from the cloud of particles that had covered him.

"I don't like spiders and snakes."

Millicent tried to lift the bicycle, but it wouldn't budge, so she traded places with Ned who had to remove a metal mounting that had been screwed into a beam.

By early afternoon, they had a nearly full dumpster, a stack of donation material on the other side of the driveway and a smaller pile of toxic waste. The three of them began loading the toxic materials into Millicent's trunk. She held one jar out at arm's length as she carefully deposited it, wondering if she should purchase a hazmat outfit for this job. By the time the Goodwill truck arrived at two, they had the garage empty and the floor swept clean.

Goodwill took most of the items, rejecting a few pieces of furniture deemed too old and poorly built. After the truck left, Millicent, Ned and Ray lugged these remaining items to the dumpster.

Millicent slammed the dumpster gate and called the waste disposal service to schedule a pickup.

"Quite a day," Ray said. "Much more exciting than golf or bridge. I saw my whole life flash in front of me when you threw that box at me."

"I didn't throw it. I accidently dropped it."

"That's right—spiders."

"Dad does a great crazy routine about spiders," Ned said.

"You'll have to put on a performance for me sometime, but not now." Millicent stepped back and rubbed an aching wrist. "We're done, and it's only three o'clock."

"I'd offer to take everyone out for a late lunch, but no one would let us in looking like this," Ray said.

"No, it's time for a shower," Millicent said. "And I don't know if I should wash my clothes or burn them."

"I'd suggest turning on a sprinkler and running through it, but we'd make too much mud in the yard," Ray replied. "Still, let's go get cleaned up and meet for dinner since I bet you two haven't eaten much today."

"Sounds good to me," Ned said. "Millicent?"

"I guess."

"With that resounding endorsement we're on. Let's meet in an hour."

"I'll need two hours," Millicent said. "I have to unload the hazardous waste before I head back to my condo."

Ray regarded his dust-crusted watch. "In that case, Millicent, Ned and I will pick you up at your place at five-fifteen."

After Ned and Ray drove off, Millicent shouted into the house, not wanting to track dirt inside.

In a moment Jean appeared.

"We're done. I'll send you a thumb drive with the pictures of the donated items along with my invoice."

Jean gawked in disbelief. "Wow, you cleared out the whole garage."

"How are things going inside?" Millicent asked.

"We made progress but not like you did out here. We'll have a tough time finding buyers for the dolls. It's a shame the owner put out all the money."

"That's why I encourage my clients to not accumulate too much stuff."

"Too bad this woman didn't have you around to advise her earlier. Her estate would have been in much better financial shape."

"I need to get going," Millicent said. "Let me know if I can be of service again."

"You'll be the first one I call," Jean said. "Thanks for the great job."

*****

By the time Ray knocked on her door, Millicent was ready to eat the wallpaper.

"You clean up pretty good," Ray said with a bow.

"You don't look so bad yourself. Not a speck of dust."

"No, but I must have coughed up enough dirt to fill a pot for a houseplant."

Millicent laughed, remembering her adventures with houseplants.

Ray took her arm, and they headed out to meet Ned.

Once they settled into the back seat, Ned said, "I'm chauffeuring you two around entirely too much."

"It's the least you can do for your old man," Ray replied. "Giving me a chance to sit next to this young chick in the backseat."

"We'll have no hanky-panky back there. I also take my chaperone duties very seriously."

"Let's get this bus going," Millicent said. "I'm famished."

"Yes, ma'am."

At the restaurant, Millicent perused the menu for all of ten seconds before deciding on the wild salmon filet. Equally eager to dig in, Ned ordered southwestern-grilled natural chicken and Ray the grilled marinated ahi tuna. Ray raised his glass of iced tea. "To a successful day of clearing out forty years of trash and surviving Millicent throwing boxes of baby bottles and clothes at me."

Millicent held up her glass of lemonade. "Just remember if I had been aiming for you, you wouldn't be here."

"I'm sure of it. Don't mess with the lady."

After their main courses had arrived, Millicent eagerly began decimating her salmon. She heard footsteps stopping beside their table and looked up to see Fred Langley from the bridge tournament standing there.

"Hello, Fred," Ray said.

Fred glowered. "Ray. Millicent."

"Fred, how long have we been playing against each other in tournaments?" Ray asked. "Ten years or so?"

"Nine and a half to be exact," Fred answered through clenched teeth.

Ray turned toward Millicent. "And I'm still waiting to see Fred smile."

"I'm not the happy-go-lucky type like you, Ray. Will you be playing in the upcoming Boulder Sectional at the County Fairgrounds in Longmont?"

"Wouldn't miss it."

"And you, Millicent?"

"No. Not again. I've retired from tournament play."

Without any more chitchat, Fred turned and stomped away.

"Strange man," Millicent said.

"Yeah. His whole life revolves around bridge. He definitely needs some outside interests like ducking from flying boxes hurled from rafters."

*****

After dinner, they drove back to Millicent's place.

"Would you two gentlemen like to come upstairs for a cup of coffee?"

Ray smiled, and Ned said, "For a short while. Then I need to head home to make a phone call."

Ray reached forward and jabbed a finger in Ned's neck. "His fiancée is traveling again, and they need to check in. Ah, young love."

"I'll drop you two off in front, search for a parking place and then meet you upstairs," Ned said, ignoring his father.

"It's becoming harder and harder to find a parking place around here," Millicent said. "I think the condo complex must be nearly filled, and people seem to have lots of visitors."

"I'll find something and be up shortly."

Ray leaped out of the car, jogged around to the other side, opened the door and held out a hand to help Millicent.

"My knight in shining armor."

"I need to stay on your good side, so I can help with another organizing gig."

"What makes you think you'll be invited back to assist with another project?"

"Hey, how can you turn down free labor? Besides, someone needs to protect you from spiders in rafters . . . and snakes like Fred Langley."

"Spiders, yes, but I think Fred's pretty harmless."

"Unless you're playing against him when he has a no trump contract to make. Then he can be vicious."

"I actually set him at three no trump in the tournament," Millicent said with a firm nod of her head.

Ray's eyebrows shot up. "See, that's why you'd make a good tournament player if you had the inclination."

"In my next life."

Millicent unlocked her two locks, and she and Ray stepped inside. She turned on the lights and started to push the door closed when she saw a man standing in the living room pointing a gun at them.

Chapter 35

Millicent recognized the intruder immediately as the other man she had seen at her garage sale. "What are you doing in my home?"

He wagged the gun at Millicent. "I'm the one to ask questions here, lady. Where's the signet ring?"

"What's so important about it?" she asked.

"Like I said, I'm not answering any questions. You two sit on the couch." He motioned to Millicent and Ray and came to stand in front of them with his back toward the door.

Millicent noticed that the front door had not closed completely. What would happen when Ned arrived? She feared that the man might be startled and shoot him when he came through the door.

Think like an organizer, she told herself. Group, reduce and reorganize. Put all the pieces together, eliminate what isn't necessary and then move forward. First, she needed to stay alert and assess the situation, putting the facts in the right place. The man was about six foot two and over two hundred pounds with dark menacing eyes and a jutting jaw. She and Ray couldn't risk trying to overpower him, and she didn't want Ned to blunder in unaware. Second, she needed to reduce the effects from her emotions so she could act clearly. She took a deep breath to calm her nerves.

Now, put the pieces back together. She would alert Ned by speaking loudly so he'd be sure to understand the situation before stumbling in.

The man loomed over them still waving the gun. "Now, one more time, lady. Where's the signet ring?"

Millicent sighed. "It won't do you any good."

"Maybe you'd like me to put a bullet in the kneecap of your friend here. Start being more specific or he may never walk again."

Millicent watched Ray, who didn't flinch. Her heart raced. What should she say? Ned should be approaching by now. "I'll tell you if you quit threatening us with that gun!" she shouted.

He lowered the gun and gave her a snarling smile. "Okay. Out with it."

Ned peeked his head through the door. The intruder was focused so intently on them that he didn't notice. Had Ray seen? What could she do to distract this thug?

Ray clutched his chest. "I think I'm having a heart attack." He pitched forward and rolled onto the floor.

"What the—"

The intruder never had time to finish. In the commotion of Ray thumping to the floor, Ned raced into the room. He tackled the man, knocking him down. Ned whacked the guy's hand, but the gun didn't dislodge.

Millicent jumped off the couch and reached for the blue vase on the end table. Without an ounce of regret, she brought the vase crashing down on the man's head, showering the room with glass fragments.

The man collapsed, and Ned removed the gun.

Ray hopped up. "Good work, son."

Ned gave his dad a high-five.

Millicent viewed Ned with an open mouth. "How did you know Ray wasn't having a real heart attack?"

He chuckled. "That old buzzard will last longer than I will. He's outlived two of his doctors. Maybe death by box-dropped-from-rafter but not a heart attack."

"Do you have some duct tape?" Ray asked.

"In my kitchen drawer. Let me get it for you." She dashed into the kitchen and returned with a nearly-full roll.

Ray proceeded to tie the man's hands behind his back and bind his feet together. He stood back to admire his work. "That should hold him." Then he bent over and patted the man's cheeks. "Wake up, Sleeping Beauty."

The man didn't stir.

Ray went into the kitchen and filled a glass with water.

"Do you mind if I splash a little water on your rug?" he asked Millicent.

"As long as it's only a small amount."

Ray put his fingers in the glass and sprinkled water on the man's face. In a minute he stirred. Ray splashed a little more until the guy's eyes opened. Then Ray pointed the gun at the downed intruder.

"I thought you had a heart attack," the man mumbled.

"Yeah, but I had a miraculous recovery. I probably lost some more brain cells which makes me pretty jumpy right now. What the hell are you doing here?"

"I'm not saying nothin'."

"I think you better come clean," Ned said. "My dad's a little unbalanced."

Ray put the gun against the man's head. "I think I should put him out of his misery right now."

"Don't do it," Ned pleaded. "If you shoot another man, they'll send you back to the institution for good. We can't have blood spattered all over the living room again."

"Again?" the man exclaimed, eyes wide with alarm.

"He's shot two people before," Ned said. "Right through the head. You better cooperate. He's insane, and if people don't do what he asks, he kills them."

"Why are you here?" Ray asked again.

The man opened his mouth but didn't say anything.

"There's a spider on his forehead." Ray gave an insane laugh. "I'm going to shoot that damn spider." He pointed the gun right between the man's eyes.

"Not the spider!" Ned wailed. "Once he starts seeing spiders, he really gets trigger-happy. You better answer his question, or we'll have some real bloodshed here."

"Wait! I'll tell you whatever you want to know. Don't shoot."

"You better talk quickly." Ned made his eyes go wide.

Ray hopped around, cackling and waving the gun. "The spider. I'm going to shoot the spider."

Millicent fought to keep a straight face.

"Please, I'll tell you everything. Just don't let this madman shoot me. I was hired to come here to find the signet ring."

"We already know that," Millicent said. "Who hired you?"

"I don't know. It was a blind drop. Somebody paid us in cash, and I never knew his name or what he looked like."

"You said 'us.' Who else is involved?"

"Three of us worked together. Two of them are dead. I have to get the signet ring or I'll be killed."

"The man who took us hostage and your friend who came to my garage sale with you. He ended up in a dumpster."

"Yes, that was a message to me from the boss man to act quicker. And a message to you to give up the ring."

"And did you trash my apartment and put electronic surveillance devices in here?" Millicent leaned toward him, grabbed his collar and shook him.

"Yeah. I found out about the microdot and took it, but it isn't what my client wants. He still expects me to find the signet ring."

"And I take it you're very proficient with picking locks?" Millicent asked.

"Sure. It's no sweat getting into this place."

So much for the deadbolt.

"Did you by any chance steal a stamp collection from my son in Indianapolis?"

"Yeah, that was another of my assignments."

"And what became of it?" Millicent asked.

"I left it for my contact. We had set up another blind drop, so I assume he has it now."

Millicent pursed her lips. "Do you drive a Prius by any chance?"

He wrinkled his brow. "No way. Always a gray BMW."

Millicent tried to put the pieces together. She remembered the BMW from before, but who had been following her in the Prius? She eyed the man warily. "And if I had given you the signet ring, what would you have done with it?"

Sweat appeared on the man's forehead. "I can't tell you that."

Ray leapt forward. "I see the spider! It's a black widow!" He pointed the gun at the man's forehead. "I'm going to nail the bugger right now."

"Don't do it, Ray!" Ned shouted. "Maybe he'll reconsider."

The man gulped. "Okay. Okay. Put the gun down. I'll tell you."

Ray danced around, pointing the gun at the man's head, then at his chest and then at his groin. Finally, he lowered it and crossed his eyes.

"I'm supposed to put it in a Safeway bag and drop it in the trash bin at the parking area at Sawhill Ponds."

"And when will this drop take place?" Millicent asked.

"Tomorrow night at ten-thirty."

"Convenient place," Millicent said. "There's only one road in, so it's easy to watch to make sure someone isn't followed."

"Exactly. I'm supposed to park my car on the dirt road right off of Seventy-Fifth and walk to the parking area."

"But what if you don't locate the signet ring?" Millicent asked.

"Tomorrow I have to send a message to confirm that I have the item for the drop. If I don't, my contact will assume the drop is called off."

"What kind of message?"

"I need to Tweet the message, "Dad's coming to visit.'"

Ned shook his head. "The wonders of crime in the electronic age."

Millicent looked thoughtfully at the bound man. "And I bet your name is Reed Eggleston," Millicent said.

He wriggled. "How'd you know that?"

"A little spider told me." She winked at Ray. "Now, I think it's time to call Detective Buchanan."

"Good idea," Ray replied putting the gun down on an end table. "This gun gives me the creeps."

"You mean you weren't going to shoot me?" Eggleston asked.

"Not today."

"Great insane act, Dad," Ned said, giving him another high-five.

"Yeah, I missed my real calling. I could have been Jack Nicholson's right hand man in *One Flew Over the Cuckoo's Nest.*"

"And you're not insane?" the man asked, his eyes bulging.

"No, but you never know when someone like you might push me over the edge."

*****

When Buchanan arrived, he admired their handiwork. Then he replaced the duct tape with handcuffs.

"I'll tell you whatever you want, but get me away from these loony people."

Two police officers arrived to take Eggleston to the County Jail, and Buchanan asked Millicent, Ray and Ned to sit on the couch.

"Now the rest of the story. Let's begin with you, Mrs. Hargrove."

Millicent took a deep breath. "When we arrived back here after dinner, Eggleston was waiting inside my apartment. He threatened Ray and me, but Ned jumped him, and I hit him over the head with my favorite blue vase." She pointed to the shards littering the rug. "We tied him up with duct tape and when he came to, we asked him some questions in a fashion that you wouldn't be able to do."

Buchanan coughed. "Probably something I don't want to know about."

"Well, Detective, let's just say that he confessed to breaking into my apartment, bugging the place and trying to get the signet ring, which he is supposed to leave in a Safeway bag in the trash can at Sawhill Ponds tomorrow night."

"And do you have this ring, Mrs. Hargrove?"

Millicent stood, sashayed into the kitchen, dug her fingers into the amaryllis plant and retrieved the ring. Washing her fingers and the ring, she brought it out and handed it to Buchanan. "Now you can catch the culprit behind this whole mystery."

Buchanan shook his head. "I'm not going to ask you how long you've had this ring, Mrs. Hargrove."

"Good. Just like you wouldn't ask a lady her age. What's the next step?"

"I can have someone Eggleston's size drop the ring tomorrow night. We'll set up surveillance to see who picks it up."

"Oh, and one other thing. You'll need to use Eggleston's smart phone to send a Twitter message to confirm the drop using the phrase, 'Dad's coming to visit.' "

Buchanan wrote down the wording and snapped his notepad closed. "I'll get that all taken care of."

"What else can we do to help?" Millicent asked.

"You can wait patiently to see who we catch."

Millicent knew she couldn't do that.

Chapter 36

After Detective Buchanan left, Millicent sat on the couch, gnawing on her lip. "I want to go watch what happens tomorrow night."

Ray rolled his eyes. "Miss Marple in action. Well, you can't do that alone. If you're going to do something dumb, you better include your spider-crazy friend."

"And don't forget me," Ned said. "I want to see this through as well. Besides, you'll need a chaperone. I can't leave you and Dad together in the dark."

Millicent smiled. "Then it's all settled. We'll do our own stakeout. I have bridge tomorrow night from six-thirty until nine. Let's meet back here at nine-thirty. I have an idea for how we can watch without interfering with the police."

*****

The next evening, Millicent was the first guest to arrive at Katherine's apartment for bridge. She brought an amaryllis plant for the hostess to replace the one that had been dropped.

"I promise to take better care of it this time," Katherine said.

"Good. I don't want to be searching through your trash again."

Diane appeared, and once again Allison dashed in last.

"I called you an hour ago to see if you wanted a ride, but you weren't home," Millicent said to Allison.

"I know. I took a trip up Boulder Canyon this afternoon, and the time just flew by. I had to rush back to my apartment, wash my face and grab my gift for Katherine before driving here. I visited a wonderful antique shop in Nederland where I always find interesting things."

Millicent wagged a finger at her. "Remember, living in your condo you can't be adding items too often. You need to watch the clutter. Staying organized is an ongoing activity."

"I know. I have to unstuff my stuff. You'd be proud of me. I only bought one little knickknack."

Millicent crossed her arms. "You know the rule. If you add something, you have to get rid of something else."

Allison smiled. "Not get rid of, instead pass on something of value." She handed a box to Katherine. "You always liked my little Greek urn. I've decided to give it to you."

"Uh-oh," Diane said. "Now to follow Millicent's guideline of offsetting what you add with something to purge, Katherine must get rid of something."

"No," Katherine said. "Presents follow a different rule. You only have to eliminate an item when buying something for yourself."

"Enough dilly-dallying," Allison said, rubbing her hands together. "We have some serious bridge to play."

They filled paper plates with fruit and sat down at the bridge table in the living room.

After the cards were shuffled and Millicent dealt, Allison asked, "How's that boyfriend of yours?"

Millicent scowled. "Ray's only a friend, and he's fine."

"I bet you're going to hook up with him after bridge tonight."

Millicent gave a Cheshire cat smile. "Actually, Ray and Ned and I plan to get together tonight."

"Going out somewhere romantic?"

Millicent giggled. "Ray and I will be out under the stars with our young chaperone. And, Diane, I want to thank you again for suggesting Ned's moving service. He's been most helpful."

"To say nothing of providing an opportunity for you to meet his dad," Katherine added. "I watched him when we played bridge last time. Ray couldn't take his eyes off you, Millicent."

Heat spread to Millicent's cheeks. "As Allison said, let's get on with the bridge. Who dealt?"

The other three laughed, and Katherine said, "See, it's always the person who dealt who asks, particularly if she gets flustered."

Millicent and Allison made game at five diamonds, and they proceeded to the next hand.

"Did you ever see Matthew Kramis again after you met him at my house?" Diane asked.

Millicent grimaced. "He called me once, but I put an end to that quickly."

"You two didn't hit it off that well, huh?"

"He's not my type."

"I think Ray is more your type," Katherine interjected. "He'd be a good catch, Millicent. And remember, if you decide to play possum, give me the signal so I can go after him."

"Will all of you play bridge and quit trying to run my personal life?"

"She's getting kind of testy in her old age, don't you think?" Allison gave a demure smile.

"I think she likes Ray but doesn't want to admit it," Katherine said.

*****

Later after the bridge game broke up and Millicent returned to her condo, Ray and Ned arrived. She had changed into black slacks, a black blouse, black sweater, black flats and an old black Rockies baseball cap with the logo faded to gray. Ned and Ray also wore dark clothes, both sporting black turtlenecks and black slacks. They looked like they were ready to rob the national bank.

"Does everyone have a cell phone?" Ray asked.

"Check," Ned replied.

"Yes, I have mine," Millicent added.

"Okay let's program in each other's numbers," Ray said, "in case we get separated."

After completing that task, Ray and Ned paced around her living room while Millicent sat quietly thinking. Her stomach churned as she considered what they would be doing tonight. Not illegal but certainly not something Detective Buchanan would approve of. She wished she could figure out this whole sequence of strange events—so much that she didn't understand tied back to George. She castigated herself again for not noticing any signs of George's hidden career. He had to have slipped up sometime. Had she been that oblivious? No, apparently George was very good at what he did. He had always been open with her about his business career and their life but somehow he had compartmentalized this one other aspect.

So many things that had never happened to her before. People had been following her. The BWM and Prius tailing her, as well as Eggleston with the other guy, now dead, lurking at the garage sale. Then of course being taken hostage by the man with the gold earring. Then she remembered someone else—the strange, tall, emaciated man who had been at the funeral and garage sale. But who was behind all this nonsense with the signet ring? Why couldn't she solve this puzzle?

"A penny for your thoughts," Ray said.

She paused a moment before answering. "I'm reviewing in my mind all that has occurred. I'm trying to put it together."

"Have you reached any conclusions?"

"No, it's still a muddle. Give me a minute to think it through."

"We'll leave you alone," Ray said. "Mind if I help myself to something to drink?"

"There's iced tea, water and orange juice in the refrigerator."

Ray grabbed Ned's arm. "Come on. Let's give the lady some privacy to do her cogitation." They disappeared into the kitchen.

Millicent chewed her lower lip. She felt close to something here that she couldn't quite put her finger on. She breathed out heavily.

After five minutes, Ray shouted from the kitchen, "Okay if we come back in?"

"Yes, I haven't reached any conclusions," Millicent said.

As the men rejoined her, Ray looked at his watch. "We better hit the road if we're going to do this crazy thing."

Millicent grabbed her black jacket and they headed outside.

As they drove, Ned said, "You mentioned last night having an idea on how we could do this stakeout unobtrusively."

"Yes," Millicent replied. "We can't show up at Sawhill Ponds. We can go to Walden Ponds next door and then walk to a good observation point to watch whatever unfolds."

"Okay, Miss Marple," Ray said. "But we'll have to stay out of the way. The police won't appreciate it if we interfere."

Millicent smiled. "We'll stay well out of the way."

A burst of air escaped Ray's lips. "Women."

"And don't you forget it."

Ray groaned. "I won't."

They took the road into Walden Ponds, passing an unoccupied black sedan parked along the access road. They spotted no other cars before pulling into the empty parking area.

When they got out of the car, Ray stretched his arms and said, "Look at all those stars."

"Hush," Millicent admonished. "We don't want anyone to hear us. And let's put our phones on vibrate."

"Yes, ma'am," Ray whispered.

They quietly hiked along the dirt road until they came to a sign that said, "Duck Pond."

"Do you know which way we go?" Ned asked.

"Yes," Millicent replied. "I've taken walks out here many times. To the left."

They tiptoed along a fence that separated the public trail from a construction site and came to another pond.

"Let's head around to the right here," Millicent said. They passed through a fence opening that separated Walden Ponds from Sawhill Ponds. Millicent pointed. "You can see the parking area where the drop will be made across this pond."

Ray checked his watch again. "The drop should be made in fifteen minutes. We'll find an observation point. I have my binoculars so we can hunker down to watch."

They stepped quietly along the trail, proceeding to a dirt berm that gave a good view of the parking area across the pond. They settled in there, and Ray took out his binoculars, adjusted them and watched the parking area.

"I can barely make out the trash can," he said.

They waited. Millicent zipped up her jacket and squirmed in the grass as she watched nothing happen.

"There's the guy coming to make the drop," Ray whispered. He handed the binoculars to Millicent.

She adjusted them and saw a man come up to the trash bin, lean toward it and then walk away.

"Do you recognize him?" Ned whispered.

"It's too dark to tell," Millicent replied. "Now, I guess we wait to see if someone picks it up."

"And then spy on the cops nabbing him," Ray added.

They took turns with the binoculars as it was difficult to watch for more than five minutes at a time. Thirty minutes became an hour.

"How long will we stick this out?" Ned asked.

"You young pups are so impatient," Ray said. "We'll stay all night if necessary."

Millicent moaned. "I hope we don't have to wait that long."

"Besides, we're out under the stars on a sparkling night, and I'm with a beautiful woman," Ray said. "What more could I ask for?"

Millicent's cheeks grew warm, and she grabbed the binoculars, thankful that it was too dark for anyone to see her blush. "Keep your voice down. I'll take my turn now." She gave up after a few minutes, her eyes becoming blurry.

She closed her eyelids while Ned took a turn with the binoculars. She wanted to drift off to sleep but forced herself to stay awake. She'd see this through and find out what the police would accomplish. With nothing better to do, she once again started thinking back over all that had happened.

She opened her eyes, peered into the sky and spotted the Big Dipper. She flinched at the recollection of the last time she had noticed this constellation—right before she found . . . George dead. How could she solve this puzzle? She focused in on the two stars that pointed the way to the North Star. She needed to figure out a path that led to solving this puzzle. Then it occurred to her. It was back to her organizing skills once again. Group, reduce and reorganize. GRR. She needed to group all the facts together. First, everything connected with George. The cryptic messages he had left that, when deciphered, led to the signet ring. The microdot that she had sent off to the address George had left in his instructions.

Next on her mental list—the government man who had given her an address different from George's instructions to send the signet ring to. And he had handed her the huge check, which she had used to buy the condo. She smiled to herself at the thought of her new place. She loved it. Sure, it had been difficult moving out of her house after all those years, but she needed new surroundings that didn't remind her of George's death.

Then the three hoodlums. The one who had held her, Ray and Ned hostage, now dead. The other one who turned up as a body in Allison's dumpster, and Reed Eggleston who had been captured.

Next, the matter of George's stamp collection, which had subsequently been stolen from Jerry.

She had also been followed by a BMW and more recently a Prius.

There had been the tall, skinny man at the funeral and the garage sale.

And the microdot that had been found in the poetry book, stolen by Reed Eggleston when he overheard her conversation with Ray through the planted electronic surveillance device. But Eggleston had indicated that whoever remained behind all of this wasn't satisfied with that microdot.

Consequently, he still sought the signet ring.

The key question remained unresolved—who hired the three thugs? She didn't know. Detective Buchanan would be trying to catch that person tonight.

Now to reduce these things. Clearly, she could eliminate the two dead men, now out of the picture. One had committed suicide by police and one had been dispatched in the dumpster. Eggleston wasn't the prime mover, only a pawn. The second microdot didn't prove to be of value to the prime mover so she could purge that from her mental list. That left the microdot from the signet ring as the key item being sought. She had sent that off as George had instructed, but the prime mover didn't know that and still wanted it. Someone had hired the three thugs, with only Eggleston still alive. Eggleston had been driving the gray BMW, so that could be eliminated. The stamp collection had been stolen by Eggleston in an attempt to find the signet ring, but when that proved futile, Eggleston came back looking for the signet ring again.

Now to reorganize. Putting the remaining pieces back together . . .

"You're awfully quiet," Ray whispered in her ear.

"I'm pondering all that has happened."

"And what new insights do you have?"

"I'm getting close. Give me a minute to think it through."

Millicent's forehead crinkled in concentration. So, how did all the pieces fit together after being grouped and reduced? Then the image of the black sedan they had passed near the Walden Ponds parking lot popped into her mind. Black sedan. Her eyes grew wide. Yes. She could reach only one conclusion. She reviewed it all in her mind once again.

She grabbed Ray's arm. "I need to call Detective Buchanan."

"This isn't a good time to be making phone calls," he said.

She looked down as she reached into her jacket pocket for her phone.

Suddenly, a bright flash appeared followed by a loud boom.

"Ow," Ned shrieked. "I'm blinded."

"What happened?" Millicent raised her eyes and grabbed the binoculars.

"I can't see anything," Ned wailed. "I was watching and this explosion went off."

"I'm seeing star bursts," Ray said. "I wasn't looking directly at the drop spot, but the explosion affected my vision."

"I'm not having a problem since I was looking down," Millicent said. "There's smoke all over the other side of the pond. The prime mover must have discovered the police stakeout and set off that explosion and smoke screen to get the ring and escape." She scanned the other side of the pond. "Look. Off to the side. There's a figure running along the pond heading toward the fence we walked by. We have to get back to our car. Ray, has your vision returned enough to help Ned?"

"Yeah. Spots are dancing in front of my eyes, but I can lead him along."

"I still can't see anything," Ned said.

"And I bet the police who were watching can't either," Millicent said. "Come on. It's up to us now."

They staggered back toward the car. Ray helped Ned into the backseat and hopped in the driver's seat. Millicent jumped in the passenger's side, and had buckled her seatbelt when she heard another car starting.

"That black sedan we saw along the road," Millicent shouted. "Follow it."

"Yes, ma'am." Ray started the car, jammed it into reverse, swerved out and around, and slammed the gear shift into drive.

Millicent spotted the tail lights of the other car up ahead. "Can you see well enough to drive?" she asked Ray.

"A little late to ask that, but yes."

The sedan turned left on Seventy-fifth, and Ray followed.

Millicent reached for her smart phone and called Detective Buchanan. He actually answered.

"Detective, this is Millicent Hargrove," she gasped. "We're following the man who picked up the signet ring. We're heading north on Seventy-fifth. Do you have any police cars nearby?"

"I'll have a car follow you, but what are you doing in that area?"

"Never mind. I figured out who picked up the signet ring and caused all of these problems."

"And this person?"

"I'm convinced it's the government man who gave me the check and asked me about the signet ring at George's funeral."

Chapter 37

Detective Buchanan asked Millicent to stay on her phone so she could relay information about their location.

"You know this guy we're following?" Ray asked.

"Yes. I finally put the pieces together. A man approached me at George's funeral. When he left, he got into a black sedan. This recollection only clicked a little while ago. We saw the black sedan parked along the road when we arrived at Walden Ponds. This man wanted the signet ring, claiming to be working with George. He must have hired the three thugs to steal it from George, having him killed in the process, and he tried to get the ring from me. Then he showed up at Sawhill Ponds tonight to claim it. Because he needed a diversion, he created the blast and smoke screen. We have to catch him."

The car turned left on Jay Road, and Ray followed. Barely braking, the car crossed Sixty-third, racing along at sixty in a thirty-five zone.

Ray stuck with him like an annoying gnat.

The car turned right on Twenty-eighth Street and Ray careened around the corner.

As Millicent slammed into Ray on the turn, she said, "Where'd you learn to drive like this?"

From the backseat came, "Dad always wanted to be a NASCAR driver."

"Jewelry, bridge and NASCAR?" Millicent's mouth dropped open. "Those don't all seem to fit."

"Hey, I merely have a variety of interests."

"What don't you do?"

"I don't do dishes."

Millicent glared at him.

He ventured a glance her way as a streetlight flashed past. "Just kidding. Actually, I do a lot of dishes, being a single fellow and living on my lonesome."

Millicent conveyed their location to Detective Buchanan.

"I wonder where this guy plans to go," Ray said. "He's trying to shake us, but he won't get rid of me. Just call me Dale Earnhardt Junior."

"Stay with him but don't get us killed in the process," Millicent replied. "We should have some police assistance shortly."

As they approached the red traffic light on the corner of Lee Hill Drive and Broadway, the black car didn't even slow down. Two cars swerved and blasted their horns as the sedan shot through the intersection. Ray waited until the traffic cleared and then gunned the engine to race across the street. The tail lights showed a quarter of a mile ahead. Ray gained ground as they headed onto Old Stage Road.

"Good thing you kept this old clunker in top condition," Ray said.

"It's only seven years old, and I service it regularly," Ned replied.

Millicent shouted into her phone to let Detective Buchanan know of their route heading toward Left Hand Canyon.

They breached the hill and headed down the other side, now within a hundred yards of the black sedan.

"Tell the police they can cut him off at Left Hand Canyon," Ray said. "There's no turnoff before we reach it."

Millicent relayed the information and waited for the response.

"There's a sheriff's deputy in the area," Buchanan told her. "He'll be at the intersection of Old Stage and Left Hand Canyon."

"Uh-oh, a slow vehicle ahead," Ray warned.

The black sedan swerved to the left and passed a pickup truck chugging along.

Ray repeated the maneuver as an oncoming pair of lights appeared around

219

the bend. Millicent shrieked and covered her eyes. She felt the car lurch right, and when she opened her eyes, they were on the tail of the sedan again.

"Sorry," Ray said. "That was close."

"You almost turned us into road kill," Millicent shouted.

"But we didn't lose him."

They took a sharp turn to the left, and Millicent crashed into the door. An equally quick turn to the right followed, and she bumped into Ray.

"Millicent, this is no time to snuggle," Ray said with a chuckle.

"It was purely accidental," she said, straightening a misplaced strand of hair.

As they approached the bottom of the hill and the road leveled out in Left Hand Canyon, Millicent spotted red and blue flashing lights. The black sedan swerved to avoid the cruiser that blocked the road. It careened up the hillside and flipped. Then it spun 180 degrees on its roof as sparks shot from the pavement.

Ray slammed on the brakes. His car skidded to a stop, missing a collision by inches.

The overturned vehicle came to rest on the side of the road ten feet past the sheriff's car.

The deputy raced over to look into the upside down car as steam blasted out of its radiator.

The door flew open and struck the deputy, knocking him flat.

The man they'd been chasing crawled out of his disabled car, stood and started to limp across the road toward the other hillside. Suddenly, headlights appeared as a car turned from the canyon onto Old Stage Road. Its driver never saw the escaping man until the bumper made contact. The driver jammed on the brakes as a body bounced over the hood and landed on the road.

The sheriff's deputy recovered and staggered over with Millicent and Ray to see the unconscious figure. He felt for a pulse. Blood seeped from the man's mouth, but he continued to breathe.

Millicent still had the smart phone in her hand. "Call an ambulance," she screamed to Buchanan. "The perp was hit by a car. We're at the intersection of Old Stage Road and Left Hand Canyon."

Chapter 38

Millicent stared at the body on the road.

"Is that the man you thought it would be?" Ray asked.

"Yes, it's the government man who approached me at George's funeral."

The driver of the car, a woman in her forties visibly shaking, came up to the deputy, wringing her hands as the red and blue pulses shone on her tear-filled face. "I never saw him. He jumped right in front of my car. What am I going to do?"

"Please stay calm," the deputy replied. "Nothing was your fault."

"Is he all right?" the woman asked.

"He's unconscious. I can't tell how badly injured."

"An ambulance will be here shortly," Millicent said.

"I've never hurt anyone before." The woman sobbed. "What will happen to my insurance?"

Millicent put an arm around the sniffling driver. "As the deputy said, you didn't cause this accident. This man is responsible for a number of deaths and tried to escape. You've done nothing wrong."

The woman sagged but gave a grateful, wan smile to Millicent. "Thank you."

The ambulance arrived and carted the government man away.

"I wonder who he really is," Millicent said to Ray.

"If he recovers the police will try to determine that. Now we should all go get some sleep."

Millicent reached for the still-connected smart phone to inform Buchanan that they were heading home.

"Not yet," the detective told her. "I'll need to get statements from the three of you. I'll meet you at the police station right away."

Millicent relayed the information to Ray and Ned. "It's a good thing I don't have an organizing job tomorrow."

"And I guess I'll have to put off any more NASCAR events until the afternoon," Ray replied.

They climbed in the car.

"How are the eyes?" Ray asked Ned.

"My vision's coming back, but I'm still seeing spots. I could recognize the flashing police lights. Give me a full report on what happened."

Millicent filled him in as Ray started the car, and they headed to the police department. When they arrived, Detective Buchanan met with each of them individually, starting with Millicent.

"First of all, Mrs. Hargrove, what were you doing in the vicinity of Sawhill Ponds tonight?"

Heat spread across Millicent's cheeks. "I guess you might say I'm a snoop. I wanted to see what transpired."

"Not a wise thing to do. And you talked the other two into accompanying you?"

"Yes. They didn't want me going on my own."

Buchanan exhaled loudly. "I should chew you out for going there, but, on the other hand, I'm grateful that you helped apprehend the culprit. Now talk me through the events."

Millicent recounted going to Walden Ponds.

"And why did you choose that location?"

"Because I didn't want to interfere with your operation at Sawhill Ponds. I'd hiked there enough to know the trails connecting the two recreation areas so figured it would be a better place to park and then walk to observe the drop."

Buchanan shook his head. "You amaze me, Mrs. Hargrove. Why didn't you stay home and read a good book instead?"

Millicent's eyes flared, and she shook her right index finger at Buchanan. "Don't put me in the category of women who only watch television and knit."

He held up his hands as if to ward off an attack. "I can assure you I'd never do that, Mrs. Hargrove. So you decided to observe the drop at Sawhill Ponds. Continue."

"Yes, as I was saying before you tried to pigeon-hole me, we left the car in the Walden Ponds parking area. Along the road we noticed a black sedan."

"And did you recognize that car?"

"It didn't click until later, but I had seen the government man get in a black sedan at my husband's funeral. That one clue helped me put it all together. I went through all the things that had happened since my husband's death—the three thugs who confronted me at various times, two of them dying and the one captured, being followed by a BMW driven by one of the thugs, Eggleston's confession that he worked for someone else, and the whole mystery of the signet ring. The government man wanted that ring and gave me a different address to mail it to than in the instructions George had left me. I finally realized that the government man was working at cross purposes to George and was the person behind all my problems."

"And after you parked at Walden Ponds?"

Millicent recounted finding an observation point, the explosion, seeing a man running out of the smoke along the other side of the pond, getting back to their car and following him to the car crash on Old Stage Road.

"One thing still puzzles me," Millicent said. "I haven't figured out how the Prius following me fits in. I've accounted for the gray BMW and the black sedan but not for the dark blue Prius. I'm concerned that someone else might be still involved in this whole sordid affair."

"I'll have an officer keep an eye on you. We'll also have to see if the injured man regains consciousness."

"I'd like to speak to him if he does."

"Only after we've questioned him. I'll let you know if he recovers."

Millicent was kept in a room by herself until Ned gave his statement. Then she rejoined Ned while Ray was questioned.

"Pretty exciting evening, huh?" Ned said.

"Too exciting for me," Millicent said. "I'm ready for a little calm time without thugs, espionage, signet rings, abductions, guns and car chases. How are you doing?"

"I have my vision pretty well back now. I couldn't see a lot of the action when tossed around in the back seat of the car during Dad's wild drive. I think he fulfilled his NASCAR fantasy tonight."

"I'm sure glad we weren't the ones to crash into the hillside."

Ned chuckled. "Actually Dad's a pretty good driver. He's never even had a ticket."

"That's more than I can say. I've had several speeding tickets."

"See, it just goes to show how wild you are."

Millicent patted Ned on the arm. "Thanks for not classifying me as a little old lady."

Ray finished his interrogation and sauntered in to join Millicent and Ned.

"I've been grilled by the good detective and spilled my guts. I told him it was all your fault, Millicent."

Millicent's eyes widened. "Oh?"

"Just kidding. I told him that Ned and I insisted on going to Walden Ponds. We couldn't leave you unprotected, and besides, we wanted to see what happened as well."

"There." She gave her head a determined nod. "You're as snoopy as I am."

"You got me there."

The three of them went out to the car.

"Millicent, we'll drop you off first," Ray said.

When they pulled up in front of her building, Ray hopped out and circled the car to open the door for her. He held out a hand to help her out.

"I have to admit that I'm tired," Millicent said.

"I'll accompany you up to make sure everything is copacetic."

When they arrived at Millicent's door, she unlocked the two locks, stepped in and turned on the lights.

"Let me take a quick scan through to make sure no one's here," Ray suggested. He scurried though the apartment and returned to announce that all appeared safe.

"Thank you for an exciting evening," Ray said as he headed for the door. "I'll check with the detective in the morning to see if our bad guy recovers."

"Yes, let me know. I'll be waiting."

"I figured as much. I'll come along with you. We'll let Ned off the hook as he has a moving job in the afternoon."

Millicent laughed. "I'm getting such personal attention."

"Hey, until everything is resolved, you need someone watching your back. And it's a very attractive back, I might add."

Millicent put a hand to her warm cheek.

Ray waved his arms wildly. "Besides, after my experience tonight I'll be ready to evade any pursuit if the bad guys start shooting."

"I'm hoping the government man is the last bad guy we have to deal with." Millicent watched as Ray reached for the doorknob. He bowed and exited.

Millicent remembered the one unresolved problem. Who had been following her in the dark blue Prius?

Chapter 39

Millicent awoke to the sound of the phone ringing. She grappled to find the receiver next to the bed. "Hello," she croaked.

"You sound bright and wide awake," Ray's voice came over the line.

"Why are you calling me in the middle of the night?"

"Look at your clock."

Millicent rubbed her eyes and regarded the alarm clock. 11:45 a.m. "What? How'd I sleep so late?"

"I guess you crashed after all the excitement last night. I have some news for you."

Millicent still felt groggy. "Yes?"

"I spoke with Detective Buchanan a few minutes ago. He gave me an update on the guy we chased last night."

Millicent's eyes popped fully open. "Did he survive?"

"Alive and kicking. He woke up this morning and has been giving the hospital staff and the police grief. He didn't even have any broken bones, only bruises."

"Do they know who he is?"

"Nope. He apparently had no identification and has refused to answer any questions. He's being kept under guard at Community Hospital."

"I need to speak to him."

"Exactly. And Detective Buchanan is willing to let you take a crack at him since he hasn't said anything useful to anyone else. How soon can you be ready for me to come pick you up?"

Millicent set her feet down on the floor. "I want to drive over on my own since I have some errands to run today."

"Okay. But let me come over and follow you. Until this is resolved, you can't be too careful."

"Okay, give me an hour."

"At which time, I, your humble bodyguard, will be there."

Millicent took a quick shower, put on slacks, blouse, sweater and dress boots, downed a glass of orange juice and munched on two frozen waffles that she had warmed in the toaster. She washed the plate and had finished brushing her teeth when the doorbell rang. Peeking through the peephole, she verified it was Ray and let him in.

"Let's go so you can interrogate this guy," Ray said, offering his arm. "You can use your female wiles to wheedle information from him."

Millicent groaned. "Don't tell me you're a wannabe poet as well as NASCAR driver?"

"Hey, remember I like Baudelaire."

"That's right you're the eclectic gentleman—jewelry, bridge, NASCAR *and* poetry."

"And now organizing." Ray winked at her. "I've been trained by an expert."

As they strolled to the elevator Millicent said, "You're entirely too cheerful today."

"Why not? It's sunny outside, we survived our wild adventure last night, and I'm in the presence of a beautiful woman."

In spite of trying to ignore his comment, Millicent's cheeks turned warm. "I guess I can't share your enthusiasm. I still have unanswered questions concerning this supposed government man wanting the signet ring."

"Your turn to get him talking, Miss Marple, or should I say Grand Inquisitor?"

Millicent scowled as they entered the elevator. "I don't know what good I can do, but I certainly have some questions for him."

"I'll be waiting outside to follow you to the hospital."

Millicent pulled out of the parking structure and drove past Ray's car. She looked in her rear-view mirror to confirm he was following. As they headed east on Arapahoe, Millicent glanced back again. She flinched. Ray's car followed her, but she also noticed a dark blue Prius behind Ray. At the stop light at Foothills Parkway she reached in her purse, pulled out her smart phone and selected Ray's mobile phone number.

"Ray, the dark blue Prius is following us."

"Okay, I see it in my mirror. I'm going to let it pass me and see if I can get a look at the guy. Don't worry. I'll keep right behind you."

"What should I do?"

"Go to the hospital. Pull into the parking lot, and I'll see what this guy is up to. Stay on your phone."

When the light changed Millicent took off and watched in her rearview mirror as Ray changed lanes and let the Prius go past him. Then he changed back.

"Did you see him?" Millicent asked.

"No, I couldn't get a good look. I could tell it's a man. Keep going to the hospital."

Millicent continued with the cavalcade behind her. Who was this guy, and what did he want? She tapped her fingers on the steering wheel as she came to a stop at the intersection of Arapahoe and 48th Street. Her stomach tensed. Would she ever get all of this resolved?

She turned left and pulled into the hospital parking lot. The Prius and Ray both followed. She parked and noticed that the Prius pulled in next to her with Ray's car on the other side. She stepped out of her car as Ray dashed around to the Prius. He yanked the door open and dragged a man outside.

Millicent blinked. The man held a bouquet of daisies in his hand. She recognized him immediately as Fred Langley from the bridge tournament.

"What the hell are you doing following Millicent?" Ray shouted.

Millicent raced over to where the two of them stood.

"I—I wanted to give her some flowers," Fred stammered.

"Why have you been stalking her?" Ray shook Fred.

"I—I wanted to talk to her."

"I'll handle this, Ray," Millicent said. "You can let him go." She pointed her right index finger at Fred. "A gentleman does not go around following a lady. You need to apologize."

Fred hung his head. "I'm sorry." He held out the flowers without looking up.

She took the flowers. "Fred, I'm not interested in you, so stop following me. Do you understand?"

He looked up. "Yes."

"Now go home and don't follow me again."

He let out a resigned sigh. "Okay."

She and Ray watched as Fred got into his Prius, backed out and drove away.

Then the absurdity of the whole situation hit her, and she broke out laughing. "After all the criminal types following me, in the end the last one turned out to be Fred Langley."

"I told you he was a snake," Ray said.

"I don't think I need to worry about him anymore." She looked at the bouquet in her hand. "Besides his flowers will serve a useful purpose. Come on. Let's go visit this mystery man."

They were directed to the room where an armed police officer stood guard.

"Detective Buchanan gave us permission to talk to the prisoner," Ray said.

The husky policeman looked at his notepad. "I have instructions only to let Mrs. Millicent Hargrove into the room."

"I'll wait out here," Ray said. "Have at it, Millicent."

Millicent straightened her sweater and entered the room.

The man lay in bed with an IV tube in his arm. When she approached him, he said, "Well, if it isn't Mrs. Hargrove."

"I've brought you some flowers." She set them on the table next to the bed. "But it's difficult to speak to you without knowing your name."

"You can call me Rick."

"Why did you give me the money at my husband's funeral, Rick?"

"That was my assignment."

"But you wanted the signet ring."

"That's correct."

"What's so important about that ring?"

"I'm not going to answer that."

She glared at him and held up a finger. "First, you hired three men, one of whom killed my husband." She held up a second finger. "They tried to steal the ring." She held up another finger. "Third, you pretended to help me but only wanted to get your hands on the ring. You expected me to come across the signet ring and mail it to the address you gave me." She added a fourth finger. "When that didn't happen, you had those thugs continue to harass me, hoping to scare the ring out of me. That's why this whole thing has gone on so long." She showed all five fingers. "Finally, you had Eggleston under the threat of his own death come into my apartment in one more gambit to get the ring. Why did you want the microdot hidden behind the stone?"

His eyes jerked to the side momentarily, and then the stoic expression returned. "I don't know what you're talking about."

"Yes you do. You wanted that microdot. Well, it's gone and you'll never get your hands on it. All your efforts were to no avail. All you've done is cause the death of someone I loved. You are a vile man. I hope you're locked up for the rest of your life."

A menacing smile crossed his face. "That will never happen." He ripped the IV out of his arm, jumped out of bed, grabbed the IV tubing and before Millicent could react, wrapped it around her throat.

Millicent let out a choking gurgle.

"Now listen carefully," he breathed into her ear. "You're going to accompany me out of here. If you want to live, follow my directions. Nod your head if you understand."

Millicent gave a small nod that didn't constrict her throat any more than necessary.

"We're going to the door. You open it and tell the guard to drop his gun on the floor." He pushed her to the door, and she pulled it open. "Now." He thrust her in front of him as a shield and loosened the tubing.

"He says to drop your gun on the floor," Millicent rasped.

The policeman pulled his gun out and pointed it at Millicent and the man. "Let her go and you won't be killed."

The government man tightened the cord around Millicent's neck.

She wheezed.

"Drop the gun or she dies," he ordered."You move an inch toward me, and I'll snap her neck."

At that moment Ray came racing up. "There are spiders everywhere." He threw his hands in the air. "They're all over the walls; they're crawling on me." He started swatting all over his body.

"Get that crazy man out of here," the government man bellowed.

"Spiders everywhere," Ray shouted.

Millicent felt the cord loosen slightly around her neck. She had one thought. She raised her right leg and brought her boot down with all her might on the bare foot of her captor.

He screamed and stumbled, loosening his grip on the tubing.

Millicent thrust her head to the side, giving the policeman a clear shot.

He fired.

The tubing fell away, and Millicent and the government man crashed to the floor.

Ray rushed over and helped Millicent up. "Are you all right?"

She put her hand to her throat. "I'll be sore for a while, but other than that I seem to be fine." Then she looked at her arm and saw it covered with blood. She shrieked as Ray pulled her away from the blood-spattered body.

He held her closely, and she burst into tears.

"It's okay, I'm here for you," Ray said, comforting her. "You're not bleeding. It's from the dead man."

"I've seen enough dead men to last me a lifetime," she whimpered as she shook.

He rubbed the back of her neck.

The gesture and the feeling calmed her.

People rushed in, and two attendants checked for vital signs before carting away the government man on a stretcher. Then a young man in a white coat helped Millicent into a wheelchair.

"I'm fine," she insisted.

The young man started to wheel her away. "I'm taking you to the emergency room. You need to be looked at."

*****

A doctor peered down her throat and carefully ran his fingers over her neck. Then a nurse gave her a wet towel to mop up the government man's blood. Within an hour she was released and found Detective Buchanan and Ray waiting for her.

"I'm sorry the man attacked you," Detective Buchanan said.

"It all happened so quickly, I couldn't defend myself." She smiled at Ray. "Fortunately, Ray did his insane act to distract the man long enough that I could stomp on his foot and duck out of gun range. Your officer did what was necessary to save me."

"In all of this I have one piece of good news for you, Mrs. Hargrove."

"I'm ready for some good news."

"In the trunk of the black sedan we found albums of United States stamps. They match the description on the insurance claims your son filed in Indianapolis for the stamps that were stolen."

"My grandson will be very pleased."

"I have a question for you, Mrs. Hargrove. Did you learn anything before the man attacked you in the hospital?"

"He had George killed to get a microdot hidden in the signet ring. He said I could call him Rick but gave no further name. I don't have any idea who he worked for."

Buchanan shook his head. "We may never know."

Chapter 40

Back at her condo, Millicent called Jerry in Indianapolis. Drew answered the phone. "Hi, Grandma. How are things in Colorado?"

"Very busy. Is your dad around?"

"Nah. He's not home from work yet."

"I have some good news for you. The stolen stamp collection has been found. You should have it back in a week or so."

"Cool. Dad and I can start working on it again."

"That's right. And no one will be messing with it again."

*****

That evening Millicent attended the tribute to George at his stamp club. Primarily men with a smattering of women, comprised the group. After she took her seat, she noticed a tall, thin man slink into the room at the last minute. Her eyes went wide. She recognized him as the man she had seen at George's funeral and the garage sale. She wanted to go speak to him, but at that moment the moderator stood up to begin the meeting.

"We're all here tonight to remember one of our favorite members, George Hargrove." A loud round of applause followed. "In addition to being an outstanding philatelist, he was a wonderful human being and friend."

A number of tributes followed and by the end of the evening, Millicent's eyes filled with tears. When the program was over, she dried her eyes and rushed over to speak to this other mystery man. She held out her hand, "I'm

Millicent Hargrove, and I saw you at my husband's funeral and my garage sale."

"I'm . . . uh . . . Herbert Sacks." He gave her a limp hand, never making eye contact.

Millicent decided that with this man a direct approach might bring the quickest results. "I meant to speak with you at the funeral and the garage sale but never had a chance. Out of curiosity, why where you at both places?"

He finally looked up at her. "Your . . . your husband, George, was always friendly to me. I . . . I'm a little shy and most people don't pay much attention to me. I went to his funeral because he was a kind man. Then I stopped by the garage sale hoping there might be some stamps for sale." His face reddened. "I hope that doesn't offend you."

"Not at all, Herbert. Thank you for speaking with me."

*****

The next morning Millicent climbed out of bed determined to try one last thing to unravel the mystery of the supposed government man. She drafted a letter telling exactly what had happened the last two days, including a description of the government man. She closed with, "Because of all the service that George provided to you and the nature of his death, please help me find closure on who this man was and what George had been involved in." She signed her name and sent the letter off to the same address where she had sent the microdot from the signet ring.

*****

Two weeks later, Millicent returned to her apartment after an organizing project. An eighty-seven-year-old woman had hired her to unclutter her home so that she could stay there rather than going into an assisted living facility. Millicent had brought in people to install a walk-in shower and safety rails in her bathroom, had reduced the mess throughout the whole house and arranged for an in-house monitor should she need assistance. It gave her a feeling of satisfaction that she had addressed the woman's wish to remain safely in her own home. She realized how much she enjoyed this job. Sure, there was a lot of hard work and she had to lug boxes and bags of stuff around. She patted her stomach. But it sure beat going to a gym for a workout. Then she chuckled at the memory of almost hitting Ray when she dropped the box from the garage rafters weeks before. This job also had its light moments and provided the satisfaction of delivering a meaningful service to her clients.

At that moment, her phone rang. Millicent answered it to hear her daughter Karen on the line.

"I have some good news," Karen said.

"This has been a good day, so I'm ready for something else positive."

"I'm pregnant!"

Millicent almost dropped the phone. "That isn't just good news, it's fantastic news. I'll have to schedule an extended trip to Memphis."

"I want you here to help out. We'll have the guest room ready along with the baby's room so you can stay for as long as you like."

"Probably not more than a week. You know the saying about dead fish and relatives being around too long."

After hanging up the phone, Millicent floated around her apartment before deciding to pick up her mail, which she sorted through at the table in her second bedroom office. She found one item addressed to her with no return address. She inspected the envelope and made out a postage mark indicating Washington, DC. She carefully opened it and extracted a neatly typed letter that read:

Mrs. Hargrove,

Thank you for informing us of the events that transpired in Boulder, Colorado. The man you identified was once an employee of our agency who became a rogue agent to work against the purposes of the United States government. The money he gave you was sanctioned by this agency and rightfully deserved for the service provided by your husband. Unfortunately, the other actions this man took were not directed by this organization. We thank you for the item you sent to us earlier, and it is now safely in the appropriate hands. We want to express our deepest regrets for the death of your husband, a man of talent, who provided a much-needed service for his country. Unfortunately, we're not at liberty to tell you anything more in regard to his responsibilities in our agency. You can be assured that no one will be bothering you further. We're sorry for all the pain this unfortunate set of events has caused you.

That was it. No signature, no letterhead, no indication of the name of the agency or what George had been doing. She decided she'd save the letter to show to her son and daughter the next time she saw them.

She sat there in thought. She knew that George had been involved in some type of espionage but hadn't learned any particulars. He'd been killed for some information he had obtained, and the ex-government man had hired three thugs, one of whom had killed George. They had harassed her, she had been held hostage twice, she had been followed, her apartment had been broken into and bugged, but she had survived. She understood the sequence of events since George's death, but his past hidden life still remained a mystery. Maybe some day she would discover more about it.

"George, I miss you so much," she said out loud. "What did you get yourself into?"

Of course, there was no answer, but she felt the need to keep speaking to him. "We're going to have a new grandchild. I wish you were here, so we could share together the new addition to our family."

She was seized with a feeling of hollowness in her chest at the loss of George. But she was only sixty-eight years old. She remained in excellent

237

health and with no one trying to choke her to death, she should live for many fruitful years. Now she had her own life to live, and she needed to move on. She'd never forget George, but she didn't intend to sit around and be depressed either. She tapped her fingers on the table for a moment and with determination straightened her back. She had a purpose in life. She would continue to help people unstuff their stuff—group, reduce and reorganize.

Just then the phone rang, and she picked it up. "This is Millicent."

"Millicent, Ray here. I thought I'd check in to see how my favorite young lady is doing."

Millicent felt a warmth course through her chest. "I heard from my daughter that I'm going to be a grandmother again."

"That's super news. That will be one lucky grandchild with such a beautiful grandmother."

The heat spread to her cheeks. "I also had a great job today where I helped a woman who didn't want to be forced out of her house. She was upset over the possibility of going into an assisted living facility and is now delighted to be staying in her house."

"Sounds like a good reason for a celebration. Would you consider a dinner tonight?"

"You and Ned?"

There was a pause on the line. "Actually Ned's tied up. His fiancée is back in town for a few days before her next trip, and they have plans to spend time together, just the two of them."

"I still haven't met this mysterious woman of his I keep hearing reference to."

"Oh, I'm sure you will. She travels so much, but one of these days he'll get the two of you together. So how about it? Are you ready to go out with me . . . without a chaperone?"

Millicent thought for a moment, and then a smile crossed her lips. "That sounds like a wonderful idea."

About the Author

Mike Befeler is author of six novels in the Paul Jacobson Geezer-lit Mystery Series, two of which were finalists for The Lefty Award for best humorous mystery. He has six other published mystery novels: *Death of a Scam Artist, The V V Agency, The Back Wing, The Mystery of the Dinner Playhouse, Murder on the Switzerland Trail* and *Court Trouble;* an international thriller, *The Tesla Legacy;* and a nonfiction book, *For Liberty: A World War II Soldier's Inspiring Life Story of Courage, Sacrifice, Survival and Resilience.* Mike is past-president of the Rocky Mountain Chapter of Mystery Writers of America. He grew up in Honolulu, Hawaii, and now lives in Lakewood, California, with his wife, Wendy. If you are interested in having the author speak to your book club, contact Mike Befeler at mikebef@ aol.com. His web site is http://www.mikebefeler.com.